I0741687

THE DARKER SIDE OF
LUST

A collection of short erotic fiction

By

ABIGAIL EKUE

5th Anniversary Edition

Published by Native Creative Press
www.abigailekue.com

Printed in the United States of America
Second Edition.

ISBN-10: 0982732724
ISBN-13: 978-0-9827327-2-4

To the members of my inner counsel who supported and inspired me and endured the flooded inboxes and late night messaging

Mother Nature hath endowed us with the gift of pleasure and we must use it at every chance we get, for it is a virtue not a vice.

-Aphra Behn

As a matter of biology, if something bites you it is probably female.

-Scott M. Kruse

Table of Contents

INTRODUCTION

It's been 5 years. And what do I do to commemorate my first book? I write it again.

Some stories from the first edition of *The Darker Side of Lust* are gone. I've grown as a writer so it was an easy decision to scrap them. If those stories were your favorites—my condolences. I hope you will find a new favorite in this collection.

New to the 5th Anniversary Edition are also versions of the stories from my mini collection, *Exhaust Pipes* and a few new erotic adventures that I wanted to share.

There are threesomes and foursomes.

There are 2 Morgans – they are not the same person. I guess I just love that name.

Thank you again for letting these characters show you who they are and who you are.

THE DARKER SIDE OF
LUST

The Charmed Life

"Good Morning, babe," she cooed.

"Good Morning, Queen."

She smiled half-expecting a kiss or pat on the ass, fully aware that wasn't going to happen.

The charmed life – many hope for it. They strive for drama-free, sheltered bliss. But every unhappy family is unhappy in their own way.

They had made love in their king-size bed. She had given birth to all five children in their living room. She fed and sometimes changed them in the kitchen. Now she was showering alone in the bathroom. He placed his wife on a pedestal so high that now he didn't touch her. He suppressed daydreams of bending her over the kitchen table and diving into her body. He told himself he didn't need to inhale her scent or taste her like he had after her workouts. It was wrong he told himself to miss the feel of her warm, damp skin against his after she was done with the last rep. He scolded himself for watching her heart-shaped ass as she walked their second youngest into the house from the car. Instead he trained his gaze on their held hands by her hip.

The children ran around like chickens without their heads but she remained cool. He admired how well she handled the children. The three older children were already eating at the table. She negotiated with the younger ones about how much broccoli versus cheese sauce should be on their plate. The children made it to the table without a disastrous mess but did have a minor spill. When she bent down to wipe it up he watched his wife's cleavage. Although she wore a bra, her breasts swayed just enough to excite him as she wiped back and forth. The memories of his wife pressing her breasts together as he rode her chest excited him even more. She wore the decorations he left on her warm flesh with pride. They'd joke about who could leave the bigger mess on whom because she also had the ability to leave the bridge of his nose down to the bottom of his chin slippery and shiny.

She knocked on the door only out of habit because she had no intention of waiting to be let into her oldest's bedroom. They had music playing and their body language screamed that they were studying each other and not the AP Calculus they were supposed to be. The teens were mortified at her intrusion. Why they were shocked at her Mom etiquette was lost on her. She didn't bat an eyelash; they were doing nothing she hadn't done before yet hadn't done recently.

"Ma!"

"We weren't doing anything, I swear!" The boyfriend blurted out. The daughter widened her eyes at him. Saying they weren't doing anything just admitted guilt.

"Do you have condoms?" she asked the teens.

"Ma!"

The mother continued, "The extra large seem to be popular now, even with the white guys." Her daughter's boyfriend chuckled a little.

Her daughter rushed to the door. "Oh my god! Get out!"

"*Eleven o'clock*..." she emphasized the curfew as she made her exit. "And make sure that door is unlocked!" Her daughter closed the door behind her as she made her way down the hallway to the master bedroom. There was no concrete evidence, but even her sixteen year-old daughter was having sex, or rounding the bases, or merely had someone in her bedroom who *wanted* to get physical. Reality checks like that can make a woman wonder where it all went wrong.

Her husband got an erection at the sight of her undressing after a day's work or the basketball games, hapkido tournaments, capoeira rodas and piano recitals. As she spoke about her day, he admittedly had moments where he wasn't

listening because he was too busy watching her lips. He thought
about caressing her cheek and kissing her. His penis responded
to his thoughts of her lips on it. How wet and warm they felt
every time she kissed the head and licked the shaft. Just as
quickly, he would snap back to reality and listen to how the
second graders at her charter school were learning the South
African National Anthem.

Yes, his wife loved to share her day with him, but
spending all day mired in juvenile energy made raw adult
behavior exactly what she needed to feel like herself again. To
feel anything. But her husband inquired about the ins-and-outs
of the expansion of the community arts program she was
spearheading and wasn't sliding his body in-and-out of her. She
appreciated his listening to her but he could shut her up with a
breathtaking kiss every now and then. He *could*, but she kept
talking about her day. And the children.

When the couple first bought their bed for their new
bedroom in their new house, it seemed too small since they used
every angle of it. Their level of kink dropped after each child.
The last two were conceived during ten minutes of missionary
sex with the lights out. Now during their nightly rituals he
watched her silently as she readied herself for bed. He did a very
good job hiding his glances and excitement. More nights than
not, one or more of the kids beat her into the bed, lying in her
spot next to her husband. She felt guilty for wishing he would
send the children to their own beds so he could be her lover and
give them a reason to change the sheets.

She learned soon enough that wasn't going to happen.
She let him have his playtime in bed with the children and she
had solo playtime in the shower. Her lengthy showers seemed to
go unnoticed by her husband. She hoped he would invite
himself in again and press her back against the slippery shower
tiles while he thrust up into her. She never locked the bathroom
door but he wouldn't know since he never paid his wife a visit.
The shower massager beat away the tension in her neck and
shoulders or from her thighs after a long run on the Brooklyn
concrete. She put her fingers deep inside and did to herself what
she wished her husband would. Once she aimed the massaging

streams of water between her thighs, it was the ultimate release.

Yet after her orgasms she still couldn't sleep because she wanted to be held by her husband. Little did she know, as she lay looking at the back of his head that he slowly stroked his erect body aching to be inside of her. She wanted him inside of her. She wanted his gentle rhythm to cause that flutter in her belly, his touch to make her thighs open while her inner walls closed around him, gripping him with a warm pulse. She wanted to lock her ankles around his waist, keeping his penetration slow and deep. She wanted her hands to slide in the sweat that beads up on her husband's brown back, her breasts to glisten in response.

Instead, under the covers, she spooned him, brought her belly to his back and draped her arm over her husband's body. She wanted him to feel her nude body against his. The last time she climbed into bed without any clothing on was a distant memory to both of them. She traced his thigh and hip then moved forward to his penis. She maneuvered his penis through the slit in his boxers and released it. It was filling with desire and hung in the air. Her fingers traced the length of it and it throbbed. She ran her fingers up the center of his stomach like she was playing a piano, in and around his navel. She noticed his breathing getting heavier because his back pressed more firmly against her breasts. Her hand found her husband's penis again and she stroked every inch, ran her palm over the head. It grew in her hand to its full length. He put his hand over hers and brought her massage to a complete stop.

"Good night, love," he said placing his wife's hand back into her space. He climbed out the bed and unlocked the bedroom door. That ended the possibility of another night writhing on the bedroom floor. The unlocked door meant any of the children could barge in. He used to joke that he and his wife would have to give their kids the birds and the bees talk at some point but didn't need to give a demonstration. So locking the door became their thing, until it wasn't their thing anymore.

She took the cue and threw on a nightshirt. She got on her side of the bed creating the usual chasm between their bodies. Even if none of their children filled it, it would remain.

He climbed back into bed and pulled the covers up to his chin.

Sleep lost out to her frustration. She rolled over, "What's wrong with you?"

He stirred, but immediately readied himself to go back to sleep.

"Don't go back to sleep. We need to talk."

He rolled onto his back. "Now? Now's not a good time, babe. We need to get some sleep. We both have long—"

"Fuck the long days. We need to talk about what's going on... what's *not* going on between us."

"I don't know what you're talking about." He kicked himself for opening himself up to more questioning but silently hoped she'd believe the lie.

She propped herself up on her elbow. "I'm talking about what just happened. I was getting things started and you stop me? What the hell?"

"Everything... it's... not about sex."

"So what is it then? Are you just too tired? I can get on top, that's not a problem."

"I don't want you on top of me..."

"Well, excuse me, then."

"I didn't mean it like that, babe."

She sat up straight and crossed her arms. "Point blank, I'm horny and I'm tired of fucking myself. I want to have sex with my husband. I'm not wrong for that."

"Come on, don't make a big deal about it."

"It *is* a big deal!"

"Keep your voice down."

"Don't tell me to keep my voice down. What, you don't want the neighbors to hear that you *ain't* doing me?" She turned her shoulder to him. "We're husband and wife. Sleeping in the same goddamn bed and you won't touch me. You don't let me see you. You don't even look at me anymore!"

That made it clear he'd done an exceptional job of hiding his lustful stares.

"Babe, we really should get some sleep." He did his best not to fidget.

She climbed out the bed and locked the bedroom door.

When she climbed back onto the bed she kneeled next to him and lifted her nightshirt. He kept his gaze trained on the ceiling. She grabbed his hand and placed it on her breast. "Look at me!" She held his hand on her body and with her other she reached into the slit of his boxers again. Her fingers grazed his testicles before wrapping around his shaft.

"Don't!" He threw her arm off him. "Just, don't. Don't touch me like that."

She straddled his hips and slid her hand back into the slit of his boxers. If she got started, he wouldn't be able to resist. He pushed her off and jumped out the bed.

She didn't recognize the man standing in their bedroom.

He paced alongside the bed. She chuckled before her sounds erupted into a full laugh.

"Sweetie...?"

She caught her breath, "It's either I laugh or I go crazy..." She laughed for a little while longer before the room descended into a marked silence.

"You might as well just tell me." she said.

He stopped pacing but didn't speak. He looked at her seeking gaze.

"Are you fucking someone else?" Before he said anything she continued. "Is that it? You're fucking someone else and you're too tired for me? Are you fucking a man?"

"No! Why would you even ask me that?" His eyes didn't drift from hers.

"Well what is it then? What did I do?" She took off her nightshirt and flung it at him. "It's *me*. I'm here. Breasts, ass, pussy and you don't fucking react... and when I touch you, you act like I'm fucking diseased."

There she was—breasts, ass, pussy. He shook his head clear of the lustful thoughts and resumed pacing.

"Tell me! Do I stink? Am I too soft now?" She grabbed at her body. A pang of guilt and self-consciousness washed over her. She'd developed a taste for dessert since her sex life ceased to exist. She no longer fought with her children to finish the food on their plate, she did it for them. She ate to celebrate a good day at work and when she was faced with a night without her husband's touch at home.

"You're fine, beautiful... You're beautiful."

Her rage came back. "Ok, so it's *you*."

He let out a short sigh. The sight of his wife kneeling in bed was too much to bear. Her nude, brown skin begged to be touched. There was anger, yearning and disappointment etched on her face.

"Does it work?"

"What are you talking about, babe?"

"Your *dick*! Does your dick work?"

"Yes!" he composed himself. "Yes, it works. There's nothing wrong with *me*..."

It was too late to change to tone of his statement.

"Oh, so there's something wrong with *me*? I'm wrong for wanting to have sex with my husband. Got it."

"No, that's not what I meant..."

"Fuck you. You know, if I *didn't* wanna fuck you, you'd be breaking my back right now." She reached across the bed and grabbed her nightshirt. "You know how many men would tear this ass up if I said 'go'?" She backed off her side of the bed.

"What is that supposed to mean?"

There was a knock on their bedroom door. "Mommy? Daddy?"

"Go to bed..." she said over her shoulder at the door.

"But I wanna come in..." they pleaded from the other side of the door.

"No!"

"Let's just let him in." He walked around the bed and picked up an undershirt.

"He comes to our bed almost *every night* 'cause he knows *you're* gonna let him in."

"Why wouldn't I?" He slipped the undershirt over his head. "He's probably scared."

"Who cares!" She was angrier than he'd ever seen her. She stood at her side of the bed. "I'm sorry. That's not what I meant. Of course I care, but he'll be OK. But you know how we got those kids? We fucked, baby! We had sex!"

"Keep your voice *down*."

She glared at her husband. He noticed her hand was in a fist and so was the one that held her nightshirt. He watched her breasts heave with each breath. Those same breasts were pressed against his back not long ago and that fist wrapped around his warm body. His body tingled. He wasn't worried that she'd hit him but he was terrified of what she might say next. The more he thought about whether she'd notice how aroused he was becoming, the more awake his penis became.

He dipped, bending his knees slightly to adjust himself. The front of his boxer shorts weren't in a full tent but not completely flat either. Her gaze dropped to the front of his boxers then shot back to his eyes. She took a few steps in his direction and he took a few steps back. He adjusted the waistband of his boxer shorts unnecessarily and broke their gaze.

"We're not done. We have to fix this."

"You're tired. You're irritable." He walked past her to the bedroom door, "I'm gonna go check on him."

"I swear to God if you walk outta here..."

"What?" He leaned in so their son wouldn't hear, "*Force* me to have sex with you?" He opened the bedroom door and scooped up the boy.

"One man's trash..." she said to his back and slammed the door shut. She was pissed off enough to lock the door and put in her earplugs so she wouldn't hear him knocking in the morning. But she didn't lock the door. She wanted her husband to come back to bed. She threw herself across the bed in a tantrum.

Her husband stayed with his son. They checked his kid-sized room for boogeymen. Even when his son was ready for sleep he stayed and read him a story. He was in no rush to return to his bedroom to argue with his wife or worse yet, have make-up sex.

When he returned to their bedroom the next morning, his wife was laying across the bed in the same spot she threw herself the night before. Her taut back and the soles of her feet greeted him. One of her knees was bent slightly to the side allowing him a view of her bush. He closed the door quietly and walked towards the bed. He studied her curves. He thought about it for a while before he ran his finger along the back of her thigh, up and down from her knee to her butt and back again. She stirred a little in response to the tickle of his fingertip.

But he didn't stop. He pressed every inch of his palm against her skin and ran it along her leg and this time spent more time on her rear. He pressed harder each time he ran his hands up to her lower back causing her cheeks to spread. She glistened and he dipped his finger in the pool before he could think to stop. Her hips responded, drawing his finger in deeper. He kissed her body and licked the crease of her thighs. Once he got three fingers inside her, he pulled her hips off the bed and buried his face between her cheeks, tasting her from front to back. She squirmed and moaned.

He blinked and that snapped him out of his daydream. His wife let out a rousing sigh. The first thing she saw as she rolled over out of sleep was her husband. She smiled before the memories of their fight came back. She climbed out the bed.

"Good Morning, I... I didn't want to wake you." he said. She went into the bathroom and locked the door behind her without a word.

She took a little longer than usual getting ready that morning. When she finally joined her family in the kitchen her oldest daughter told her mother to "get it" because she was looking "right" that day.

"Who you tryna look good for, Ma?"

"Don't worry about that. Get your butt to school." They kissed each other on the cheek and off her daughter went.

"You have to get them on the school bus this morning, remember?" The first words she said to her husband regarding their youngest children were icy but he was relieved she was speaking to him.

"Yeah... yeah, I remember." He looked at her, taking in how polished she looked that morning. She didn't acknowledge him. She said goodbye to her children and headed out.

A silver Mercedes-Benz S-class with three passengers was waiting for her at the curb. She climbed into the front passenger side seat next to the handsome male driver. Her husband had to wonder who his wife was trying to look good for that morning. Many of the executive staff members at her school were attending a family and early childhood development symposium at Rutger's University. That could explain her dressier than usual attire. Hopefully she wouldn't be "getting it" elsewhere.

That evening the family of seven sat at the dining room table and ate dinner just like any other night. Once the younger children were tucked in and the older children were tucked in with their iPads, the husband and wife retired to their bedroom.

He propped himself up on his two pillows and the extra throw pillows while he read. His wife spent her usual alone time in the shower. This night she came out the bathroom wearing a sheer nightgown and a pair of thong underwear underneath.

He looked up from his Kindle. "Wow," the word slipped out. "What are you wearing?"

She shrugged, "I bought myself something nice today. Figured it's something we both could enjoy."

"That wasn't necessary, babe."

"So I should take it off?" she pushed the straps off her shoulders and the light fabric fell to the floor.

There she stood; her nipples stared back at him.

"Babe, you should—"

Her actions interrupted him. She ran her hands down her stomach and her fingers stopped between her legs. She circled her clit over the tiny patch of silk. She wouldn't be told what she should or shouldn't wear or that she shouldn't want what she wanted. "I'm your wife. I'm a woman," His level of discomfort was visible. "I'm a sexual person..."

"What are you doing?"

"Touching myself. You know I do this. You used to love to watch me do this all the time."

"I did... I *do*..."

His wife's fingers pushed aside the panty and her masturbation grew more intense. She squeezed her breast with her other hand. His wife self-pleasuring had an effect on him he couldn't deny. It was time he exorcised himself from whatever held him back from his wife. Her two first fingers disappeared and reappeared shinier. Her toes on the foot she propped up on the bed curled. She was in another place. Without him.

He scooted to the foot of the bed. He took her by the wrist and sucked the fingers that were just inside her. He ran his fingers along her wet slit and tasted his own finger. He placed her on the edge of the bed and stood over her for a few moments. He leaned down and kissed her and allowed his body to react to the feel of her lips and her hand on his cheek. He dropped to his knees and spread her legs, throwing one over his shoulder. He held the crotch of her panty to one side and lost himself in the sight of her body for a long time, for the first time in what seemed like an eternity. Going back wasn't scary as he'd made it out to be in his mind. Her scent ignited latent memories in his entire body.

As did her taste. He tore the thong off her body and let it land where it saw fit on the floor. His wife's hips seesawed against his mouth and nose and chin. He hoisted her hips up in the bend of his arms to meet his face. He remembered where to flick his tongue and with how much pressure. Her reaction was as melodious and gratifying as he remembered.

Their youngest daughter opened the bedroom door with her baby doll in hand. "Mommy?"

Her parents scrambled to cover up. "No!" "Sweetie, go back to bed!" they shouted. He scrambled off his knees to the door.

"Why you not wearing your pajamas, Mommy?"

"Go!" He ushered her out the doorway and closed the door. He looked at his wife teetering on the edge of the bed clutching the sheets over her body.

"Did you lock it?" she asked.

He locked the door with exaggerated flair. After a few seconds they burst into laughter. Things were finally back to normal.

* * *

The Good Night Kiss

I left four tracks in the tightly packed shea butter with my fingers. Clumps of the paste stuck to my fingers. Without second thought, I smeared the yellow onto my damp cheeks and forehead. I let the streaks sit there and stared at my face, transformed to warrior. For centuries my ancestors used this butter to protect the many complexions of Africa. The slippery massage ended in a sheen that was intense. My expression brightened, my deep eyes studied the vision of my high forehead, arched eyebrows and full lips in the partially fogged mirror.

Next I took down my hair. I'd had my two-strand twists up in a French braid for the better part of two weeks. I didn't realize how much I missed my hair cascading past my cheeks and over my shoulders. I instantly felt taller as my hair reached for the ground. Tomorrow, I'd pamper my hair and scalp with a hot oil treatment.

My body had a thirst that needed to be quenched tonight. It was midweek. Roho, my weekend lover, was unavailable. Since the first time we experienced each other's bodies, he initiated and I was always willing. My body responded to him, unconsciously opening for him. I was his finger puppet. His fingers spent endless moments inside me. He controlled me.

I was going through a thong-free phase, or maybe I'd outgrown them all together. My cotton panties were so comfortable. They made me feel cleaner. My camisole hugged my breasts and waist.

Ovie was already in bed when I went to the bedroom.

He was facing away from me, but I knew he wasn't sleeping. Peeling back the covers so I could climb under them with him revealed his strong brown body. My skin barely touched the sheets before my hands were touching him. He rolled over to face me and kissed me. He was ready to end the kiss when I put my hand in the scruff on his face to keep his lips pressed to mine.

I loved the manual labor he completed during the day, the body it helped to sculpt. I wanted some of the love we make. Tonight, that labor sapped him of his energy. He was kissing me good night. I didn't worry to pick a fight. I wanted to de-stress and let go. He gave me an excuse to touch myself. I didn't always need him around when I came, or even want him. I opened the drawer of my nightstand and the smooth sound of the wheel in the track was arousing. My body knew what I stored in that drawer.

Climbing out the bed, I took out my curvy, slender dildo and a packet of lube. He patted the bed next to him urging me to stay but I wanted to spread out. I wanted to feel the energetic air swirling throughout the apartment against my dampness.

I rarely used the plush, beach towel I chose from my linen closet. It was still practically new and always ready to use for special occasions. I spread it out on my couch. I slid my panties down to my ankles and stepped out of them. I kept my camisole on. It fit like a dress five inches too short and my full ass peeked from under the bottom hem. The fabric tickled my nipples. My entire breast swelled, anticipating.

The fiber of the towel cradled my ass the way my panties had. It complemented my skin tone with its second chakra color. I rest my feet on my ottoman. The soles of my feet nearly touched and my knees lay open to the sides. I was at home in the asana of the Goddess. My back was propped up by the oversized pillows on my sofa.

Enthralled by the diamond my hips and legs formed, I ran my hands along my inner thighs, then out to the front of my thighs, the pull on my muscle opening my lips slightly. My faint scent tickled my nostrils and I took a long deliberate inhale. I was fleshy sweet. My scent made me picture how my pussy looked as it blossomed. There was a subtle pulse at the mind's eye vision of my glistening.

I tore open the corner of the packet of lube. The cool lube dripped down my mound and I shivered slightly as it trickled over my clit. I squeezed more out of the packet and it coated me further. The lube intensified my touch. I swirled my fingers around my clit and my black hole opened, my body craving something with its intense gravitational pull.

Drop after drop of the cool lube landed on my hot lips. My nipples reacted to my touch below the waist. My inner lips spread apart as I swelled. I teased my hole with the tip of my finger, teasing myself by not exploring my insides.

I slid my toy along my slippery space. I eased it inside against the slight resistance of my inner walls. I threw my head back; the sensation of being filled up was intense. The toy was smooth with a narrow tip, wider in the center, narrow again, with a wider base, like a woman with the coveted hourglass shape.

My pussy closed around the waist of my dildo. I exhaled as silently as I could. I wish I had put on some music for some aural privacy, but didn't want to disturb the silence coming from the bedroom. Not even Ovie's faint snoring was heard. I imagined strolling into the bedroom and climbing on top of him, knees next to his ears as I clawed at the wall and headboard.

I fucked myself with the dildo at a gentle pace. Where a man would slow down upon feeling me tighten, I keep fucking, the ridges of my G-spot grabbing the toy. My clit was the size of a tiny sixth finger. I could feel a wave of warmth inside me. This was my body and there was no guessing what I wanted.

The angle of my thrust was down and in now, my massage was a rhythmic down and around, back and forth like windshield wipers across my clit. My ass clenched sending my hips slightly higher. This was the "don't stop" moment; my fingernails dug deep into Roho's ass steering his strokes, my pussy squeezing around him while it grows stiffer and deeper.

A long sigh escaped my lips just as I heard Ovie stir in

the bedroom. I could hear the doorknob turn and the latch slip out of the lock. I could feel him standing there watching my form in the candlelight. He didn't say a word. The clock seemed to tick every half-second.

My desires conjured the vision of Roho kneeling in front of the sofa as I lay open before him. He explored my insides knuckle deep with a four-finger width. Ovie sat next me on the couch and slipped a finger down the top of my camisole. My nipple reached up to greet him. The added sensation made me moan. He slipped his finger under the straps of my camisole and pushed them off my shoulders exposing my breasts. He glided over my skin with feathery touches. I pressed my head deeper into the pillows, my neck stiffening.

Ebb was now flow. Another wave filled me. I was sure my imagery of Roho was bright enough for Ovie to see. I know Roho would be watching me with a pleased expression. I tensed around his fingers as he made this motion of scooping out my insides, leaving his four-finger track marks. I couldn't grab hold of his wrist, so I gripped the hips of my dildo tighter. The wet sucking sound of my dildo fuck was syncopated with the second hand tick of the clock. Ovie moaned against my neck as he sucked it, my body's sounds making him ache. His hot breath washed over my shoulders and breast. He massaged my scalp through the parts in my hair, gripping and tugging on it.

I was silent until my orgasm washed over me, letting out a passionate cry. My pussy took control of the dildo as it spasmed. I slowly eased up on rubbing my clit as I brought my knees together, shuddering. A few moments passed before I slowly pulled the dildo out of me. It was covered in my cream and I felt some dripping down onto the towel beneath me.

I stood to go clean myself and my toy. I spied Ovie's hard dick as he touched his balls. My legs were wobbly and I only took a few steps before he grabbed me by the waist. He bent me over and ran his finger from my ass to my clit, making me shiver. I could feel the wetness sticking to my ass cheeks as I spread them apart for him. He took the dildo from me and pressed it against my asshole. He was met with little resistance. My ass was ready, my engine was warmed up. He guided it into my ass slowly. I could go from zero to an anal orgasm in five minutes if he wanted to take me there.

But he didn't. He wrapped the dildo in the edge of the towel and put me on my back on the couch. A sound of surprise and wonder and pleasure came from deep within him as he penetrated me. He'd felt my wetness before, but I was flowing like the Nile right now. He'd never entered me right after a creamy orgasm; the warmth, the throbbing, the wetness. I ran my fingers down his tense chest. He rode me high, so he'd rub against my clit, and slow for intensity. It wasn't long before I was sucking him into my black hole.

I recalled hearing different vowels sung by Ovie at various pitches as he slammed into me with more force at the end of each long slow descent into my body. I could feel his dick pulse as he lay deep inside before starting the upstroke. My pussy tugged on the head of his dick and he came hard. His release rocked me. I smiled at his face strained in pleasure. I knew he'd catch a second wind.

*   *   *

GAME NIGHT

ABBIE: So we made plans to finally meet...
"At his *house?*"
"Nah, a bar a few towns over. Just to be safe."
"Finally. All this buildup better be worth it."

Abbie sat with her hips relaxed and her knees far apart enough that she could place her laptop on the seat top, had she brought it with her. She had the window seat. The aisle seat next to her was empty. As was most of the train car she rode in. She nearly missed it at Penn Station. The rumble of the train, the periodic ringtone from the smartphone of other commuters and her thoughts entertained her on the journey. She didn't frequent Long Island often. She was from New York City. Emphasis on the city; that meant Staten Island and parts of Queens weren't graced with her presence much either. She went on a date with a smart aleck who got into it with her over the semantics of geography—you know Brooklyn is on Long Island. She knew that. But to be honest, how many claimed Long Island? It stuck out like a genital wart on the back end of New York. Last word to him. Last date with him.

Her phone buzzed in her hand. It was then she realized how tight she was clutching it. It buzzed again. She stopped staring at Josh's contact icon and answered the call.

"Hey..."

"Hey... where are you?" Josh's question came over the phone in hushed urgency.

She peered out the window looking for a station sign.

"Just got to Mineola."

"Ok that's two stops away. I'm here in the parking lot." His excitement couldn't be denied but he tried to play it cool.

"Ok, great, thanks..." She wasn't sure what to say. She still wasn't used to hearing his voice.

ABBIE: Girl what I wanted to say was, 'Just take off your clothes and wait for me in the back seat' but you know, I kept it classy.

When she ended the call there was no way to stifle her smile. The ticket collector made his way up the aisle and they locked eyes. Her mind was still on Josh but her smile beckoned the LIRR employee.

"Someone's happy to get home..."

She shook her head, "Visiting a friend."

"Well I hope they're as happy to see you."

Abbie realized he was commenting on her beaming grin. "Oh, yeah, I think so."

"So who is he?"

"A friend, I said."

"You can have more than one friend...?"

"No, thanks. He's enough."

The collector straightened up from his flirty stance with his ego bruised. He took his elbows off the back of the seat in the row in front of her. "Have a good evening."

She didn't encourage him with another word, only nodded.

Her thoughts reverted to Josh's intense gaze, which she only knew from pictures. Their meeting was a combination of a blind date and a reunion. They knew a lot about each other but had never met. They could pick one another out of a line-up but were deprived the aural stimuli of their voices. She wondered how he'd hug her, how warm his lips and tongue would be, how he'd fill her body with his. He asked her not too long ago if it was weird that he often wondered what she smelled like. Not at all, she assured him because she often thought of similar things. The sensory-deprived nature of their relationship brought to light every base yearning and keen intuition.

Over the past nine months they fell for each other through emails and texts. Replaying particular exchanges in her mind made her very aware of her pussy in the present moment. It did flips and a trickling made its way to her white cotton panties. It hit her that she hadn't shaved. It was winter and she was sporting a full fur coat. Josh liked her full fur. He'd used that visual to get him through some solo sessions. He'd seen it all—the hair, the birthmark, the flood after she's come, the pucker in the back—everything in the gynecological grade photos she'd sent him during their sexting marathons. They did enough writing as it was, and on two occasions he thought it best to show her the conclusion of said sessions with a video message. She wanted to become acquainted with his pink buddy that had a staring role in the motion pictures.

But there wouldn't be time for that tonight. Just a couple of drinks, the game... unless there was someplace they could sneak off to. They'd be on his turf so she had no clue where they could go. *Breathe, Abigail, Breathe.* You don't want your first hookup to be in the bathroom of a sports bar anyway. She read the text he'd sent, a few minutes ago, for the third time -- I'm parked in the center of the lot. A Black Jeep. I'll flash my lights.

Josh sat in his black Jeep, in the center of the parking lot, waiting, as patiently as he could. He flipped his phone -- right-side-up, upside-down, right-side-up, upside-down -- in his palm. He finally stole some time from his daily life to meet her. *Where was the fucking train?* He didn't want to waste one second. Upside-down, right-side-up. He could almost feel her sitting in the passenger seat already, looking over at him smiling *that* smile. He turned off the radio to quiet his thoughts. Right-side-up. He checked the time on his phone. Judging from where she said she was when he called, the train was pretty much on schedule that night. That was the first time her number showed up in his call log. None of their Skype dates came to fruition. He stared at his phone as the hours ticked by, working up the nerve to call her, until it became too late to call. His feelings for her terrified him. *If I talk to her, if I see her face, it'd all be too real. I can't deal.* He'd kick himself because those were nights when everyone else in the house was asleep. Her "what happened?" texts the next mornings were a punch in the gut. He felt like a disappointment. He was tempted to call her a second time to tell her to get off the train at a different stop. If they were seen together by a family friend, he'd be fucked.

He read through the last few texts she'd sent that day -- My hair's in a 'fro today. And you'll finally get to meet little red. She punctuated her text with a smiley. His thumb swiped the trackpad on his Blackberry and like the big wheel on *The Price is Right*, it landed on one of her texts from a couple of days earlier. A photo. He'd hit the jackpot. He knew which body part was in that picture text before he opened it and his pants fit tighter instantly. He imagined reaching over the parking brake and feeling the warmth of that body part through the hair...

Or entering her with only the tip, thrusting ever-so slightly teasing her until she begged for him. He leaned his head back against the headrest. After a few seconds, he turned the car radio back on, to quiet his thoughts.

The train pulled into the station and one by one, passengers made the exodus down the stairs to the parking lot and street below. Abbie followed the other passengers towards the exit.

Josh watched the newly-arrived; some greeting families at their cars, others driving off solo, some making the trek down the street deeper into the suburbs.

She was crazy to travel out to buttfuck Long Island to meet this man. But she was crazy about him.

He peered through the windshield, tapping the bottom of the steering wheel. This *would* be the night everyone wears a red jacket he thought. That one was too long. Too short. That one's too fat. Too Chinese. Then he saw her. Little Red. He understood instantly why she gave her jacket that nickname. It fit... her, her aura, her energy.

Abbie noticed how quickly everyone else found their way leaving her alone in the parking lot. *Josh couldn't work up the nerve to call me before, what's stopping him from standing me up tonight?* She suddenly felt a heavy sense of dread at being stranded in that parking lot.

Josh watched her look at her phone. When she looked up again, he could've sworn she locked eyes with him but she merely looked in his general direction. He flashed his lights and he saw the exact moment of recognition on her face.

Her walk became more focused now that she had a destination.

Josh exhaled and turned off the radio again. He rubbed his hands together and tried to warm them up by blowing on them. He climbed out the jeep and circled around to the front passenger side. Her bag bounced off her hip and he eyed her compact frame.

ABBIE: It took everything in me not to break out into a full sprint when I saw him.

He straightened his already straight coat. All the tension left his body when she flashed her infectious smile.

Her nerves made her strides shorter and her steps quicker.

JOSH: She was so cute. That hair, those legs...

It struck her that this was the first time she'd seen a full smile on his face. And it meant the world to her that he had good teeth. She couldn't wait to run her hand over his buzz cut.

He was taller than she expected. A definite plus.

Their bodies crashed together. As though they'd rehearsed this countless times before, her arms went up and around his neck and shoulders and he held her by the waist in the crook of each elbow. This was months in the making. Josh's chest heaved. Hers hoed. His shoulders were broad and strong. She perched her chin on one. She was real. He was actually holding Abbie in his arms, her hair tickling his cheek. Each kept their hands where they could be seen, in case they were seen by

anyone. It wasn't their intention to be exhibitionists. The least
amount of attention they could draw to themselves, the better.
To the outsider, it looked like two friends hugging after a long,
long time apart, just out of the beam of the streetlight.
　　　She could feel his heat radiating off of his body. As she
memorized his scent her lip grazed his neck. Josh let out a
sound so low in frequency she felt it louder than she heard it.
Her moan in response escaped her lips without thought.

ABBIE: He just kissed me.

Soft and slow.

　　　Their kisses intensified. His hand traveled up, down and
around her back. She couldn't get any higher on her tip-toes but
she tried so she could press her hips into his as he pressed
forward. Abbie's tongue slinked deeper into his mouth. She
lightly raked her fingers down the back of his head as she
sucked his lip.

JOSH: I haven't been kissed like that in forever...

　　　The last car drove out of the Seaford LIRR station
parking lot. The two remained passionately embraced and
oblivious to the world.

　　　Josh abruptly ended the kiss and let go of her. Not a
word. She was still taken with the heat of their exchange and
watched him bleary-eyed. He walked to the driver side of the
Jeep and climbed into the back seat. He opened the passenger
side door. The invitation was accepted.
　　　Abbie threw her bag over the back of the front
passenger seat and began to work her jacket off as she slammed
the door closed behind her. This must be his car, not the family
car, she thought, since there was no car seat. She barely
formulated the thought before Josh kissed her, pressing the back
of her head onto the window, flattening her hair. She pushed
back with the force of her kiss and worked her jacket all the way

off and straddled him in one motion. Her hands were cold against the skin of his chest and stomach when she slipped them under his shirt. His nipples hardened under her touch.

The rustling of their clothes and movements against the car interior,

Their breaths,

The only sounds. From across the parking lot, the two figures could barely be made out. It looked as though there was a struggle or a violent dance going on in the back of the Jeep.

Josh scooted his hips out from under hers and forced her on her back. He pulled his lips away from hers just long enough to take off his shirt. She eyed his pecs, the round of his delts, his abs. She subconsciously mirrored his physique by sucking in her stomach. She tugged at his belt buckle in haste but wasn't making any progress. He undid it himself so she focused on undoing her own clothes. Josh's jeans hung open. She reached up and ran her fingers along that spot under his belly button looking him in the eye the entire time. A smile crept onto her face. In the first photo he'd sent her, in which he wasn't wearing a shirt, she noticed that spot, under his belly button and above his "man-goods", and instantly wanted to play with it, kiss it, lick it. This was a moment of firsts, a moment of finally being able to experience all they've wanted to.

He leaned over to kiss her, one hand on the back of the seat, the other working off his jeans and underwear. Abbie reached down to touch that spot again. Her finger didn't feel the waistband of his boxer briefs so she ventured lower and there he was, firm, warm, throbbing. She raised her hips as he tugged her jeans down her legs. She worked one of her sneakers off so she could take her pants all the way off on one side.

Josh, nude from the waist down.

Abbie, in panties with her jeans around one ankle. *She remembered how much I fucking love the way she looks in white panties.*

ABBIE: He looked so fucking sexy over me like that.

JOSH: She looked up at me with that look on her face like 'fuck me already'.

Her nod was almost undetectable but Josh saw it. She was saying yes to him. Yes to all of it. He hadn't been in the back seat of a car since college. The monotony of suburban life had dulled him, but she reinvigorated him.

He used both hands and revealed more and more of her brown from under her white panties. He combed his fingers through her bush then over her lips and clit. She closed her eyes as he slipped two fingers into her, swirling them around and in and out at a delicious pace. She was ready.

Abbie held him and stroked lightly. He was ready.

He pulled his fingers out of her. She shifted her hips slightly under his for entry.

"Wait," he whispered the first word either of them had spoken.

She searched his face.

"What?" she whispered back. He changed his mind, she thought. He couldn't go through with it. Shit. Moving too fast? She let go of his bare skin... *we should use a condom...*

"Just wanna look at you." Those words sounded exactly how she heard them in her head when she read them.

He hovered over her for what felt like an eternity. He studied the coils of her hair, her smooth skin, noticed the way her eyes' focus darted back and forth to his right eye and his left. There was no turning back from the beautiful woman lying underneath him. His body twitched against her opening. The heat from her body taunted him. His arms were tense from holding himself over her.

He finally pushed into her. Her warmth surged across the base of his spine and sent a charge down the back of his legs to the soles of his feet. Neither broke their intense gaze. She fought the urge to close her eyes as he eased in deeper. The faintest gasp escaped her. They were finally skin-to-skin.

ABBIE: Definitely my puzzle piece. He fit perfectly.

He stopped when he couldn't go in any deeper. He could feel her heartbeat and a pulse around him. They both let out moans of yes and no as he began his retreat from her body. After a few thrusts, they fucked each other fast and hard, rocking the vehicle housing them.

Abbie braced her foot against the headrest of the driver side seat, using the leverage to buck her hips higher and harder. She grabbed his ass and bit his shoulder. He slowed his pace. She slowed too. He stopped.

"What?"

"Your hands... They're cold."

He couldn't be serious.

He was. He fought back a smile.

"So let me warm them up." She smiled and grabbed two handfuls of ass again. He sucked in some air sharply. All that racquetball and time on the ice really toned his ass and made it extra cute. His half-smile, half-wince let out a moan as he sunk deeper into her.

It wasn't much longer before she whispered 'Josh'. The next time Abbie said his name it came out in a longer, harsher whisper. "Josh..." she said with more force, his name shortened. The time between each utterance of his name also shortened. He pinned her wrists against the door and showed her no mercy. He also punished himself with his intensity. He rode her high and hard. *To the left*. Her thighs trembled in waves. 'Oh god', 'fuck', 'keep going', 'yes' accented the calls of his name. Her ass clenched and her insides clenched him. She arched her back then slammed it back down onto the seat.

His pace quickened.

Point of no return

"Ohhh...." Thrust. "Fuck..." In. Out. "Did you just come?" the question didn't stop his strong, deep thrusts. Her natural lube coated him, stringy remnants of it attached to both bodies.

"Yeah," she managed to say through aftershocks.

"I'm about to too..."

Josh shuddered on his first burst. She felt it flood her insides. He forgot where he was for a moment but made a quick enough retreat to decorate her pubes, inner thighs, his hands and shaft.

He gave himself two last milking strokes, his stomach quivering; Abbie ran her fingers down his center and onto his thigh. He looked up from studying the mess he made and right into her eyes. She brought her knees together against his ribs and squeezed. He smiled. She winked and bit her bottom lip.
He carefully reached his upper body between the two front seats. He opened the glove box and took out a pack of baby wipes. He only had one clean hand so she opened the pack and took out the first wipe, handing it to him. She sat up to clean herself off. Josh remained kneeling. As he wiped his hands, Abbie held a balled-up baby wipe to her inner thigh but was too busy staring at Josh to give herself a proper cleaning. His hands slowed. Next thing they knew they were lips-to-lips again.

Abbie gripped Josh by the cheek and ear. His hand was on her lower back after trailing down her breasts and around her waist. Next thing they knew they were horizontal again.

Josh came up for air. "We gotta get dressed."

"Yeah, for real this time."

He started up the Jeep. Music from the radio filled the vehicle cabin. He rubbed his hands together then cupped them over his mouth and nose and blew on them to warm them. He bent the fingers of his right hand under his nostrils and inhaled Abbie. There was a twitch in his pants.

Abbie climbed in the front passenger side and closed the door. She extended her hand. It took him a split second but he played along and shook her hand, firmly, and she loved it. This was a man who had her yearning for his strong fingers with short, clean fingernails that held his phone when he took selfies in the mirror.

"Hi Josh, I'm Abigail. Nice to meet you." She was beaming.

"Hi. It's nice to meet you too. I hope it's ok but I'm gonna call you 'Abbie'."

She nodded and began to fluff her hair. "Excuse the hair. This dude just gave it to me *good* in the back seat of his car."

"Oh yeah?" He dug for the truth with his question.

Her eyes widened. "*Oh yeah...*" Afterglow was truth serum.

"Lucky you."

"Lucky dude."

They smiled at each other. Josh stepped on the gas.

"So where are we going?"

"There's this great bar, about 5 minutes from here. They have about 20 screens, they're huge. Comfy booths. Lots of beer."

"Heineken?"

Josh belched a sound of disgust. "I don't know how anyone can drink that piss."

"Some could say the same about Oban," she taunted with a smile. She watched him sidelong waiting for his response.

The bass and drums of Exile came on the radio. "Yo, this is some crazy timing that this song would come on now." It wasn't officially their song but the bridge and chorus summed up the past few months between them. She shook her head in amazement at the synchronicity. These sorts of coincidences never got old to her. She was hoping this would never get old. It felt easy being with him.

Abbie began to sing along in a false baritone:

...gonna wrap my arms around you, hold you close to me, oh babe I wanna taste your lips, wanna fill your fantasy...

She was real. She was real, Josh kept thinking to himself. She belonged in that seat next to him being silly and singing in fake voices. If she could be with him all the time, he'd have no complaints. They'd talk and laugh and learn and do more of what they just did in his back seat. But that wasn't reality. In the morning he'd be back to babysitter drop-offs, rush hour commutes to and from work and terse conversations at the dinner table.

After he pulled into the parking lot of the sports bar and cut the engine, the silence enveloped them. Abbie turned her hand palm-side-up and laid it across the arm rest between them. Josh put his hand on hers and they interlocked fingers. Their silence was loud and comfortable.

"It started already?"

He nodded. "But we didn't miss much. They're still in the first period."

Silence

Josh squeezed her hand...the way he squeezed her breast. Abbie squeezed his hand in response...the way she squeezed his butt.

"We should probably go in, right?

"Yeah, I guess." Josh conceded.

Neither of them moved.

"If we stay in this car, you know what's gonna happen."

"Yeah..."

He let go of Abbie's hand and rubbed her cheek with the back of his finger. She touched Josh's thigh. His fingers traveled under Abbie's ear and behind her neck. She rubbed her hand higher and higher on Josh's thigh.

They made eye contact.

Their eyes widened.

Gotta go. Yeah, we should get outta here.

They made a quick exit out of his Jeep and headed towards the bar. Josh walked slightly ahead of her and she watched his hockey-toned butt. He opened the door and held it for her. The loud din of the bar crowd and the signature *eau de sports pub* spilled out. He checked out her ass as she slunk by him.

Abbie clapped rhythmically as she entered the establishment. "Let's Go, Rangers!"

* * *

Touchdown

"In your fucking face!" Karin parades around the living room doing her victory dance taunting her belittled husband at the final whistle. The home team, "her boys" as she likes to call them have just defeated their arch rivals, her "husband's team".

Willie could never stay angry with his wife, not while she shook her ass like that – his team could lose every week. She reverts back to her cheerleading ways from Grambling, high kicking all over the room. Moments like this took him back to his college days, lusting after his Bonita Applebum. Now secure in adulthood, he could boast that he'd won. He's the one with the hot wife... or a "Hot Thing" as Talib Kweli puts it. He tries to catch glimpses of her pussy through the space between her thigh and the leg opening of her shorts. The terry cloth sticks between her ass cheeks, emphasizing her onion booty as she pops her hips back and forth.

Their teenage son can only look on with adolescent derision when he comes to the living room. Every week during football season and he's still not amused. He watches his mother celebrate as she holds the waist of a bent-over imaginary partner. "Take-that-mother-fuckers!" She emphasizes each word with a thrust of her hips. She turns to her son. "And I don't ever wanna hear you use those words." Her husband, on the other hand, is encouraged to use those words. Willie gets carried away during sex sometimes and talks to Karin like she's turning a trick. The words he spits and his grunts turn her on, making her soak the sheets on some nights.

"And you can add this," she strips off her Number 14

football jersey revealing her baby tee underneath, "to the mountains of laundry you'll be doing for the next three months." She throws the jersey at Willie. "Ruin it, and die."

Abdul Kelly, Number 14, wraps his arm around Banks' shoulders, Number 82. Asses are being slapped by open palms or helmets that have been removed. Wet, manly kisses are planted on foreheads, cheeks and full-on the lips during the post-game celebration, all which are sticky from sweat or sports drink. The field is hectic with reporters and photographers jockeying for position in front of the quarterback, head coach, kicker, wide receiver and tight end, Kelly and Banks, respectively. "This dude right here... I gotta thank him. He's an amazing tight end. And when the quarterback wasn't tryna get the ball into his hands," Abdul puts his other hand on Banks' chest, "I got some great blocks from him."

"Yes, the season is only half way through, but I'm sure sports enthusiasts are going to be talking about that catch you made at the end of the fourth quarter for years to come," the sports reporter recaps. She has the stoic sex appeal of Angie Harmon, certainly hired by the network and granted access by the league for her looks and brains...and looks.

"Exactly! Both of us were in double coverage but somehow he was able to draw the corner and safety off me so I could go up for the catch! Brilliant." Abdul flashes a million-dollar contract smile at Banks and then at the camera.

The sports reporter turns to the camera to wrap up the interview. Abdul uses that opportunity to survey her backside.

"Yo, thanks for the shout," Banks says once they're no longer on the air.

"Man, listen, we teammates. You know what I'm saying? And I meant what I said. If it wasn't for you, I wouldna got the numbers I got today." Abdul pats him on the chest once more then turns to walk into the locker room only to be stopped by another broadcast team in the media gauntlet.

They eventually make it to the locker room. Teammates are lobbing cheers at Abdul when the coach approaches him. "We embarrassed those fuckers! They making you look like a star!"

"Play-OOOFFFS!" Abdul's battle cry starts a call and response in the locker room.

The coach tries to reign in the excitement. "We still have 8 more games to—"

"We going to the playoffs, then to the motherfucking Superbowl, my nigga!"

The white coach, ten years past middle age, grabs Abdul in an enthusiastic congratulatory hug. He acknowledges Banks with a smile and pat on the shoulder. "Great job out there today... protected our guy. Great job."

The euphoria mixed with testosterone in the locker room is palpable. Abdul strips off his Number 14 jersey. Many of the football players are half or completely naked, sweat beading on their skin, jock straps cupping ass cheeks of some players, and on other players, dicks and balls reacting to gravity, the excitement of the game or the sight of their teammates. They're male thoroughbreds with badonkadonks. Abdul joins the ranks of the completely nude. He doesn't show off in the locker room as much as he does on the field, he lets his proportions speak for him. He heads to the showers wrapping a towel around his waist midway through his cock-strut across the locker room. Banks watches him, memorizing his muscles and movements. His preference is known to most of the players and they notice that he's looking at Abdul longer than is acceptable to the extremely macho, pussy-bounding members of the team.

The dryer tumbles a load of whites and there's a pile of clothes in the laundry basket to be folded. Willie loads dirty clothes into the washing machine. Among the clothes is the pair of panties his wife wore on their night out on the town earlier in the week. It's her favorite pair – sheer black panties. She always wears those when she's really feeling herself. They sit low on her waist but cover her ass without being granny panties. Much of that night out is fuzzy to him thanks to the Hennessy but he has memories of taking those panties off of her when they got home. Karin was especially eager with the head she gave him that night; he had no choice but to give it to her good. His dick stiffens while he's reliving the night in his mind.

His favorite pair of Karin's panties is in the load of laundry too—a red lacy boy short. The bottom of her ass cheeks hang out and the lace just makes it pretty. He has to use so much self-control when he sees her in them because all he wants to do is rip them off her and fuck her when she's wearing them but he loves the way they look on her. He even likes the way they feel against his lips and tongue when he eats her out while she's still wearing them, "taste testing" as they like to call it. He's always extra careful not to snag any of the lace when he's taking them off her with his teeth. Willie holds up the red panties and studies them before sniffing them.

"This is supposed to be punishment for you. Stop sniffing my goodies."

He looks over his shoulder at her, half-embarrassed but shrugs it off, "You caught me." He throws them in the washing machine.

She shakes her finger at him pretending to scold him. She grabs a towel out the laundry basket, twirls it and towel snaps him across the ass. Karin would blend in seamlessly in the boy's locker room. All the trash talking and ribbing—she can dish it out with the best of them.

"What'd you do? Come in here to abuse me?" Willie asks.

She rubs his ass, "Aww, poor baby... Did I hurt your booty?" she pouts.

"Quit it..."

"Does your booty hurt?" She pokes her finger into his butt crack.

"Stop." She's hit a sore spot with her husband. He's a member of Team No Homo So Don't Touch My Butthole. The one time they got carried away and Karin was able to get a few licks in back there still haunts him because it felt so good he couldn't contain himself. It was his wife doing it, but it was his ass. He couldn't reconcile the two.

She holds her hands up in mock surrender. Willie continues to load the washing machine and she wraps her arms around him from behind, presses her face to his back and inhales deeply. "I love the way you smell too..." She inhales again. "I wanna sleep in this shirt tonight."

He turns the machine on and water pours in. He reaches for the detergent; she lowers her hands and reaches for his dick. He adds detergent to the load and closes the machine. She slips in front of him and hops onto the washing machine.

"Got about twenty minutes before this enters the good part..." Karin's eyes bug out and she shakes her body like she's being electrocuted, "the rinse cycle." She slides forward and spreads her legs tugging on his t-shirt. "We've had some fun on this machine."

"Yeah, and we busted up the other three." The contour of Willie's dick is visible under his sweatpants. He slips his hand into the leg of her shorts and finds her clit nuzzled between her cushiony lips. Her involuntary moans mean he's touching it right. She leans back on her elbows and opens her legs wider allowing him easier access. His fingers slip right into Karin's snug pussy. She pulls the leg of her shorts aside so she can watch her husband's fingers dip in and out of her. When he pulls them out her natural lube forms a bridge between his fingers that sags when he spreads his fingers slowly.

He goes back in and is turned on even more at the sight of his hand up against his wife's body, only one finger pointing back at him. Her fleshy fragrance mixes with the mountain breeze detergent and her juice acts as fabric softener for the seat of her shorts. She sighs when Willie thumbs her clit over and over. She's almost flat on her back, her hips hanging off the front of the washing machine. Perfect position for a repeat performance of the last time they rode the machine. Her calves rested against his shoulders, he held her hips and her lower back was sore for days. All for a good cause, they agreed.

Karin uses her toes to climb his thigh and curls them around his dick. She rolls her foot back and forth and when a small wet spot forms on his sweatpants she sits up and pushes the band of his sweatpants down. His cut, brown-on-the-top browner-on-the-bottom dick makes an appearance.

"I want your penis in my pussy," she sing-songs, popping each "p" sound with extra emphasis. The "fuck me now" demand is in her eyes. She serves herself to him, leaning back and pushing her shorts to the side.

"Ma? Dad?" Willie pulls his sweatpants back up. She hops off the washing machine and grabs a shirt from the laundry basket and starts folding it. They roll their eyes at each other. "He has *got* to go away to school soon."

Their son appears at the door of the laundry room. "Hey, I'm going out for a ride with Luis. I'll be back." The words come out sounding like 'Ah be back' thanks to his teenage tongue.

"You better be home before me." She hands him the shirt she just folded.

"Yeah, yeah. I'll be home." He rushes out.

Banks and Abdul soak in adjacent ice baths in the training room. The players' wet brown skin is a stark contrast against the chrome of the tubs, the lucidity of the ice and white tile of the room under the fluorescent light. Abdul has the complexion of a creamy milk chocolate at a melt-in-your-mouth temperature. Banks' skin color matches the dark brown of aromatic Blue Mountain coffee beans. Their toned arms hang limp over the edge of their tubs. The high of the game is wearing off their worn muscles.

"So what you getting into tonight?" Banks asks.

"Hopefully I'm getting into some honeys, nah mean?" he laughs. "It's why I love home games. I get it *in!*" Abdul's expression makes no secret of his thoughts of sugar plum pussies and apple bottoms, two things Banks has no interest in. But he'd love to put that same satisfied smile on Abdul's face himself.

Another player finishes up with his treatment and walks past Abdul. "I'm getting outta here now. You good, man?" He asks Abdul while eyeing Banks.

"Yeah, I'm cool. I'm hurting a bit today."

"Aight..." He's reluctant to leave the two men alone. Banks reaches out and caresses Abdul's arm. He looks their teammate dead in the eye and blows a kiss at him. The player swallows his anger and rushes out the training room.

"You ain't even right for that," Abdul smiles.

"You saw how dude was grilling me."

"And you just had to fuck with his head like that?"

Banks merely shrugs off his actions. "I've never pushed up on him. I don't know what he's so concerned about."

"You know how it is, they around a gay nigga and they think he's gonna wanna fuck or some shit."

"And how stupid is that?" Abdul doesn't answer. "Besides it's all in how they look at me or how much eye contact I get before they look away. Believe me, I know who I can get on the team." Banks takes his hand off Abdul's arm finally.

"Word? Who?"

Banks shakes his head 'no'. He has no intention of spilling to Abdul which of their teammates' ass is furry and warm. "I like to deal with men who like men. Let's just leave it at that."

Abdul sinks lower into the ice bath, taking his arms with him under the water, resting his head on the edge of the tub and letting the ice water slosh around his chin. "I hear what you're saying but I'm telling you straight dudes don't be thinking that way," he says with his eyes closed.

"I fall into that thinking sometimes too. Just because I can. I mean in general, folks mess with gay men or homophobes... and I'm talking about gay or straight on both sides. Men mess with each other. It's all about power. Being gay kinda gives me something over them."

Abdul opens his eye closest to Banks at the sound of the word 'power'. "That shit's about power?"

"No doubt. Got nothing to do with sex."

Abdul sits with what Banks just said. "You ever had sex with a chick?"

"I haven't." He answers like he's at a deposition.

"You ain't never been in a pussy..." Abdul trails off into incredulity.

"I've always been attracted to men. Of course, growing up, I knew that men had sex with women. But I never wanted to."

"That... wow. I was gonna ask if like fucking a dude's ass feels like a pussy but you can't tell me."

"No. I can just tell you that," Banks dons his best Abdul voice, "fucking a dude's ass feels amazing."

Banks' imitation is completely lost on him because his mind is on backdoor loving. "All ass probably feels the same..." Abdul's mind is miles away.

"You've had anal sex with women?" It's more confirmation than question from Banks.

"What? Been in booty balls deep, my nigga!" his trademark gleeful grin returns.

Banks shakes his head. "So yeah, I guess *you* got something to compare it to." Banks rises from the ice bath, his movement slowed by the cold and the aches and pains. The water cascades off his body. His Under Armour shorts live up to its second skin reputation. Banks sports a bulge that's bigger than you'd expect after being submerged in ice cold water.

"You done?" Abdul blurts out. Shit, it was too late to take back sounding like a thirsty nigga.

"Contrast bath. Maybe..." he smiles. The temptation to skip treatment and go to sleep in their own beds was always strong after home games. Banks steps out the tub and stands in the space between the two. "How much longer you got?"

"I think like ten more minutes but I might stay longer." he fidgets in the tub. "I can still feel this knot in my neck," he stretches to one side and hangs his arm out the tub again, "and this arm still ain't strong again."

"You got hit hard today? Sounds like a stinger."

"I don't know. Probably. You know how we don't feel shit till like a week later." Abdul continues to slosh around like a fussy infant.

"Let me check it out." Banks stoops next to Abdul's tub his thighs spreading out as they rest on his bulbous calves. Water drips from the ends of his body – knees, heels, seat – to the tiles. He presses his fingers into Abdul's delts, feels around on his traps and down on to his rhomboids.

"What you know about this?" Abdul challenges. "You read books about this?"

"Sure did. And I'm always asking the trainers to explain what they're doing when I get treatment." Abdul flinches. "Right there?"

"Dude..." substitutes for 'yes that fucking hurts'.

Banks takes Abdul's arm closest to him and manipulates it into different positions and gets his answers from Abdul's low frequency whimpers. He places his hand on his teammate's head and pushes it down slowly so his chin is pointing towards his shoulder, exposing Abdul's strong neck that's begging to be sucked. "Feel that down in there?" Banks presses on a spot on Abdul's back.

"Yeah..." he moans, "right there..."

He releases his now patient's arm and it absentmindedly rests on his lap, his fingertips a fingertip away from Bank's crotch. He palpates various spots on Abdul's pecs using the pads of his four fingers. He feels around some more on his back until Abdul flinches again.

"Spasm. Right there. Gotta work on getting that out. You should def get some heat on that."

Banks, who should be on his way to the warm soak, doesn't move, remaining at eye level with Abdul. The result of a stare down like this is usually a fight or a fuck. Fucks are often on Abdul's mind.

"Does it hurt anywhere else?" Banks challenges Abdul to tell him about his sore groin.

Abdul's gaze is promising while he takes inventory of his bumps and bruises. "Nah, just my back." Banks nods. "You could keep working on that?"

"Sure." Banks shifts closer to the tub for more leverage.

Abdul half opens his mouth to say something then shakes the thought out of his head.

"What, nah, say what you want to say."

"I wanna ask you something... about... you know... gay sex."

"Ask me. If it's something I don't want to answer, I won't."

"Bet. So... like only one dude gets off? Or you gotta jerk dude off while you fucking him? Or you gotta switch off getting it up the ass?"

Banks chuckles softly at Abdul's ignorance. "Dude who's getting fucked, the bottom, he comes too. He can jerk off if that's what he likes. But you can get off without even touching your dick. Hit that spot right and it's a wrap."

"Hold up," he flinches as Banks hits his sore spot on his back but quickly regains his focus, "You can fuck a dude in his ass and it makes him come?"

"Best fucking nut he's ever had."

Abdul sits up straight in the tub so quickly a few ice cubes spill out of the tub. His chest and shoulders are heaving from the cold and the excitement. The pulse at the base of his dick this time is stronger than the one when he was talking about fucking pussy. He's looking at Banks, expecting a 'psych!' that Banks never delivers. "That's fucking insane."

"And incredible. It's the P-spot. Like a woman's G-spot." Before Abdul can even grill him on how he knows about the G-spot, "Yes, I know about the G-spot. I read books."

"You really are a nerd nigga."

The teammates laugh heartily breaking the air of adolescent sexual curiosity. Their faces are so close together they can feel the heat of the others' breath. There's more than water slicking the inside of Banks' shorts. The silence following the outburst punctuates the sexual thoughts on each man's mind.

"You ever turned a dude?" Abdul asks.

Banks stop the work he's doing on Abdul's back. "You thinking about getting fucked in the ass, ain't you?"

"My dude, the best fucking nut in my life?" he huffs. "Yeah, I'm thinking about that!"

The smell of Biofreeze, hydrocollator water, and wet towels slaps the coach in the face when he enters the training room. His view is of Banks stooping with his arm behind Abdul. The top of Abdul's head can be seen but his face is eclipsed by the back of Bank's head.

"Everything OK in here?" The coach's jaw muscle twitches at the discomfort of walking in on his star player alone with Banks, wet and practically naked. Banks takes his hand off Abdul's body and stands, now blocking the coach's view of

Abdul with his bubble butt. Abdul has a full view of Banks'
body for appraisal. He alternates his gaze between the eyes and
crotch of Banks, who mercifully doesn't call him out on it.

"Everything's good, Coach." Abdul answers from the
tub. As Banks walks away from the tubs, Coach notices Abdul
scanning his teammate's body.

"Is there something I should know?" Coach asks. Banks
walks out of the training room flashing, for the first time, a
predatory smile.

"Nah. Why you ask that?" Abdul counters.

"Um, babe, you *gotta* come see this..." Willie sits in "the
throne", his oversized armchair that is placed at the optimal
viewing distance from the television. Karin comes to the family
room from the kitchen, drying her hands with a dish towel. She
takes a seat on the arm of the throne.

On the television there's footage shot from a distance of
Banks and Abdul leaving the arena via the player's entrance.
Both athletes are dressed in designer suits that are mandatory
for travel. The silk drapes over their bodies like butter. There is
a slight pull across the shoulders when they give one another a
bro-hug. The sportscaster insinuates meaning to the bro-hug,
questioning why the two men were just leaving the arena when
all the other members of the team had long since gone home
and perhaps this is the reason the city's beloved Abdul Kelly
was the perpetual bachelor. The only thing missing from her
report was the *um-hum* and the neck roll.

"Your boys dipping like that?"

"He can't be gay!" Karin's mouth hangs open.

"Look at dude though..."

The news report was rerunning the footage of the men
leaving the stadium and bro-hugging. The footage cut to a
screenshot, zoomed in on the video. The focus was the grainy
image of the men's heads while speculating if they were in a lip
lock too.

"It looks like they're kissing to me," Willie taunts Karin
but is also drawn in to the report. The circumstantial evidence
mounts.

"Nope, can't be." Karin shakes her head vehemently. Willie rubs her back to soothe her. Her rage causes her scent of vanilla and the citrus dishwashing liquid to radiate off her body. He can still smell her arousal from earlier on.

Now the footage on the screen is a freeze frame of the two football players from right after the game when Abdul gave props to Banks. His arm is around Banks' shoulders and his other hand is on his chest. What was a split-second smile of gratitude now reads of the loving adoration of post-coital bliss the longer the image remains on the screen.

"Yo, I wouldn't be surprised if they were a lot of DL dudes in the league. And cause of what happened with Sam, they probably gonna wanna stay in the closet so they don't get cut from their teams."

"He's not on the down low." She glares at the television screen.

"Looks like Abdul is playing for *that* team to me. Banks is probably recruiting!" Willie jabs Karin with a chuckle. She shoots death rays at him with her eyes. Abdul is known for sampling and displaying his new flavor of the month. Banks' sexuality was never a secret from the public but he didn't swordfight in public either.

The sportscaster's report quickly devolves into a TMZ parody. "Perhaps number 14 and 82 are turning their 96 into a 69." The original footage of the men leaving the stadium and hugging is replayed on the screen. Karin huffs and puffs from the arm of the chair.

Willie runs his finger along the path he loves to run his tongue – down her back and into the back of her shorts. Karin stands and swats his hand away with the dish towel. "You were ready to throw down when I was doing laundry a minute ago..."

"I lost my appetite for that."

"Why, cause of this?" he motions at the television with the remote. She rolls her eyes. "What does it matter if he's gay, you still have a winning record."

"Seven and one..." she boasts.

"Right. So who cares if he's DL or whatever." Her annoyance returns and she walks away. "Hey! Where you going?" he calls after her. No answer from the kitchen. "We all have secrets, babe." Willie hears the water in the kitchen sink running.

Once he's done flipping through all the channels and feasting on the media frenzy of the Banks-Abdul gay scandal, he joins Karin in the kitchen.

"Book club tonight?" Willie asks.

"Yeah, book club," she stresses the words acknowledging the non-secret. "You know damn well we just sit around drinking wine talking about sex." The women of the book club are known for comparing notes on their one-hit wonders and marathon men.

"I'm shocked," Willie feigns disbelief. She smiles. "What do you tell them about me?"

She raises an eyebrow, "I look like I kiss and tell?" She rinses the soap off a plate and places it in the dish rack. "I would never kiss and tell how good your dick is. I gotta keep that to myself."

"So we don't share in this house?"

"No we don't..." Naughty is written all over her face.

The mirror in the master bathroom is foggy as it usually is on a Sunday evening. Karin does her beautification routine to make sure her black don't crack.

Willie enters carrying a cordless phone. "Babe, Joyce said she's running to the store to pick up some ice cream. But she should be back home by the time you guys start coming over."

Among the girls of the book club, ice cream is code for sex. Karin knows Joyce is getting hers right quick this Sunday night. The tight knit group of women is mainly old friends from high school or Deltas from college. Joyce has been doing her dirt for so long she didn't know if her husband or her side piece was the father of her kids.

"Ok," Karin answers over the sound of shower. "When you're done on the phone, can you come back in here?"

"Sure," he says to the curtain.

Karin places her foot on the inside edge of the tub and

shaves her leg. She makes sure she's completely smooth below the knee and maneuvers over the bend of her knee. The razor travels lithely up the curve of her thigh right to her crease.

"I'm done. What's up?" Willie asks from the bathroom door.

She pokes her head from behind the shower curtain. "I need a little help." Karin moves the curtain aside and holds up the razor. "In case I missed anything..."

Willie smiles and takes the razor from her. "Sit."

She sits at the very edge of the tub and spreads her legs. He squeezes some of her liquid soap into his hand and lathers up her 3 week old bush. He deftly removes the hair from her mound in four passes of the razor. He rinses the hairs out of the blades under the shower stream. He cups his hand over her pussy, flattening the lip so he can carefully remove all the hair from the crease. As he slowly reveals her smooth pussy, the glide of the razor turns her on and watching her husband with his intense gaze directed at her body is arousing.

His strong hands take extra care with her most delicate of parts. Willie uses soap suds and her slippery juice to lubricate his shave as he cleans up the area at the bottom of her lips and around her asshole. He runs his finger slowly up and down each lip making sure he's left a smooth finish. He can't resist her pink wet hole and sticks the tip of his finger in, pulling it out slowly and watching the sticky trail of Karin's juice connecting his finger to her pussy. He raises his finger until the "rope" breaks. He stands and takes the shower massager off the hook and rinses her off.

Willie runs his fingers along her pussy, admiring his handiwork. "Good enough to eat." She raises her eyebrow asking with her eyes, "Am I gonna get it?" He waves the shower massager spraying her with water. "Later..." he says. Karin looks like the fat kid who didn't get a piece of pie. "Come straight home after book club and you'll get the rest." The couple lived for this sort of prolonged foreplay.

In the bedroom, Willie enjoys one of his favorite pastimes – watching Karin rub cocoa butter all over her body. He has convinced himself that it makes her skin browner, like she's actually spreading cocoa on her skin, which only makes him want lick and suck her Hershey kiss titties.

"Hey, babe, wear these tonight," he holds up the red lacy boy shorts he loves.

She shrugs and walks over to him, "Aight, I was gonna wear my sexy black ones but..." she holds onto his shoulder for balance and steps into the panties. He slowly pulls them up, making sure they sit just right on her body.

Karin sits demurely in the back of a town car after a skillful wardrobe change nearly half an hour later. The driver stands at the back passenger door. Her pencil skirt reaches mid-thigh. She's not wearing any stockings, showing off her freshly shaven legs and her pedicure visible in her peep-toe pumps adds an extra hint of femininity to her appearance. Her blouse is buttoned up to the third button. Just the right amount of cleavage peeks out. She could easily pass for a reporter who dressed nicely because she could afford to and because she had to maintain her woman status in the boy's club...all while wearing red lace boy shorts.

The driver opens the back door and Abdul climbs in. The driver closes the door behind him.

"Great game today," she coos shifting her body so her knees point towards his muscular thighs.

"And you came here to tell me that in person?" he asks. His frame fills his half of the back seat. "That's some impressive PR work."

"You know I'll always be your number one cheerleader." She puts on her 'let's be serious' expression. "We gotta talk about you and Banks."

"You don't believe that shit do you? I just spent like an hour with Coach trying to convince him. I don't know why niggas was even out there waiting for us like that!" The future ramification of the scandal aggravates Abdul and his voice raises a few decibels but Karin doesn't flinch.

"You just had an amazing game. Of course they're gonna hang around looking for a story. That's the way shit works. And you just hand-fed them this one. It's more believable that *you'd* be on the DL. The media would never spin it that *you* were trying to *convert* Banks. That's not PC."

Abdul's short, bassy chuckle fills the car. "That nigga is *gay*."

"Right. And *you're* the team. You. Outside of the quarterback, you're *it*." He sinks into the truth of her words. "And everyone likes you – men and women." Abdul's rage returns. He's not trying to hear about how men want him. She gives him a reassuring rub on his thigh. "Not like that... I mean the quarterback is married, two kids... he even has a dog. But you're the successful bachelor. Men wanna be your best buddy, party with you, wingman you, and women just fucking *want* you. Hard truth is, if you're gay, all that goes away."

Abdul's eyes fall to her hand on his thigh. She removes her hand after one last caress. He gazes out the window. "So I could hold a press conference..."

"I don't know if that's gonna do anything... This thing is on *all* the networks." He turns his face to her with eyes wide. She answers with a sista girl nod. "And the memes are crazy..."

"Word?"

"...all over Instagram, Twitter and Tumblr..."

"Damn. Now I know how Drake feels."

"The only time you need to be linked to Banks is on the field. Don't stop doing what you're doing during games. You're a star there. We need you to be Number 14. Off the field, we gotta get you a girl. And you two need to be booed up in public for like the next six months."

"And what are you gonna do?"

"I guess I'll just have to fuck my husband," she winks.

In one motion he kisses Karin and slips his hand under her skirt. They kiss each other wildly. He pulls Willie's favorite pair of panties down around her knees. They stop kissing just long enough so he can take her panties off all the way. He puts them on his face and takes a long drawn out inhale of laundry detergent and Karin's scent while she opens his pants and whips out his dick. She runs her tongue up the underside of it, wraps her tongue around the head and hits the top of his dick with the back of her throat.

Abdul opens his window and signals to the driver over the top of the car. The driver climbs in and gets settled behind the steering wheel. They make eye contact through the rear view mirror and Abdul nods. Karin is skillful with the pleasure she gives Abdul while the car navigates the gravel by the new stadium construction site.

He reaches over her back and pulls up her skirt. He slaps her hard on the ass. "Come here..."

She steals a few more sucks before she straddles him with her skirt hiked up. She wraps her fingers around him, holding him in place so she can slide down onto him. It doesn't take long before they get into a serious jungle sex rhythm.

"Wait, wait, shh..." He points to his Bluetooth. "Hey, yeah dude, we headed to the hotel right now..." He makes eye contact with Karin, "You wanna party tonight?" She bites her bottom lip and does a quick calculation in her head – it should take Joyce about an hour to get ice cream and the book club meeting lasts about three hours. There was enough time to party. She nods and leans in to suck his neck. "Yeah, she's down...aight, meet us at the hotel."

Abdul and Karin walk into the hotel like they own the place.

"Good evening, Mr. Holder. Great to see you and the missus again," he types on the hotel registration POS, "Your room's already been turned down for you," and hands him the key card and winks.

"Thank you."

While they're waiting for the elevator, he takes a red ball of lace out of his pocket and passes it to her. "You might wanna put those back on."

Karin slinks out of the bathroom in the opulent penthouse like a video vixen, decked out in her bra and panties and pumps. Her jaw drops likes she's just seen a ghost. She loses her confident strut, tripping over her own feet and nearly breaks her ankle. She stops dead in her tracks.

"Look at those pretty red panties," Willie says, lounging on the bed with his back against the headboard and his legs crossed at the ankles. "My favorite..." She turns to escape but

Abdul is over to her in three bounds and blocks her way like a fullback. She pleads with him with tear-filled eyes. Willie climbs off the bed and stands behind her.

"Thought you wanted to party," Abdul squeezes her tit and spins her around to face Willie, making sure she stays put with an aggressive slap to her ass.

Willie stoops in front of his wife. Usually when he assumes that position in front of her it's the prelude to ecstasy. Now there's malice in his eyes despite his smile. Where she'd usually cradle the back of his head, she's scared stiff, her arms frozen by her sides. Tears stream down Karin's face.

He pulls down the front of her panties. "Yo, check this out, dude," Abdul peers over her shoulder at the front of her body while Willie runs his fingers over her bald bikini area, "I hooked her up just the way you like it, dawg."

* * *

Keep Me Warm

The makeshift ashtray was almost full. Cigarette butts and ashes mingled like brown limbs and kinky hair. He puffed away, tapping his cigarette into the heap in the ashtray. He stared out the window, his gaze fixed miles away through the snow that blanketed the city.

My gaze was fixed on him. There was no telling when I'd see him again. And the sight of him always quickened my pulse rate, heating me from the inside.

We sat together in the family room, the old metal radiators clanging. His powerful thighs sat apart. The live bulge between them emanated heat, an invitation. I wanted to strip him bare. He threw his head back and blew out a plume of smoke.

I longed to kiss his lips yet my mouth landed on his powerful neck. The vibration from his throaty sigh buzzed against my lips. I loved his flavor. The scent of cigarettes mingled with his testosterone. His beard tickled my upper lip and his fingers tickled the small of my back. He made me feel so safe in his masculine hands. I wanted to take my time with him but I ripped off his clothes. He had unbelievably smooth brown skin I could feel just by staring at it.

My eyes traveled up his thighs to where he saluted me thick and strong. I wanted to spread him out across my bed and please him for hours, he wouldn't let me. He was focused on my body and my pleasure. He licked me from all angles, joined with me in all positions.

The snow swallowed my echoes. He placed me on my back and I lay waiting for him with my thighs parted, wanting to taste the wet cream I left in his beard. When he entered me we dared each other to make it good. I grabbed his ass and the feel of his muscles powering his thrusts made me wetter.

His powerful body carried his powerful personality. His voice penetrated my ear demanding to know if I approved of his dick, his touch, the way he savored me with his mouth and dived into me with his fingers. He whispered in my ear that we'd never wait so long to lie together again. I clawed at the soft wool on his head and responded with deep kisses that made my pussy leave wet kisses on his dick.

He displayed his dominion over me and withdrew just long enough to make me beg for it. I didn't close my eyes and lose myself in the sensations as I have with past lovers. When he pierced by body again, I spread my knees so I could watch his broad chest and abs. I loved to watch him. He looked amazing dancing deep inside me. So powerful, holding up my legs, bending me in half so I leave footprints on the wall over my head.

He stretched my wet pussy with his thick dick. I could feel his throbbing through every inch of my insides, in my back, in my toes. I reached down to rub my clit. He let out an appreciative sound and slowed his stroke so he could enjoy the view. He was using his body to help recreate my moments of self-pleasure.

His moans were deep, timed to the tugging from my pussy as he slid out right to the head. My knees opened wider, pressure built up; my pussy got tighter pushing him out. I quaked. The feeling was unbelievable as he forced his way back in along my fault line.

I came around him and I could feel the early waves of his orgasm. I put all my trust in him that he would pull out in time. And he decorated my face and breasts with his release. His body jerked as the last of it oozed out of him. I sucked the rest of the juice out of his body until he stopped me. He remained on his knees rolling and stretching his neck. His sculpted shoulders and arms slowly relaxed. He claimed his territory over me with his knees on either side of my hips. I scanned his body at the speed of REM. This wasn't a dream.

* * *

Puppy Love

There weren't enough hours in the day for me to stay in the shower. I used some of Amari's body wash for my first rinse. I was abusing my skin with water that was too hot and with the lather, rinse, repeat. But I still felt so dirty. For my second sudsing, I used his Black soap. That would explain his flawless skin. I lost myself at moments but my overzealous sucking and raking fingernails didn't leave a mark on him. The stains the soap left on the tile of the shower stall were eerily similar to streaks of mascara-stained tears.

I could barely make out my outline in the fogged mirror. The ceiling and walls were damp from the humidity. In my haste to get away from him, I left my clothes in the bedroom. I finally crept out the bathroom. He had spread my clothes out on the bed. I could tell he probably even shook them out for me, picking off any lint too. I'd also forgotten to ask for a towel when I hightailed it to the shower. He had one waiting for me when I eased into the room. It was fluffy and smelled laundry fresh.

Amari offered to dry the spot on my back where droplets remained and to apply lotion to my body again. I lied and said I was allergic to that brand. Petroleum or dimethicone or hydroxy-whatever. He hadn't put on any clothes. I wanted to study his body again but I resisted. The thought of laying my eyes on his chest, muscular thighs and dreadlocks draped over his shoulders sent a surge of blood to my clit. He held my panties so I could step into them. I tried to convince myself that only young boys do stuff like that thinking that's what women like. Yes, I really liked that he did it. I really liked the care, the intimacy but it wasn't...right.

"That... that was really great," Amari said.

"Of course it was." That came out with an arrogant sting I didn't intend. I just couldn't imagine he'd been with women of my experience before. "Sorry, I'm not good at modesty."

He smiled. And his age shone through. "You know, I was thinking, when you were in the shower," yeah, I was in there a long time, "I think we should be together," he declared.

I just stood with my hand up my butt. I ran the gamut of shock, confusion and then annoyance. "Why? What makes you think we should be together?"

He got off the bed and stood in front of me. I kept my eyes above his waist. "Two people don't have that kinda fun together unless—"

"Don't say it," I interrupted.

"...unless they love each other."

I finished pulling out my wedgie and took my hands out my pants. "I really shouldn't have fucked you." I thought I'd said that in my head but I actually said it out loud. Amari shrunk right before my eyes. His shoulders slumped, his chest collapsed, his balls retracted. He took a few steps backward and practically fell onto his bed.

"Wow." The word hung in the air. "You're telling me you felt nothing?" he sat there, his eyes pleading with me for an honest answer.

I felt a lot, including feelings. Amari was some of the best sex I've ever had. With a boy fifteen years younger than me. This 23 year-old shared roughly three hours of lovemaking with me and that's what I was running away from. I imposed the no-younger-men rule on myself once I hit 30 and was convinced any man not older than me "wasn't ready". Many of them proved not to be. I reinforced the rule when all those stories hit the news about teachers sleeping with their students. Women teachers, many not even older than me, who apparently were so desperate for sex or a connection that they were seducing high school boys and falling in love. I vowed that would not be me.

Amari was not in high school. He played sports in high school though. And in college. His healthy, active lifestyle showed in his physique. He's legal but would still be charged extra to rent a car and have higher insurance premiums. On occasion he showed his age, like when he flashes that smile at me, but otherwise he's very mature. He matches me wit for wit in conversation. He could quote the Koran, Bible and the Pyramid Texts and sing along with Gang Starr or Nina Simone.

He also didn't believe men shouldn't show emotion either. Guess that's how he was raised. Shit, he was still being raised. That night when we finally hooked up, we didn't stick to just telling each other how we felt. We acted on the emotion and sexual tension. With his face buried between my thighs I could hear his moans almost as loud as mine. He took my cues and knew when to flick my clit with his tongue, when to travel around it or lap the length of my pussy repeatedly and slipped the tip of his finger in right when I needed something to pulse on. I was on my elbows so I could watch him. I was still quivering and he didn't jump right in me or straddle my face for his. He kissed my inner thighs until I stopped flinching and my tight grip on his locks subsided to a caress.

I tasted sweeter on his lips when we kissed. Our tongues danced while he slipped into me. With our mouths still pressed together, we took each other's breath away. In reflex, I wrapped my legs around him. When his flesh pressed against the back of my thighs each time he slid in and out of me, I reached back and raked my nails along his thigh. I danced while I straddled his hips with his body deep inside mine. He gave my breasts gentle attention with his palms or sat up to kiss and suck them. He held my hips when I neared my finish line. We hugged when I collapsed onto his chest after I came. I kissed his neck; he tickled my back with his fingertips. Amari remained stiff while I came around him, because of him.

That was the love we made that sent me running.

"I truly believe we'd be great together," Amari said.

I dug deep into my brain for the right words but all I came up with was, "We have fun together."

"That's just part of it," he countered. "You are a

beautiful, intelligent, caring woman." His words penetrated me as he did hours earlier. "I tell you all the time how happy you make me, but you have no idea."

Amari had the wide-eyed optimism of youth. He fully believed that together we would be amazing. We'd support one another and help each other grow. We'd never be afraid to argue because that would only deepen our understanding of one another. I was older. I didn't want to go back and wait for him to catch up. Or worse yet, feel like I was raising him.

I wondered if he foresaw all of this when he approached me at the African Flea Market. I sure didn't. I was carrying a drum and a Kenyan giraffe sculpture, but it was a struggle. The idea that he was one of those dollar van drivers quickly ran through my mind. I rolled my eyes when he said he saw a sister who needed help and couldn't just stand by and watch. Here it comes, I thought, but I accepted the help anyway. He took the drum and sculpture from me and walked the five blocks to my apartment carrying them with ease. When we got to my door he placed them on my welcome mat and didn't take another step.

Amari asked for my number so we could keep in touch and then he was gone. He released the knot he had made in his locks when we were walking to my apartment and they cascaded a few inches past his shoulders. He looked sexy either way. I remember watching him take the stairs for as long as he was in eyeshot.

I wasn't expecting his call that night, but he called. We talked with ease about everything and he asked me out. A week after we met, we went out to dinner at a soul food restaurant. It was a choice between that or an Ethiopian spot I really liked. Amari took charge and decided the whens and wheres for our evening. I found that sexy. I could hear his baritone in my head while I got dressed that night. I dabbed oil behind my ears. The next dab of oil on my finger ran from my neck to the center of my cleavage. I couldn't wait to feel his hot breath on my neck while I ran my fingers through his locks. Yes, I had those fantasies but never considered acting on them.

He kept his age a secret until our first date. I guess I can't totally blame him since I didn't ask. I nearly choked on my cocktail. "You're 23?"

"Yeah, I'll be 24 in May." He stated a fact and that was that.

"Damn, you're a *baby*. You know how old I am, right?"

"You're probably 37, 38. I don't know. Doesn't matter to me." He was dead on. But how could it not matter to him?

"Ok, so... this is just a dinner thing, I guess..." I wasn't even sure if I was saying so or asking him. I was still reeling that I had let myself get caught up for a while with a 23 year-old kid. I didn't see any red flags and wasn't on the look out for any youth flags either.

"Why would this just be dinner? I like you. I want to see where this goes."

I was shaking my head the entire time he spoke. "Where do you think this is gonna go? You're 23." I took a sip, then a swig of my cocktail. I felt stupid for putting in the effort to look nice for dinner. He morphed before my eyes—he suddenly looked younger—and I felt like everyone in that restaurant could tell I was "the older woman". Couldn't I get a man my own age? If I did, he'd come with an ex-wife, children, and issues if he's never been married.

"What cocktail did you order again? You've been sucking that thing down. It must be good." he said. I took the glass away from my mouth but had nothing to say. I looked down at the menu instead.

"Hey," he placed his hand on mine, "you okay?"

I pulled my hand away. "I'm fine." He looked at me like I took away his favorite toy. "I'm just hungry. I get irritable when I don't eat," I added to soften the blow. He was staring at me, waiting for me to tell him the truth. My lips were sealed.

Throughout dinner we had conversations like we had over the phone only this time I could see his flirty eyes and had to hide mine. I needed some comfort. Dessert would be had. I was torn between the banana pudding and the peach cobbler.

"You should have the peach cobbler. Banana pudding might mess up your stomach." I questioned him with my eyes. "There's milk in it..." he waited for me to catch up.

I am, in fact, lactose intolerant. It's gotten worse the

older I've gotten. Like I'll start farting just smelling milk. I love dairy though so I do indulge sometimes and just live with the aftermath. On really windy days, you can't smell a thing. "How do know that?" I asked him.

"You said it was a good thing no one'd be under the covers when you had that pint of ice cream that day." I'm mad he knew what I meant by that. I was wowed that he remembered. I just stared at him. "I pay attention."

I shrugged it off, "Well, I could still get the banana pudding. No one's gonna be under the covers tonight either." Never mind that I suffered a canker sore from all the pineapple I ate to sweeten the pot for Amari...before I found out he was 23.

"Order the peach cobbler." He spit that at me and got me thinking how he'd sound when he ordered me to "turn around", "bend over", "open your mouth", "get on your back". It sounded like this boy had plans for me.

When the waitress served the peach cobbler I ordered she brought two spoons. "So you guys can share." She annoyed me with her presumptuousness.

"Do you mind?" Amari asked.

"No, it's fine." This time I was telling the truth. I didn't have a problem sharing the dessert with him. I had a problem with the waitress assuming we were that kinda couple who shares food. Or just assuming we were a couple to begin with. I caught myself watching him as he used the spoon to scoop out some of the peach cobbler. I noticed his short, clean fingernails and silently granted him permission to finger my pussy.

"Think you're sucking that spoon hard enough?" he asked. That question snapped me out of my horny gaze. I didn't realize how seductively I was sucking that spoon thinking about his fingers doing things to my body.

I played along with his question and licked my spoon one more time for emphasis. "That's how grown folks do it."

"Oh yeah?" He put down his spoon and took a slice of peach from the cobbler we shared and demonstrated, close-up, his pussy eating skills. "That's how *I* do it."

I was so wet and confused. How I could be turned on

by him? He dipped his finger in the cobbler and pointed his finger at me. I leaned across the table and took his finger in my mouth. The cobbler was delicious, his finger strong and I ran my tongue on the underside of his second knuckle. I let out a moan and totally lost myself in the moment. Thank god we had a booth along the wall. That way folks wouldn't notice how I was molesting his finger, treating it like it was his brown dick in my mouth, hard and stiff.

He took care of the bill that night. I offered to pay half and he wouldn't hear it. He held my jacket so I could slip my arms in the sleeves. He placed his hand low, I mean really low, on my back and said, "Let's get you home."

I sat behind the cab driver on the ride home. Amari took out his cell phone and when he started scrolling I scanned the cityscape that went by.

He chuckled to himself. "Yo, check this out..." he leaned towards me and I leaned towards him. He showed me an Instagram post of the most adorable brown baby I'd ever seen, covered in their lunch and a very pretty woman side-eyeing the camera. "That's my sister. And her son. He's a mess. I love that kid." There was so much joy and pride illuminated on his face by the glare of his phone. Twenty-three was gone and all I saw was a man who was an uncle, who clearly loved his family. He scrolled through his Instagram feed and his sister's feed sharing photos and the stories behind them.

"Do you want children?" he asked.

"Yeah, I do. Some day."

"So do I." He scrolled through a few more photos before putting away his phone. "Come here. Move closer..." he motioned for me to sit next to him. I unbuckled my seat belt and scooted my hips closer to him. I let my feet drape over the hump in the middle. Amari put his arm around my shoulder and by default my head was on his shoulder. In that moment, I was glad we went to the soul food restaurant for dinner. It was farther away from my apartment so the cab ride was longer. If we hit traffic, I wouldn't mind that either.

Like the gentleman he is, Amari took me all the way to my door. When we got to my door, I couldn't find my damn keys in my bag. I probably reminded him of his Mama just then, digging through a big ol' bag full of nothing. I couldn't believe how nervous he was making me.

"It's aight, take your time," he rubbed my shoulders. His breath lingered on my neck after he said that. He was standing so close to me. I was ready to bend over and arch my back for him right there. I chose the wrong key and I couldn't even blame that on having too much to drink at dinner. When I found the right key I kept fumbling with it and couldn't get it in the lock. Amari ran his hand down my arm and put his strong hand over mine. He guided my hand as we slipped the key into the lock.

Click

I couldn't wait to get Amari inside and see what kind of fit he'd be in me. I turned to him and smiled. He flashed that handsome, young smile at me and I nearly melted. He was too young. He stood too close to me. I kept looking at his lips and that brown skin of his chest. The first two buttons of his shirt were open begging me to touch it. There we were at my front door again, just feet away from having him on my couch where I could ride him till we were sweaty.

"Where'd you put that giraffe and drum?" he asked. That young boy was slick.

"I put them in my office." I finally opened the door. "Wanna see?"

"I would, actually." I walked into my apartment. He stood at my door, still in the hallway of the building. I turned around to him. "Aren't you gonna invite me in?"

I liked that he wasn't just inviting himself in. He would wait to be invited in. That made me smile and made me realize how tense my face had been. "Amari, please, come in."

"Thank you." he stepped into my foyer and I closed the door behind him.

"Come...my office is this way." he followed me to the second bedroom that I used as my office. The drum was next to my desk. I used it as an extension for more surface area. That evening some papers and an empty glass were resting on top of it. The giraffe statue was in the corner of the room.

"This is definitely the room of a busy woman. But one not too busy to enjoy art, or music," he took a few steps and stood right in front of me, "or the finer things in life." I took a deep inhale of his scent. When I looked up at him he was studying the frames on my wall behind me. "Is that an original Gordon Parks?" He was making his way around my desk to get a closer look.

"It's a print, yes. You know his work." I was impressed.

"Are you kidding? I love his work. He documented the African-American, hell, the American experience so honestly and stylistically," he caught himself. "Sorry, I can totally get into art and photography and go on and on for hours." Yup, I thought the same thing—Amari going on and on for hours.

"It's wonderful to have a passion. I just didn't think you'd be so into Parks."

His gaze shot right through me. "Cause he's before my time? *You're* before my time, and I'm into you." He turned and walked out the room.

It took a few seconds for me to pick my jaw up off the floor and follow him out my office to the living room.

"Did you just call me 'old'?"

"I did not call you 'old'. I said I was into you." He stroked my arm. Then he smiled. It was irresistible so I had no choice but to smile back. "And you are before my time." I tensed up immediately. "Why does my age bother you so much?" I still had my screw face on. "Or is it your age that bothers you?"

"I don't have a problem with my age. I'm not old," I blurted out.

"Again with the 'old'. You're not old. You're just older than me. And there's nothing wrong with that. There's lots of women who mess around with younger men. It's nothing new. The Mrs. Robinsons? They exist."

"I'm not trying to be a Mrs. Robinson."

Amari shrugged. "Suit yourself. You got anything to drink here?" He pointed in the direction he thought the kitchen was in. I nodded and headed in that direction.

I had tons to offer him to drink in the alcoholic and

virgin variety. Part of me wanted him to come up behind me
while I was bent over looking in the fridge. Just for a little while,
he could press his body against mine until he got hard in his
pants. I wanted heat.

"What's that?" his face was right next to mine peering
into the fridge and his hand was on my back. He pointed to a
dark bottle.

I took the bottle out. "It's sorrel. Have you had it
before?"

"Once I think. It's sweet, right?"

"Yeah, depends on how the person makes it." I lifted
the bottle. "Mine has rum in it."

Amari smiled. "Nice! I want some..."

I put the bottle on the counter. Amari only had one beer
with dinner; he didn't strike me as a big drinker. If he wasn't, a
sweet drink like sorrel was an easy introduction. It wouldn't get
me drunk but I didn't know what kind of effect it'd have on
him. I took down two glasses from the cupboard. I only poured
a little in one of them. I had him taste it first to see if it was too
strong for him.

"Nah, it's good. I'll be all right."

"Ok, cause I don't want you getting drunk and passing
out," I teased as I poured him a full drink.

"But you could take advantage of *all of this*," he
showcased his body, "if I'm drunk."

"I like my men sober, please and thank you."

"You're right though, I shouldn't drink 'cause I wanna
remember this..." Amari kissed me with his full lips. I heard him
put his glass down on the counter then he wrapped his other
arm around me, his hand landing on that same spot low, low on
my back. I was already tiptoeing to get closer to him and deeper
in his mouth. I couldn't play if off like I didn't want him
anymore.

We came up for a breath. Looking at him my eyes
almost felt like they were gonna swell up and tear. I took him by
the hand and led him out the kitchen. We were walking to my
bedroom when he stopped. He had this look on his face like he
was trying to figure out a puzzle or recall a song lyric.

"Next time..." He took his hand from mine and picked up his jacket off the arm of the couch. He kissed me slowly on my cheek and whispered in my ear, "Good night, my peach." This time he ate me with his stare like he ate that peach cobbler at dinner. He gave away a lot of his experience in his eyes. I enjoyed every second of it. There was still time for him to change his mind and follow me into the bedroom. But I guess he wasn't ready. "I'll call you when I get home." He let himself out.

I lollygagged around the apartment naked. I sipped a tall glass of wine and checked my emails with one eye. It was just an excuse to pass the time while I drank.

My cell phone rang. When I finally got to the phone that was still sitting on my kitchen counter, I saw the call was from Amari.

"Wow, that was quick. No traffic tonight?"

"Nah, I'm not home yet."

"Oh, ok, what's up?"

"Let me in." There was a knock at my door.

"What?" Things were happening too fast for me to process.

There was more knocking at my door. "Hear that? That's me. I'm outside. Open the door."

Fuck, he was ordering me around again. I put down my glass of wine on the counter and rushed to the bathroom and grabbed my towel. "Shit..." I was fumbling with the phone and the towel. Then I quickly put the phone on mute. I wrapped the towel tight. Real tight so it wouldn't fall off and rushed to the door. I stood on the other side of the door trying to temper my excitement.

"You gonna open the door?" Amari asked from the other side.

I opened the door and made sure to extend a proper invitation before he came into my apartment again. I wasn't sure how to look at him. I could easily come across like the horny old lady welcoming her boy-toy for the evening if I wasn't careful.

"So..." I trailed off.

"I didn't give you a proper good night earlier. I couldn't

leave things like that."

I suddenly got self-conscious standing there wearing nothing but a towel. "Oh, um...ok, lemme go put on some clothes."

"You were gonna take a shower?"

I nodded. I mean, eventually, I was, after more wine.

"Ok, I'll help."

He walked towards my bathroom. "What?" I rushed forward to cut him off. "You're gonna help me take a shower?"

Then he flashed this grown-man look at me, took me by the hand and led me to the bathroom. He turned on the faucet and adjusted the hot and cold knobs while checking the water until he was satisfied with it. He reached to take my towel off and I flinched. Again, he caught me with the grown-man look and a smirk. And he waited. Moment of truth I, thought. Was I gonna really let him do this? Was I gonna let him see me naked? Was he ready? Ok, fuck it, was I? Yeah, I thought about some buckwild sex with him after our phone calls and seeing his brown chest and getting whiffs of his scent but damn, was I really ready for the young lad?

His fingers worked open the knot in my towel. "Wait!" I wrapped my arms around myself keeping the towel on and backed away from him. "Wait..." I said a little more calmly. "Let me get in first." He nodded and turned his back to me. I hurried and dropped my towel and climbed into the tub. I pulled the shower curtain closed.

The water was the perfect temperature. I stood under the spray of water and got lost in it for a moment. I wasn't thinking about the fine young brother standing on the other side of the shower curtain while I stood naked and ready for him. Everywhere the water tickled me, I wanted Amari to follow with his tongue.

"Everything ok?" Amari asked.

"Perfect," I purred. "I mean, the water, it's perfect. Perfect temperature."

"I'm glad. But you know I can't help you if I'm standing with my back to the closed shower curtain."

It all happened in slow motion. I could see the outline

of his arm reaching for the shower curtain and saw it start sliding open. I quickly turned my back to him. "My back! Do my back first..."

The shower curtain was halfway open now. I could feel him standing there, staring at my back, my ass.

"Where's your soap?"

"Here," I handed him the bottle of castile soap over my shoulder. I reached for my aqua blue shower pouf and handed that to him over my other shoulder. He took it from me, reached over my body and hung it back on the hook. I could smell the sorrel on his breath when his face passed "*thatclose*" to mine.

"I want to use my hands on you." I heard the snap of the bottle opening. A few seconds later, "I'm gonna start now," and his hand touched my back. He made small, then bigger, then bigger circles with his palm. I could feel the suds multiplying but could still feel his hand. I closed my eyes to imagine what it looked like – Amari's sturdy hand being so gentle against my back, changing the design of the soap bubbles with every swirl of his hand. He washed my shoulders, letting his fingers travel forward to wash my neck, down my back, low, over and under the curve of my ass—one cheek at a time—then he did the back of my thighs and calves. He put the bottle down on the edge of the tub and started using both hands on my body. I took a quick peek over my shoulder and saw he was stooping down while he worked one leg. He had me bend my knee so he could hold my foot to wash it and work between my toes. Yes, my mind ran on him sucking my toes while he worked his hips against me. He continued to wash and massage my other leg working his way back up my body. Now that he was using two hands he could get the back and front of my thighs. His hands were reading my body. He'd spend a little more time on parts of my body that needed the extra attention.

Including my ass. On his second pass over it, I could tell it was more play for him now. Amari went up and down, around and in between. For a little while, I was hoping that my butt wasn't too jiggly for him, hoping it didn't look old to him. Then I let that go. However it looked and felt Amari was having fun playing with it.

"Aren't you glad you didn't have that banana pudding?"

My stomach was in knots as soon as he taunted me with that question. My whole body tensed up. He was behind me, face at my ass, talking about farting and what not. Yes, good thing I ordered the peach cobbler...

"Relax..." he had my ass cheek in his palm and shook it back and forth. I had that butt-clench on. And slapping my ass, lifting and spreading and what Amari was doing all cause a flood between my legs. Don't start nothing you can't finish, little boy...

"*You* should be glad I didn't have the banana pudding," I said, "considering where you are."

He carved ten tracks in the soap up my back then he ran his hands over my shoulders and down to my breasts. He held them for a little while before he actually started washing them. The heat of his palms soaked into me. I watched his hands work their magic. My nipples were hard as rocks in no time and he scissored them with his fingers. I smiled when he did that and I could feel him smile too. I could also feel his breath on my neck. This shower was gonna make me more dirty than it would clean me. He washed my stomach next. He even squeezed my softness, lingering on handfuls of my flesh. "That's nice," Amari said to himself. He ran his hands back up through the suds over my breasts onto my shoulders and down my arms. He washed and massaged each of my arms, individually. When he washed my armpits I flinched 'cause it tickled me. He liked that and tickled me on purpose a few times after that.

"Give me your hand." I reached my hand out and he held it from underneath. He squeezed a little of the soap into my palm. He dipped his head so slightly, I almost didn't notice it. "Wash yourself."

My hand was between my legs working up a lather. I was slippery as fuck. Amari running his hands all over my body had really turned me on. He was missing the best part, in my opinion. When I was done soaping up I stepped under the shower spray and washed off. There was no graceful or sexy way to do that so I just did it.

I stood straight up and let the water wash the soap off

the front of my body. Then I quickly washed my face.

"Turn around." He said that in the same grown-man tone that stopped me from ordering the banana pudding. He was so deliberate with his eyes. He studied my feet and knees, my thighs and his gaze lingered on my bush. For the first time, I wanted him to be aware of my age. I hoped he could see some my gray hairs. My body, my pussy, she's got wisdom. The things I could teach him, he had no idea.

Amari's eyes moved along to my belly, my breasts—my 38 year-old breasts, my shoulders, neck, chin, lips, nose, eyes.

We stood there for what felt like forever looking at each other.

"And you didn't want me to see you?" He stared some more at my body, looking a little overwhelmed by it all but he was doing a good job of holding it together. "You're gorgeous."

He reached towards me and held his hand under the stream of water, washing off the soap. Then he washed his other hand. He stepped away from the tub and dried his hands on one of my hand towels. He picked up my towel and held it open for me. I didn't want the shower to be over. I opened my mouth to say something slick, to invite him to get naked and wet with me but he beat me to it, "Come... let's dry you off."

I turned off the water and stepped out of the tub and into his arms. He wrapped the towel around me and tucked the corner of the top edge under the rest of the towel close to my armpit. I secured it and took his waiting hand. He led me out of the bathroom to the only room he'd yet to visit in my apartment—my bedroom.

"You sleep with the AC on?"

It was deliciously cool in my room. "Yeah, till about October, November. I like it cold at night."

"Why not just open a window? It'd be cheaper for you and better for the environment."

He was right and I had nothing to say so I just shrugged. He walked over to my dresser and scanned my products. I helped him out in his decision-making process. "I use the argan oil on my face and coconut oil or the shea butter on my body." He picked up the jar of coconut oil after he picked up the argan oil.

We stood there face-to-face; me with my eyes closed while he applied argan oil to my face with the dropper and then massaged it in. I didn't open my eyes even after he was finished. He took off my towel. I felt more naked in my bedroom than in the shower. I resisted the urge to thrust my chest forward, nipples tight with yearning, and scream, "Take me! Take me now!"

I heard him screw off the top of the jar. He massaged coconut oil to every inch of my still damp body. He even made sure to moisturize my bush and kissed me on the between my belly button and where my pubic hair starts. I put my hand on the back of his head and held it there. I let the heat from his lips radiate across my belly and wrap around my waist. He got caught up. I felt his tongue running back and forth against my skin. I finally opened my eyes and looked down at him. He must've felt me look down at him or heard the little moan I let out 'cause he suddenly stopped and peeked up at me. He gave me one last sealing kiss and stood up.

If he was gonna kiss me again, now would be the perfect time. I didn't care that I was stark naked and he was fully clothed. I knew a kiss would change that. But he didn't kiss me. He picked up the jars of oil and placed them back on my dresser. I was done trying to tempt him. I grabbed a t-shirt that was on the pile of clothes on my chair and threw it on.

"I'm gonna get going now," Amari said.

"Yeah, I figured as much."

"Thank you for letting me back in," he stepped back up to me. He took my hand and kissed it. "I hope that helps you sleep well tonight."

It did.

I moved a few of his locks off his face and kissed him lightly on his lips. I searched his face for my answer but still shook my head. "This...this cant..."

"We made love. You don't want to accept that, but that's what it was," he declared.

I took a step back from him and his dick bobbed. I

grabbed the damp towel I used to dry off and threw it on his lap. "Cover that up."

It took a few seconds, but he smiled. "See what you do to me?" Amari moved the towel revealing his hard dick. The sight of it brought on a yearning for a repeat performance. It took all I had in me not to drop to my knees and feel his mushroom top on my tongue. The image of gripping him in my hand while I tasted his balls brought me to an extreme state of wet arousal.

I still insisted on leaving. I finished getting dressed and was letting myself out. "I really wish you would stay," he confessed. He waited, took his time before having sex with me and this was his reward.

I shook my head. He wasn't going to be able to fix me. "I'm gonna go." I had to get out before he hit me with his best Al Jarreau impression.

"Lemme call you a cab then," he offered.

"I'll hail one." I gave him a kiss on the cheek.

"I'll call you, ok?" like he was asking permission. I nodded and walked out his apartment. I felt like the young one now. A boy tells me he likes me and I run because I'm afraid he's going to try to hold my hand and kiss me. My Mama always told me to never live in fear because you'll never live.

The cab I hailed was extra comfortable as is usually the case when you need some time to think. In a perfect world, the cab driver and I would be friends. We had the same taste in music. I don't know if it was the radio station or a CD but Miles Davis was on. At one point when Amari and I made love "Flamenco Sketches" surrounded us. The music had an enchanting effect. It slowed us down and we were totally present, kissed, rocked, grinded...dare I say, made jazz with our souls, and then kissed some more. I expected us to clash like jazz with no discernible rhythm or beat.

I let myself get carried away by the sax, trumpet and riffs of "All Blues" as the cab cruised down the city streets. That should be my theme song, I thought, all my decisions bring me nothing but the blues. My cell phone rang. I smiled back at the smiling photo of Amari I used as his contact icon. A rush of blood hit my belly and clit again. Just another symptom of a love hangover.

"Excuse me..." I tapped on the partition. The cab driver slid it open. "We gotta go back. I need you to go back." Then I answered Amari's call. "Hey... yeah... I just told the driver to go back..." I had some growing up to do.

* * *

Love You, I Do

Roché Jenkins never looked more beautiful than she did in her wedding dress. I couldn't take my eyes off her as she walked down the aisle. She had this unbelievable glow, that whole blushing bride vibe. To be honest, it was like she was floating towards me, being delivered like a dream, a wish come true. The best gift ever. When we finally locked eyes, I could see that she was fighting back tears. It would've ruined her makeup and I know she wasn't gonna let that happen. She still would've been the most beautiful woman in that church with her make-up smeared cause of that ugly cry face. I kept my eyes on her, to give her strength until she made it to the altar. I wanted to run down the aisle to her and kiss her, skipping over all of the pomp and circumstance and announce to every one in that church how much I loved her.

My name's Cordell. I'm 29. My brother Jason is a year older than me. My brother and I met Roché at college orientation. Wow, that's ten years ago. Jason was all about "hittin' it and quittin' it" back then. His friends and mine were always clowning me 'cause I was trying to *marry* girls. But honestly I only ever wanted to marry Roché. I just knew I would marry her one day. I've loved Roché since the first day I met her.

Jason got a lot of chicks but mine were steady. My other girlfriends...I liked them and treated them well, gave them romance. I remembered birthdays and Valentine's Day and would get porn star sex from them when I would give them flowers just because it was a Tuesday.

Then Jason told me about Steak and Blowjob Day. Any

excuse to get his dick sucked, I thought. But turns out it was an actual day that people celebrated. They were trying to get it to be the V-day for men back then. Then Roché put me on to it too like four years ago. I was like, "word?" It also happened to be a Tuesday, my just-because romance day. In school we never did anything cause of roommates in the dorm and then she moved back home for a few months after graduation. She got a job at a not-for-profit and put her change together to get her own place.

I showed up on that Tuesday with a bouquet of orchids. She was so touched. I was a little nervous though. I could feel Jason's energy and hear him egging me on to get some head. I followed her into the kitchen and she put the flowers in some water. And there was a steak wrapped in butcher paper on her counter.

"Is that... a steak?"

She gave me this sly smile and nodded. "It's a special day."

"What?" I was trying not to freak out. But I was getting hard thinking about her sucking me off.

"Steak," she motioned to the steak, "and *blowjob* day." She motioned to my piece and bit her lip.

"You *know* about that?"

"Yeah, I know about that and I know about *that*..." she looked at my bulge again and laughed. "Jason's been going on and on about steaks and blowjobs."

"Word. With me too. He's like 'get that meat, yo!'" We both laughed.

She shook her head. "Brothers." She unwrapped the steak and I saw it was a humongous T-bone. It had the right amount of white in it to make it good.

"How much did that *cost*?"

She didn't look at me. "How much did the flowers cost?"

"Never mind." I stayed in the kitchen with her while she cooked the steak for me.

I had a huge chunk of the steak in my mouth. "Damn... I'm not worthy..." I chewed some more. Roché said the man who gets to eat her steak has to be worthy. That's a guy who knows how to treat a woman, who remembers her birthday and brings her favorite flowers just because it's Tuesday.

When she finished washing the dishes, she was looking at me different. It wasn't like she was horny per se but she was looking at me like she wanted me right then and there.

"Are you gonna kiss me?" she asked.

I didn't know if she was gonna let me or kiss me back even though she asked. I always did stare at her mouth when we'd talk and when she'd smile. I was finally able to kiss her beautiful lips. If I could tell her how I felt all in one kiss, I tried to that day.

The next thing I remember she got comfortable on her knees and blessed me. She didn't let me sit. She was all into it, moaning and slurping and whatnot. The picture of her looking up at me while I was in her mouth is burned into my memory. I lost it when she did this flutter thing with her tongue. I wanted to make it last a little longer but her lips were too full and soft, her tongue was too strong, her mouth was so warm and wet.

I told her I was about to come and she didn't stop. She just nodded and swallowed every drop. After that she sucked and kissed my dick till I got soft in her mouth. I had to stop her 'cause it was too much.

That day I got to taste her too for the first time. Her lips kissed me back and she had this tight grip on my head, keeping it between her legs. I felt like I was gonna come again just from eating her out.

We got addicted to each other from that day on. We snuck around a lot. Any chance we got we were together. Inside closets, the car, her friend's home office when we were over for a BBQ, we even snuck off during a Vegas trip we took with Jason and LaShonda, his girl of that moment. We were in front of the Bellagio fountains, joking about how we need to get an *Ocean's Eleven* crew together so we could run away and never work again. We shared our big money dreams and big money schemes. Then she leaned in and whispered, "See how the water shoots up like that? It looks like you when you finish."

I was never prepared when she said stuff like that. I wanted to see the world through her eyes. Sometimes I think she sees sex in everything; that she thinks about it all the time. Yeah, we fucked a lot but we also loved to just chill and talk. I knew we could make a life together. We shared a lot of the same values and supported each other's dreams. I loved her spirit. She was so intelligent and professional and wise. She loved to help other people, she wasn't selfish at all. And she was freaky when the time was right. She also never let me forget that she wanted me, and that she loved me.

The first time she said she loved me was after we made love for the first time. I didn't really know the difference between like "slow fucking" and "making love" till that day. I was about to say it to her too but she beat me to it. I was stroking her long and slow and I could feel her getting real tight around me. I don't know how to explain it, but it was like her spirit was surrounding mine too. We were becoming one – I finally understood what that meant. She was moaning so sweet and soft. She would whisper my name sometimes. It almost sounded like she was gonna cry. Felt like I coulda cried too. I would catch myself just looking at her. I've seen her so much before this, naked too, but it was like seeing her for the first time. Her eyes were closed; she was totally in another place from how good it felt but still there with me. My lower back was getting hot and I could feel the heat going up my back. The top of my head got warm and my legs were tingling. It kinda freaked me out 'cause that never happened to me before. But it felt too good to stop.

Roché was trembling under me. I had to really concentrate so I wouldn't come too fast. I wanted to make her come. Her nose was crinkling up a little bit. When I'd get in her real deep I could feel her warm breath on my face. "Cordell..." She opened her eyes to look at me and held my face. A tear ran out her eye to her ear and she said, "I love you." She looked me in the eye for the entire time after that until she came. That was so intense and I came inside her for the first time that night. I didn't want her to think I said, 'I love you too' because the sex was good.

"I know you mean it," she said with that afterglow and

wisdom in her eyes.

My mother saw that same wisdom in her eyes when she finally met Roché. She was also happy to see one of her boys finally bring home a woman that looked like her. I had my "white bread" phase as she liked to call it. I joked that now I was down with the wheat and pumpernickel bread. My mother isn't *against* her sons being with a white woman but she would prefer we have a version of her relationship. My parents have been together for 43 years. Black love is forever celebrated in her home. And she *can't wait* for black grandbabies.

That day when Roché and my mother talked about their not-for-profits, my Pops had that "that's my boy" look on his face while me and Jason hung out with him in the basement watching the game.

"Your mother was a fine little thing just like Miss Roché when we first met." I made sure he knew I wasn't trying to hear about how he bagged my mother, but I did have to listen to tales about being a man and making sure a woman is always satisfied. "When you come home and your dinner ain't ready and she's wearing sweats you *know* you ain't getting none that night." Pops taught me to treat my Black Queens as such and then you'd always have a happy home. I was also informed that my mother's 40-year old looking skin at 60 was 'cause of good lovin'. I would love to roll over in bed and see Roché at 60 with that same afterglow and wisdom.

I didn't realize how long the wedding march was. It flew by during the rehearsal. But it's totally different when you're the one up there...on your wedding day, no less. I looked at Roché's father and we nodded. He approved. He would never give his daughter to a man who he didn't think was worthy. I would love and honor Roché forever. I would do anything for her. It was scary to think about the next phase of our relationship. I hoped things wouldn't change but I think change is inevitable.

She made it to the altar, without crying, and we smiled at each other.

"Dearly Beloved, we are gathered here to today to

witness the union of Jason and Roché in holy matrimony..."
She's going to make my brother so happy.

* * *

Woman In The Moon

She woke up with a glow. But he wasn't next to her. He was thousands of miles away but she'd hold him close to her heart. The night before was a sultry, summer night. Once the sun goes down, people release all inhibitions. And it's as if all the body heat causes the temperature to rise after sundown. He called asking what she was up to—chillin' or better yet, cooking. He loved her cooking. Almost better than his Mama's.

"There's no way I'm standing over a hot stove in this heat," she said. He smiled to himself because he could see her neck roll as she said that over the phone. "But I got some leftovers. And fruit and ice cream. We could do something with that. I don't be eating much in this heat anyway."

In a failed attempt to keep his thoughts clean, his mind ran on licking melting ice cream off her and her kissing away her sweet juices from his lips and chin. That usually made her giggle.

She wore faded denim shorts and a tank top. Her perky breasts sat high under the cotton top, her nipples confirming she wasn't wearing a bra. She tied her afro up in a pineapple. The hairstyle accentuated her high cheekbones, her neck, broad shoulders and collarbones.

His beauty wasn't lost on her either. He had his boyish half-grin permanently etched on his face and eyes you could get lost in. His lips were framed with a moustache and goatee, thicker in the middle and thinner along his jawline and sideburns. His clothes were wrinkled from the day's wear, but she knew they were probably wrinkled when he put them on.

She could smell him before they came together for their usual hug and kiss 'hello'. There was a strong possibility that there was nothing between her and him but those khakis he was wearing. She wanted to take off his shirt right there and then but knew the heat would get to him soon enough. He had already wiped his brow with his sweat rag.

She was still rummaging through the fridge. "I got some fruit together, and some cashews. And I have some cheese. I hope it's enough for the both of us." The impromptu platter she prepared was more than enough for the two of them. He never want for anything when he was with her. "And..." she said with that gleam in her eye, "I got a bottle of champagne. Mimosas? Straight up?"

"Sounds good."

"Aight. Grab that," she said pointing to the tray.

"Where we going?"

"The roof."

They lay side by side on a sheet they had spread out. The heat of the night got to him. He had stripped down to his wife beater. The stems from the grapes and strawberries littered the tray. The champagne bottle was strewn on its side. They talked and laughed and flirted. And the red, full moon lit the way.

"You know, at the right angle, you could look like you on the moon." He rolled his head to the side to face her.

"You crazy."

"Fa real, stand up."

She made her way to her feet, taking a few seconds to steady herself. "See, like right now, it's just yo' figure, yo' silhouette against that giant moon." He sunk into the moment, taking in the sight of her. "Beautiful."

She swayed, which became a full dance, seductive, and bubbly like the champagne. "Have you ever danced with the devil in the pale moonlight?" The Joker never made it sound that sexy. She twirled as if an imaginary partner spun her in a ballroom dance.

He reached up and caressed her calf and the back of her

knee. He traced the crease with his finger and she shuddered. The hum of a city bus heading down the boulevard broke their trance.

"You didn't answer my question," she said mockingly stern as she stood over him, straddling him. "Have, you ever—"

He tugged on her shorts and she bent her knees to sit on him. He ran his hand along her thigh and up her shorts. He played in that space between her thigh and lip. That tickle made her anticipate his next stop. His fingers moved to the dampness between her thighs. She sighed and raised her hips slightly so he could play. He massaged her nub and made her dance again. He dipped his finger inside her. He'd been watching every second of his physical orchestration. She took off her tank top in one motion and ran her palms over her nipples. He withdrew his finger and she leaned forward to kiss him.

He put his wet finger to her lips. She sucked her essence off his digit. Only then she was granted permission to kiss his lips. She grinded her hips against him and he grabbed her ass so he could follow her flow. She ran her hands under his wife beater while she kissed and nibbled on his ear.

Their dry hump turned urgent. She kept her mouth on his neck while she undid her shorts. With her hands at her zipper she could feel his bulge aching for an escape from his pants. He wanted nothing more but to feel the inside of her body, or her mouth.

She stood over him, nude, framed by the full, red moon. He knew she was waiting for him to free himself and he did hastily, kicking off his pants. She squat over him and took him inside. One thrust, two thrusts, three thrusts, he cupped her buttocks and helped her with her crude bounce. Four thrusts, five. She stood straight up, like she sat on something too hot to handle. He couldn't quite make out her expression, but she must've been smiling.

She bent forward, legs straight and spread, and took him in her mouth.

"You are some kinda crazy. You a sexy crazy, girl." She moaned in response and sucked and slurped. Looking up, all he could see was the slope of her back and the rise of her haunches, her head bobbing and his dick throbbing. He stopped her after a while. He wanted to get the ultimate view of that rear.

They both kneeled but he didn't enter her right away. He played in her wetness with the tip of his body. He tortured her, his dick sliding up and down between her cheeks. By the time he slid into her, she was already working her fingers around her electric knob. Her body swallowed him whole.

"Why?" she was pleading, almost crying, wanting to know why he felt so good, why her body responded to him that way. As he pumped in and out of her, he kneaded her breasts and massaged her back. It sent chills up her spine and made him cry out because she had clamped down around him. He knew he was doing her right when he got that love squeeze. The rhythm she worked her clit with grew feverish but he was the tortoise tonight; slow and steady wins the race. His spastic eruption caught him without warning. He laid his chest on her back and hugged her close as he emptied himself inside her.

They toppled over onto to their sides with giggles. They always had so much fun together. He remained inside her while they spooned, in her dream. But she woke up with a glow. He wasn't next to her. He was thousands of miles away but she'd hold him close to her heart.

*   *   *

Errare Humanum Est

(To Err is Human)

The couple sits on opposite ends of the bench while the officer fills out paperwork. The sound of a plastic bag peeling off Dominique's thigh tears through the silence. She figured she'd catch something—infection or splinter—if she sat without a layer of protection.

Her stomach growls audibly. Arturo looks at her and the two crack their stoic expressions with strained smiles. She stands and approaches the officer.

"Excuse me, Officer..." she reads his badge, "Reyes, can I eat this? I'm starving."

"Didn't eat enough earlier?" He shoots Arturo a glance.

Her jaw drops. She snaps her mouth shut before he can make any other rude remarks.

Officer Reyes looks back at his work, feigning disinterest. Dominique doesn't budge.

"Don't make a mess. Don't need the Captain knowing I let you eat in here."

She rushes back to the bench. "You want some?" She sits closer to Arturo and pulls a round aluminum container out of a brown paper bag. She uncovers a half-eaten burrito.

"No, it's ok. You eat." He rubs the center of her back. There's no bra strap to be felt. He crosses his legs at the thought of her bare breasts.

"We might be here a while..."

"No touching." Officer Reyes reminds them without looking up. Arturo takes his hand off her back. He leans forward and buries his face in his hands.

Dominique puts half of the leftover burrito in her mouth. It's room temperature and on that level of delicious when you haven't eaten for hours. The beans and sour cream will go unnoticed by her stomach of steel. But she's not immune to her nerves. Her hands are shaky as she feeds an emotional hunger as well.

Arturo can only pray he gets his guitar back in one piece. Music is his life and he made his name by singing about love and social justice. There is definitely a song in this experience. He left Argentina because he was tired of being famous for being in jail. He lost many of his music students after his last five-day stint made the local papers. 1980's New York was his next stop. Now he is facing that possibility again. He has much more to lose now in his 40's than in his 20's. He's a family man now—wife, kids, soccer games, guitar lessons. If his wife finds out about this, it will be more ammunition for her "I don't love you anymore," and "You're no good," arguments. He could find himself a bachelor again. He can't bear the thought of only having weekend visitation rights with his sons. He doesn't have an appetite for a burrito or much else.

Dominique swallows the last bite. The food sits in her chest. She needs water to wash it down or a good burp. She runs her tongue over her teeth; her mouth tastes of burrito, Malbec and Arturo.

He watches her apply chapstick to her tempting lips. His thoughts revert to the bookstore and the erotic scenes Dominique shared, the way she described a woman's lips around a man, controlling him, enjoying his moans and throbs of pleasure. Dominique is facing God-knows how many charges. She doesn't have the bail. Her friends are as broke as she is and the people who can afford to bail her out would want a lot more in return than just having the money paid back. Unless the bail bondsman accepts her disconnected cell phone, she doesn't have any real property to put up. A broke artist with this on her record—she couldn't even spin it as a public art project. A sharp pain radiates across her midsection. She squeezes her eyes shut and lets out a quiet whimper.

Arturo places his hand on her lap. "*¿Que te pasa?*"

"I don't feel so good." She holds her stomach grimacing.

"Mr. Medina," Officer Reyes interrupts, "step forward. I'm gonna go over the charges."

Dominique sat amongst the other performers in a showcase at a local bookstore in Washington Heights. Arturo Medina took the stage with infectious energy. Dominique was drawn to something about this man and not just the fact he was a musician. She'd find out what it was over a drink after the show. He encouraged the crowd to sing along while he made clicking sounds with his tongue. *To be on the receiving end of his tongue while he rolled his R's.* Arturo's black loose-fitting lounge pants gathered at the crease of his hips. She eyed his crotch under the guitar to see what filled the extra fabric that fell to the seat of the chair. The filling was soft, but noticeable.

As soon as the MC thanked everyone for coming out, she bolted from her seat towards Arturo. His bright eyes didn't leave hers.

"I'd love to hear you play again. Do you have any gigs coming up?"

He motioned for her to follow him to the checkout counter. There was a stack of his CDs by the cash register. The image on the cover was a younger Arturo Medina, sporting long rock star hair and a piercing gaze. The incarnation looked nothing like the man who stood in front of her with short hair — slightly longer in the front and swept to the side — a three o'clock shadow darkening the lower half of his face, and flutter-inducing eyes. He scribbled his info on a Post-it and handed it to her.

"What're you doing after this?" he asked.

"I'm actually looking for something to do. It's still early..."

Twelve minutes after nine on a Friday. No gentleman can let a woman go home, alone, so early on a Friday night. Without thinking, he said, "Let's go back to my place."

"Sure!" Getting to know him was going to be easier than she thought.

"I was thinking we could go back to my studio and have a jam session. I'll see if anyone else here wants to join us."

There was no denying the tinge of disappointment in Dominique's gut.

They parted briefly to mingle. In the crowd, Arturo watched Dominique hug another man goodbye, his hands sitting lower on her waist than Arturo was comfortable with. It was a good thing he wouldn't be alone with her. He didn't trust himself; his thoughts were already wandering into dangerous territory. Besides, he was a married man, albeit unhappily, but married nonetheless.

She approached him after the rest of her goodbyes. "All set?"

Arturo loaded his guitar and amp into the back of his Subaru Forester. "Everyone else already had plans." He shut the hatchback and walked to the driver side door. "It'll be just us." He did a terrible job suppressing his smile. He climbed in and opened the passenger side door for her. He caught a whiff of her subtle scent of brown sugar and fresh cotton. "I hope that's ok." His long frame filled the car from top to bottom but not side to side. He lived up to his nickname, Flaco.

"Yeah, I guess. We can have a jam session with just two people, right?" she asked.

"We can do a lot with just two people."

She smelled good enough to eat so he devoured her with his eyes.

He checked the rearview mirror, the passenger side view mirror, and Dominique's thick thighs and the warm spot where they met. His body pulsed under the lap band of his seat belt as he envisioned her thighs wrapped around his waist or shoulders. She sported a proud smile when his gaze rose to her face. "I really enjoyed your stories tonight. I couldn't read stories like that in front of people. Everyone would know what I'm thinking. Men, we can't hide that."

"Yeah, guys really can't hide that stuff," she mocked, placing her umbrella in her lap and pointing it up at a penetrating angle. Arturo laughed and she noticed the convex curve of his top row of teeth. The side of her mouth curled up thinking about a young Arturo sucking his thumb.

He pulled out of the parking space. A familiar rhythm escaped his car speakers. She tilted her ear toward the radio, "I know this song!" She listened for a few more bars, bobbing her head to the song before figuring out it was Bob Marley's "Could You Be Loved" sung in Portuguese.

Her knowledge and appreciation of music was impressive and a turn-on. He kept his eyes on the road, fighting the urge to watch her bouncing breasts as she danced next to him. He sang along in Portuguese, tapping the rhythm on the steering wheel and Dominique beat a rhythm on her thighs as he weaved through traffic on Broadway.

On a green light, he made a left turn towards Amsterdam Avenue. There was an empty parking space right in front of the building. "It was meant to be," he said.

The would-be living room was furnished with instruments, a few folding chairs and a card table in the corner. A small desk lamp and light filtering in from the hallway through decorative French doors lit the room. Dominique went to the bathroom to wash her hands before eating. There was a layer of dust in the sink, on the floors and on the empty towel bar that showed his apartment was strictly for music, not for occupancy. She rinsed off the soap then used her damp hands to sculpt her twist-out afro just-so. She studied her glowing complexion in the mirror from different angles before heading back to the other room.

Dominique unpacked the Mexican takeout they bought. He uncorked a bottle of wine.

"Awww, I don't like red wine," she pouted.

"You'll like this, it's from Argentina." He filled two red plastic cups.

"¡Salud!" Dominique raised her cup and he followed suit. They tapped cups. She took a sip and raised her eyebrows in approval of the Malbec from his hometown of San Juan. "Argentina is sweet." She winked and stuck out her tongue. Arturo placed his elbows on the table and leaned in, his hands

holding the cup close to his lips. That's when Dominique
noticed his wedding band. She never remembered to look for
one when she met a man she was interested in. Now she'd have
to put him in the friend zone—an interesting, talented, quirky
friend who she was attracted to. She'd have to make the
impossible possible and have a platonic friendship with him, like
the ones she valued with her gay male friends. She leaned back
in her chair, creating some distance between them.

They shared food and stories until his tray was empty
and Dominique showed no interest in the half of a burrito in
front of her. Damn him and those eyes, his genuine interest in
everything she said, and his affectionate touches on her cheek,
her shoulder or her knee. *Don't forget, he touches his wife with those
hands. Repeat to self, Dominique.*

He gulped the rest of his wine and slammed the cup
down. The plastic made a comically weak sound against the
table top. Arturo gave her knee another squeeze. "I want to play
for you." He carried his chair to the center of the room and
removed his guitar out of its case. She crossed the room and sat
across from him.

Arturo positioned his fingers on the frets and played a
Spanish guitar riff. Dominique swayed in her seat. He began his
song, *"La morena bailando bajo las estrellas..."* She quickly averted
her gaze to the doorway, out the window, or she'd take a sip of
wine each time he caught her eye. Between the chorus and the
second verse, he quickly said, "You should be dancing."

Dominique placed her cup on the floor and rose from
the chair. She danced salsa with an imaginary partner. As the
song's tempo picked up her movements grew freer, wilder but
rhythmic as she moved closer to him. She could feel his breath
warm against her neck as he exhaled his lyrics. Her chest
glistened with sweat. She ran her hand down her front; Arturo
could see the outline of her nipples under her top.

> *Tomó su mano y nunca la suelto*
> *La beso a la luz de la luna*
> *Juntos para siempre con mi negra*

He directed her dips and spins with the E chords of his
song. She put her hand on the nape of his neck and circled

around him. Her touch was inciting madness. The heel of her palm rested just below her belt buckle and her fingers curved under onto the warm denim. Arturo's gaze was glued to her hips carving figure-eights through the air. He bit his bottom lip in concentration as he played his song's crescendo.

Dominique, flushed, finished her performance with a sated grin. He lifted her hand and sniffed her fingertips. At the scent of her arousal he wanted to toss his guitar aside and ravage her.

She pulled her hand away from his face, grazing his lips. "I'm thirsty. More wine?" she picked up her cup from the floor and walked back to the table.

He shook his head and made a fist, with his thumb tucked under his first two fingers, resting on his wedding band.

She poured wine in both cups. "Here you go," she handed him a cup. She crossed the room back to her chair with her cup full and the bottle. She turned the chair around and straddled the seat backwards. She noticed the sudden attention he was paying his wedding band.

He felt her gaze on him, waiting.

"You know...marriage is hard. And we're struggling right now. Trying to work on it."

"I'm not exactly making this easy for you, am I?"

He shook his head during a pregnant pause.

"Monogamy isn't for everyone." Dominique didn't want that to sound like an invitation and quickly added, "it takes work. I've been there..."

"You've been married?"

"Yup. And not monogamous. That's why I'm single now." They shared a consolatory smile. He held the cup between his knees, staring at his maroon Chuck Taylors in deep thought over his sons whom he loved with everything in his being and his wife who was now simply the woman he lived with.

"So how do you handle all this? I mean situations like this," she waved her hand back and forth in the space between them.

He let out an exasperated sound with a sexual tone.

"I'm tempted all the time by beautiful women. *Everywhere*. But I don't act on it. I just drink a lot of wine." She furrowed her brow waiting for an explanation. "So I *can't*... too drunk to do anything."

"Nice try. Getting yourself too drunk to fuck. But I'm sure your fingers and your tongue still work."

"Oh, you're bad! I have to drink a lot of wine around you."

"And if there's no wine?"

"Masturbate?" he thinks for a second. "Yeah, I just masturbate. I do it a lot. I don't get much sex at home."

"Well at least you get some sorta release, you know?" She had a sly smile on her face at the vision of Arturo stroking himself, his slender torso bare, long legs stretched out in front of him. "And I'm sure music is a great release for you too," she said.

"I would be dead without my music."

"For me, it's my writing. And working out. Dancing. I need to be physical. This helps too..." She filled her cup then topped off Arturo. "Spending time with people, it's great for me."

"I thought you meant the wine," he teased.

Dominique sipped her wine. It ached to watch her lips wrapped around the edge of her cup.

"Play. I see the way you're looking at me. You need a release."

Arturo smiled and drank most of the wine in his cup, letting out an exaggerated 'Ah' as he set the cup down next to his chair. He rubbed his hands together hungry for more music. He played and they sang Beatles hits, Rolling Stones, Manu Chao, even the forgotten songs that Dominique hummed out of tune, by ear.

It was after two in the morning before they decided to head home. Arturo collected some of the garbage from their meal and took it into the kitchen. Dominique pushed the chairs back around the table and grabbed the two empty wine bottles.

"Do you recycle?" She followed him through the French doors and around the corner into the kitchen.

"Yup," he took the bottles from her. "We'll just put that right here." He placed them on the floor next to the garbage can.

"The table's kinda sticky, I'm gonna wipe it down."

For the first time that evening, Arturo wasn't listening to her. All he could think about was her scent, her ass, her lips. He scooped her closer by the waist and put his nose in her neck, her sweat mingling with the brown sugar scent. *One kiss.* Pressure built between his legs. His face remained close to hers as he crossed to the other side of her neck, barely grazing her other cheek with the tip of his nose. *One kiss isn't really giving in to temptation.* Dominique angled her lips up towards his and they finally met. His slim frame felt strong when she wrapped her arms around his shoulders. The urgency of their kiss grew, his stubble burned her. He grabbed a handful of hair, holding her head steady so he could explore her mouth at will. She sucked the flavor of wine off his bottom lip, tiptoeing and pressing her chest against his. Their hands explored one another with no rhyme or reason. He moaned into her mouth and grabbed her ass almost lifting her off the floor. Dominique's hand ran down his chest and he inhaled sharply when her fingers landed on the waistband of his boxer briefs.

"Wait…" she broke the kiss. "We can't do this." He kissed her neck and could feel her body lessen its protest.

"I want…" he kissed her swollen lips. "I want you so bad."

"We can't. You're married…"

"I haven't touched her in months." She looked into his eyes, his eyelids heavy from passion and wine. Hard with want, he pleaded for a few seconds more before releasing her. Dominique went past him to the sink. She ripped some paper towel off the roll, wet it and left the kitchen.

Arturo offered to drive Dominique home to Brooklyn. She gladly accepted the opportunity to witness his natural and sexy movements behind the wheel.

"So who's the *morena* who danced under the stars that you'll never let go?"

She watched Arturo struggle with the realization that she understood what he'd sung. "You speak Spanish?"

"*Un poquito—morena, negra, baila, beso.* I've had those words said to me before."

Who else believes she's their morena? I could be driving her right to him. He turned onto the West Side Highway.

"So, who is she?"

"You." He looked over at Dominique then back at the empty road ahead.

"I thought that was a song you already wrote."

"*Sí.* It was *bella,* but I changed it to *morena y negra* to sing to you."

"Wow..." Dominique smiled. "That's sweet. *Gracias,* Arturo. How do you say 'thank you' in Portuguese?"

"*Obrigado.*" The bass syllables were smooth on his tongue.

"*Obrigado.*" She repeated, as her small hand trailed along his thigh, her fingertips light on his inner thigh.

Arturo knew he wasn't going to be able to drive all the way to Brooklyn sitting that close to her. He exited the Highway and pulled into a parking lot. Dominique scanned the deserted scene. *This is our secret.* He unbuckled himself. Before the seat belt snapped back into position he was halfway across Dominique and kissed her wet and deep. Her quiet moans fueled him as he tasted her neck. She tangled her fingers in his hair. There was a rhythm to their quickening breaths and the friction of their skin and clothes against the leather. He freed her, the seatbelt buckle slamming against the door. He had to see her. Arturo took one breast in his mouth, the other in his hand. He heard the clang of her belt buckle and the whiz of her zipper opening and looked up at her. There was no hesitance in Dominique's eyes. He pinned her to the headrest with the force of his kiss and slipped his hand into her pants traveling through a small patch of hair down to lips that were already parted. She slid her hips forward and threw her right foot up on the dashboard. Arturo's fingers delved into her warmth and he took her sweet nipple back between his lips. The motion of his fingers and thumb was fluid. He couldn't take his eyes off her as she gripped his wrist and her insides gripped his fingers.

It took Dominique a few moments to catch her breath. She rolled her head to the side to face him as he brushed the back of his knuckles along her cheek. In the silence she tried to rationalize what was happening between them—receiving pleasure from a married man couldn't be nearly as bad as giving, but that notion wasn't convincing her. Even if she believed it, she didn't want to stop there. She wanted to please Arturo. Her hand worked on the stiffening beneath the thin fabric of his pants. She tugged his waistband away from his flat stomach and took him in her hand. She stroked him; her touch made him want to fuck her on the parking lot pavement. Her pumps made a slick sound as he grew bigger and wetter. He reclined his seat back a few notches. He twitched in her mouth at the feel of her tongue. She tasted his salt and inhaled his musk, her full lips meeting her fingers that gripped his base. She overwhelmed his stiff, curved body. Arturo's hand went into her shorts and kneaded her ass in response to the job she was doing on him. A few more moments in her mouth, her tongue massaging him and he'd explode.

There's hard tapping on the passenger side window. The front seat of the car is flooded by a beam of light. "All right, step outta the vehicle."

Dominique figures if she moves slowly enough she won't be detectable, as she raises her head from Arturo's lap. She wipes the corners of her mouth with her thumb and first finger. Arturo pulls his t-shirt down and tucks himself back into his pants.

The couple looks into each other's eyes. *Shit.* She doesn't look at the NYPD officer standing outside her door. Dominique bites hard on the center of her top lip and her eyes widen. Arturo looks straight ahead to stop himself from laughing. He shakes his head, and his chest and belly heave slightly from a silent chuckle. She turns to the passenger door and raises her eyebrows at the officer. The officer steps back as she opens the door and climbs out the SUV. "So sorry you had to see that." Her hands are up by her shoulders, her belt undone.

The officer gives her the once over and looks past her into the car. There's no movement in the vehicle. Dominique's eyes dart around to prevent herself from ogling the human landscape in front of her. There is no doubt Officer Jennings passed the fitness tests at the Academy with flying colors; his muscles strain his uniform.

"You know it's illegal to do what you were doing, right?"

Dominique shrugs slowly. "We were headed home, you know, but we got distracted. Figured we'd pull over."

"Public lewdness is a misdemeanor. Go ahead and fix your clothes," he motions to her open shorts. She makes herself decent. "Ok, now go ahead and turn around and put your hands behind your back."

Her mouth hangs open and she slowly turns her back to the cop. *Arrested for sucking a married man's dick.* She scolds herself for not keeping her hands to herself, but Arturo felt great and his hands felt great on her. The cold steel of the handcuffs does not.

Arturo springs out of the SUV and around the front of the vehicle towards them. "What're you doing to her?"

"Don't take another step." Officer Jennings' hand is on his weapon. "Don't make things any worse."

"It's aight..." She assures Arturo with her eyes. He is no match for the cop. She doesn't want to witness Officer Jennings snap 'Flaco' in two. "He's cool," she says to Officer Jennings.

"I have to detain her while I figure out what's going on here."

Arturo notices the officer's hand on his gun. His hands shoot up and he backs up a few steps. "Don't have to put cuffs on her."

"Until I get the situation straightened out, I'm following procedure. Now I need you to place your hands on the front of the vehicle and spread your feet."

Arturo does as he's told. When he spread his legs, his slightly damp balls brush against his boxer briefs. The officer pats Arturo down quickly and finds nothing on his person. Not even a wallet.

Where are you coming from? How do you know each other? Why'd you stop here?—Officer Jennings runs through the usual questions. He doesn't doubt that Dominique isn't a prostitute as she adamantly states. Officer Jennings has lost track of the number of horny couples he's interrupted, scared a bit and sent on their way. Arturo's details match-up with hers but Officer Jennings can't ignore the familiar odor on Arturo's breath. "Sir, have you had anything to drink tonight?"

"Yeah, just some wine."

"How much have you had to drink?"

"Just two or three glasses."

"So there was alcohol consumed and you drove to this location." Neither of them responds to his statement. "Ok, listen, I'm gonna have you take the breathalyzer. If it comes up that you're not drunk, I'll chalk it up to just three glasses of wine."

This cop must have a quota to fill. Dominique doesn't realize how loud she sighs until the men turn to her.

Arturo blows into the breathalyzer and the reading comes up point zero nine.

"Well, according to the State of New York, you're legally drunk." Officer Jennings appears to get pleasure in sharing the results.

"There's no way! I didn't drink that much!"

"Guess you're just a lightweight," Officer Jennings chides.

Arturo takes a second to swallow his rage. "If I was drunk, I wouldn't drive. Plus *she's* with me."

"See, now that's the thing with alcohol. It causes you to make stupid decisions, like charging at a police officer."

"I didn't char—"

Officer Jennings leans his wide frame over Arturo's back. "You could've gotten your brains blown out." Officer Jennings steps back slightly. "Go ahead and put your hands behind your back," he orders while removing the second pair of handcuffs from his double cuff case.

"I'm not drunk..." Arturo insists.

"Maybe he's diabetic," Dominique blurts out. "That could be what you smell on his breath. Right?" She opens her eyes widely, hoping Arturo will go along with it. "Do you have diabetes? Or hypo— low blood sugar?"

Before he can answer, Officer Jennings asks, "Are you a doctor?"

"No, but I know breathalyzers get false positives with diabetics." Dominique shakes her head and shoulders with authority.

Officer Jennings looks at the couple. The man stares into his SUV through the windshield. The woman stares at the officer with her piercing eyes. "Ma'am, I'm gonna need you to go and sit over there," he motions towards the far end of the neighboring parking space. She watches him handcuff Arturo as she lowers herself to sit on the concrete bumper.

"Sir, where's your ID?"

"In the front, between the seats." Arturo is a defeated man.

The officer finds what he's looking for and returns to the front of the vehicle.

"Ok, so you're not a prostitute, and you claim you're not drunk. But you wanna explain these?" he holds up a baggy containing three pills. Public lewdness, DWI and now Possession of a Controlled Substance—he's hit the jackpot, of paperwork, on a Friday night.

Dominique throws her head back and stares at the sky. Then she leans forward putting her head between her knees. She rolls her shoulders. She straightens out one of her legs and continues to fidget. She can't get comfortable as the wave of nausea washes over her.

"Are you OK?" Officer Jennings asks.

She looks up, "I don't feel so good." She drops her head back down between her knees. This must be punishment for seducing a married man. No, being seduced. Next thing she knew, the cop will find smuggled beef in the trunk for Arturo's weekend *asado*. Or she'll find out he's running a pharmacy in his basement. Those pills could be an HIV cocktail. If she gets to sleep in her own bed that night, he'll face the STD Inquisition in the morning.

Arturo interrupts her irrational thoughts, "They're not mine."

Dominique's head shoots up. She has an even sicker feeling in the pit of her stomach. *He's going to have me take the fall.*

"They were in your vehicle with your ID."

Arturo blinks away his far away gaze and locks eyes with Officer Jennings. "Is for my son." He drops words by the second. "Is sick. My son. We give him medicine."

His thin frame is now arrow straight. That isn't the same man she'd spent the evening with. And he's losing command of the English language right before her eyes.

"His head. He shake. I put like that for his coach." Arturo shakes his head 'yes' repeatedly in rapid succession.

Officer Jennings takes a half-step back and glances over at Dominique who's watching the scene with a confused expression. "So these are your son's pills. And you're carrying them around in this little baggie in your car?"

"Doctor says is brain. Santera says is devil."

"Excuse me?"

"You know Santeria, no?" he asks the officer.

Officer Jennings turns to Dominique. "You know what he's talking about? You're the doctor."

"What? No... no! I don't know anything! It looks like a seizure but I don't know!" She shrugs. Officer Jennings searches her face for an answer. She reads uncertainty in Officer Jennings' eyes for the first time.

"These pills aren't yours?" he looks at Dominique expectantly.

"No." She shakes her head.

He drops the baggy on the hood of the SUV without a word. While he studies the pills, Arturo catches Dominique's eye and winks.

She stands as Officer Jennings approaches her and turns around so he can retrieve her ID holder from her pocket. Dominique assures the officer that she's never been arrested and has no warrants before he returns to his squad car.

Dominique checks if Officer Jennings is watching.

"Psst!" she hisses, as quietly as she can. "Hey." Her eyes brighten when he looks sidelong at her.

"Hey." He winks. But the sight of her standing there handcuffed hurts. "I should've just taken you home."

She shrugs, "I didn't say 'no'..."

Officer Jennings comes back from the squad car and stands between the two detainees. "You," he says to Dominique, "you're clean." He puts her ID behind Arturo's.

"Mr. Medina, did you know your registration is expired?"

Arturo and Dominique walk into the precinct followed by Officer Jennings. At the witching hour, the precinct is a fine social scene of drunks and pseudo-miscreants. The officer motions for them to sit. The thought of her bare legs touching that surface makes her cringe. She slips the black plastic bag off of the paper bag she's carrying and spreads it on the bench before sitting next to Arturo.

"This isn't after-school detention—move over." He jabs his thumb to the right. Dominique scoots a few inches away from Arturo. Officer Jennings continues to stare at her. She quickly moves all the way to the other end of the bench. Officer Jennings greets Officer Reyes behind the desk. Both lawmen glance over at the couple throughout their hushed exchange.

After hours of waiting, Arturo is relieved to be hearing something, anything, even if it isn't good news. He approaches when Officer Reyes calls him to the desk.

"You're being cited for public lewdness and public sexual conduct," Officer Reyes points to the words on the citation with his pen.

"A citation?"

"Yup. Pay your fine and you're done."

"Ok..." Arturo reads the ticket. "And my car?"

"Your registration is expired."

"Yes, it was just last week. I was camping with my sons. I can get that fixed right away." Arturo stops rambling. Officer Reyes doesn't respond. "When can I pick it up?"

"*Llama tu esposa.*" He'd spotted Arturo's wedding band and Dominique's lack of one when they were first brought in.

"*No puedo.*" Arturo says. "Can I get a friend to pick it up?"

"You don't have to. Officer Jennings didn't call anything else in." Reyes holds up Arturo's car keys and places them on the desk. "It's still sitting in the parking lot."

Dominique thanks Reyes after he explains her citation to her. Her fine is considerably less than Arturo's but this month's what-bill-to-pay decision will be between a full rent payment and this fine by the forty-five day deadline.

"Don't let me see you back here. Do that stuff indoors next time."

"You got it." She sighs at the thought of finally being able to go home.

"*Y vaya al doctor.* Diabetes is serious." Officer Reyes flashes Arturo a knowing glance.

They walk from the 26th precinct back to the Fairway Market parking lot. His guitar is right where he left it, in the back of his SUV.

There won't be any traffic this early on a Saturday morning and the drive to and from Brooklyn will give him time to come up with a story to explain not being home for over twelve hours.

He insists on driving Dominique home.

* * *

My dick was so hard. Any little thing she did or said set me off. I'm never far from a hard-on to begin with. I excused myself from the table just so I could cool off. I went to the bathroom but didn't have to go. I leaned up against the door and did my breath control exercises I learned in Taekwondo. I even let out a *K'ihap!* The dude waiting to use the bathroom after me gave me a weird look and cast a wide berth around me when we passed one another.

I felt more in control now. I made sure I adjusted myself in the bathroom too. I was laying up and to the left and I pulled my balls way forward so they wouldn't end up between my legs. I lost all control I'd regained when I saw her applying lip balm when I got back to the table. It was in this ball. You take the top of it off and you rub the ball on your lips to apply the lip balm. She was rubbing her full lips with this ball making them shiny and more pronounced. When she smiled her mouth was the exact replica of the cartoon lips you see used when they draw smiles with perfect white teeth. And you could say I was the cartoon guy with steam coming outta his ears and his eyes bugging outta his head.

So to say dinner was going well was an understatement. Yeah, she was beautiful and I wanted her bad but I don't think we struggled for conversation at all that night. We didn't sit and stare at the walls while we waited for dinner. Instead we talked about our childhoods, families, and jobs. We got along pretty well. She had a brain in her head. She also had told the funniest stories with her as the butt of the joke but without pity-seeking self-deprecation. I laughed so hard at one point that it turned into a coughing fit 'cause my drink went down the wrong pipe. She took it in stride and I didn't feel embarrassed to have her see me like that – eyes tearing up, nose running – until I stopped coughing. We were quiet for a little bit after that only 'cause I needed to catch my breath. The coughs really hurt my chest.

"How are your abs?"

"Huh?" Maybe she said something I missed when I was coughing so hard it felt like I'd return my dinner to the plate from whence it came.

"Your stomach? How's it feel?"

Now that she'd asked, I noticed it was tight like after I do crunches. She reached over to me and put her hands on my stomach. "Sounding like you were really coughing from the gut." She gave my stomach a soothing rub that I almost purred and sucked my thumb. I also looked her right in the eye trying to use a Jedi mind trick to make her lower her hand a few inches...and to the left.

We met almost 2 weeks before our date on the website BlackSingles4You.com. We did a lot of messaging back and forth and were ready to meet each other before either of us got bored.

Over dessert we made up back stories for the other diners in the restaurant. "He looks like he likes to get pissed on after sex," she said of a tall men with a George Costanza balding pattern. My eyes were bugging outta my head. I couldn't believe what I just heard. She smiled. "Relax. Just because I know about that stuff don't mean I like to do it." I relaxed a bit but now I was thinking about the things that she might actually be into. "I don't have to piss on a man to mark my territory." She took a spoonful of her chocolate cheesecake past her dick-sucking lips. Me, I was speechless again, and praying to *all* gods that she'd mark me and make those same cute sex sounds she was making while she ate.

"What about them?" I discreetly pointed out a couple sitting across from each other at one of the two tops along the far wall. We lucked out with a four-top and it was her choice to sit at the 90-degree seat instead of across from me. She rolled her eyes at the idea of sitting on opposite sides of the table. "We've had a screen between us for long enough" was her reasoning. I was happy to hear that because I wanted to be close to her too. The dude on the 'first date' was average looking. The woman wasn't bad at all. She had a huge natural hair afro that was weighed down in the middle, making it look like the McDonald's "M". She had smooth skin and two bodies in one – her upper body looked like the after of a weight loss ad, from the waist down she was real thick. I'd hit it. I'd keep my eye on her to see how she maneuvered on the stilettos she was wearing.

"Oh they're definitely on a first date." She studied them some more. "But they didn't meet online like us. They met in a bookstore or something."

I could totally see it. "In the self-help aisle."

"Ha! She was buying and he was out trolling for desperate women."

"Yup... so now they're on an 'ok' first date, stressing about what's next."

"To fuck or not to fuck." Damn if she wasn't sexy when she said the word 'fuck'. Fuck.

"Exactly."

"She's thinking, 'if I have sex with him then I'll finally have a boyfriend!'" She throws her arms up in rah-rah fashion.

"And dude's thinking 'I'll finally get some pussy.'" We both laughed at that one. It's true that some women think it's a slut's game to fuck on the first date. We talked about that. And it's not fair that dudes think like that too but they still fuck women the first night if they can. But if two adults are feeling each other, then why not go for it? Could just be for fun, but if it leads to a lifetime of happiness then it proves that love can triumph over all.

All right, so I'm gonna come clean. I felt like she could be the one for a minute. I wasn't dating anyone else at the moment and couldn't see myself doing so if I was dating her. We seemed to be on the same wavelength too – not looking for anything too serious but willing to go with the flow. If it led to a LTR so be it. I would be willing to be her spiritual man who had a relationship with God. On her profile she checked the box marked "Christian" but admitted at dinner that she's becoming more spiritual than religious the older she's gotten. That was a relief for me because even though I checked the box marked "Catholic" in my profile, I never did go to church on the regular, only when my mother thought we needed Jesus. Now that I'm grown, I go to church for weddings, christenings and funerals. And I partake in the practice of premarital sex quite often. Praise Jesus!

"So, what do you wanna do now?" So many freaky thoughts ran through my mind at that moment, some probably illegal. I didn't know how she would respond to, "Let's go back to my crib," so I just said, "Let's take a walk."

"It'll be good to walk off this food," she agreed. I couldn't help watching her as she scooted out of the booth, all her goodies bouncing. She stood and adjusted her belt. Her ass looked right in them jeans.

It was a damp spring evening. A light mist was falling so we threw on our hoods. As we walked down Smith Street the rain started to get really heavy and she opened her umbrella. She was too short to hold it up over my head so I took the umbrella from her and put my arm around her shoulders. She waited a little then she put her arm around my waist. I couldn't help but smell her hair. She might've caught me. I saw her smile but she didn't say anything so I'm not sure.

I took another sniff of her hair when we were waiting to cross the street.

"It's almond oil, coconut and vanilla." She said looking straight ahead. The light changed and she stepped off the curb. I was a split second behind her. I settled back into my spot next to her, holding her a little tighter and closer than before. She was fast. "Those are the oils I use in my hair. I see you like my blend."

"Oh...!" Damn, she got me. How was I gonna get outta this without coming across like some pervert weirdo. "Yeah... sorry, I didn't mean to..."

"It's ok, I'm glad you like it." She finally looked at me with that smile on her face. My stomach did a flip when she did. "I use those oils on my body sometimes, too." She didn't even

know how fucking sexy that sounded. Nah, she probably did. I
could tell by her smile this woman knew a lot.

I slowed our stroll to a halt. I leaned in and smelled her
neck to find out if she'd used the oils on her body that night.
She smelled good enough to eat. She raised her chin ever-so
slightly like she was serving her neck to me. The street was
quiet, the rain was steady and we were standing real close. My
lips landed on her neck real soft. I lifted my head and saw her
eyes were closed. I kissed her lips real soft. I startled her just a
little bit, she was expecting the kiss but maybe not so soon.
Then I felt her kiss me back and she ran her tongue along my
bottom lip. I put my hand on her lower back and pulled her in
so I could press my *whole* body against hers. After that she took
charge of the kiss. I was definitely feeling that.

I'm not sure how much time passed but when we
stopped kissing, I said what was on my mind this time, "Come
home with me."

She smiled that smile again, "Lead the way."

We were standing in my kitchen drinking. I was
knocking back the Yellowtail wine but she was nursing her drink
at a torturously slow pace. Her laughs dropped down to giggles
and she didn't talk as much as she did at dinner. I leaned in to
kiss her again and she turned her head a little and I only got the
corner of her mouth. She cast her eyes down, acting all shy. I
lifted her chin and kissed her neck. She liked it when I did that
earlier. I heard her moan a little when I kissed her neck in the
kitchen so I kept at it. I kissed and licked all around. Warm her
up a bit and then I'll go for the kiss again...

Again she turned her head away when I went to kiss her.
"Come on, give me a kiss..." Now was not the time to start
acting like a goody church girl. I brought her face back towards
mine and got to taste her lips again. She was holding back. I
could hear her moan into my mouth then stop and stiffen up a
bit. I put my drink down and took the glass out of her hand and
put it on the kitchen counter behind her. I pulled her close but
she felt tense. She didn't get into it like when we were outside.

It's the kitchen. The kitchen ain't sexy to some women.

It's all about cooking and cleaning in there so they just can't get
into the mood. I was more than willing to take her to my
bedroom, do it missionary with the lights off even, if that would
make her more comfortable.

"You live here by yourself?"

"I have a roommate," I whispered as we walked past the
closed door to his room. I didn't know if he was home or not.

"Ok," she smiled and put her fingers to her lips and let
out a playful "Shhh..."

She let me undress her, piece by piece. She was standing
in front of me when I took off her shirt and her bra. She had
awesome ski jump hill breasts. Her nipples pointed up at me and
I flicked them with my tongue. With my hands on her waist I
could feel her quiver a little bit. I took her whole nipple and
then some into my mouth. Her nipples and my dick were rock
hard when I was done. I put her on the bed after I pulled off her
jeans. Her thighs were smooth and strong. All her skin was just
soft and smooth. That's that skin that you just gotta touch and
kiss. Damn, I was lucky.

I couldn't wait to be between her thighs and have her
wrap them around my waist. She had her eyes closed the entire
time I was sucking and kissing her body. I dry humped her,
hoping she'd grind against me so I could get an idea of how she
liked to fuck. I opened her pussy lips and her clit trembled when
I was rubbing it. She was so quiet, but she was still breathing. I
actually slowed down a bit to check. It hit me that she was
probably trying to be quiet cause of my roomie. Damn, dude
was cock-blocking and I didn't even know if he was *actually*
there. She was moving her hips to get away from my touch. She
grabbed my wrist to stop me. I fucked up. I went straight for
her clit without warming her up and I know better. Some
women are too sensitive for that. I stuck my finger inside her
instead. Her pussy was hot and wet. I loved the way her pussy
grabbed onto my finger. My dick was jumping thinking about
being inside of her. I took her hand and put it on my dick so we
could play with each other at the same time. Her hand was
warm and soft. Problem was she stroked it like three times and
her hand went limp. She looked sidelong at me like she was

waiting for instructions on what to do next.

Damn, what to do next – that was probably it! Maybe her pussy was so tight 'cause she was a virgin. I only took one other girl's virginity. But that chick was with it, an active participant, willing to learn all I could teach her. I don't remember if she was into church or anything, but I do remember she was cool with never seeing me again afterwards. I had to decide if I was ready for the emotional aftermaths if I took this woman's virginity. And I had to think fast because my fingers were soaking wet from getting in her up to the knuckles.

I was stroking her hair before I realized I was doing it. I would take care of her. I wouldn't do her wrong. Make sure her first time was passionate. Then once she learned what I knew, we could do more crazy shit together, but no pissing on each other. After a few seconds, she closed her eyes. When she opened them again she was looking at a corner of the ceiling.

I was careful not to put too much of my weight on her while I eased into her. Tight, and hot like fire. And so slick. I wanted to look into her eyes. To connect with her. To really be *with* her while I made love to her but she wouldn't make eye contact with me. She didn't look like she was in pain. She didn't look like she *felt anything*. I'm not laying 12-inch pipe but chicks know when I'm in them. I pulled out really slow just to the point where my head would graze her lips then went back in. A few more strokes like that and I didn't know how long I'd last.

I kissed her chin and her neck, nibbled on her ear and asked, "You ok? Does it hurt?"

She finally spoke again. "Hurt?"

"Yeah, sometimes it hurts the first time..." I uttered those words with compassion while I kissed her neck again. I was going to make sure she knew I wasn't only out to get mine.

"What?"

"It's ok if it hurts a little. You'll open up once you start having sex more."

She pushed on my shoulders so she could see my face. "You think I'm a *virgin?*" You'd think I asked to piss on her. I looked lovingly into her eyes. Her angry eyes and furrowed brow.

She was picking up her clothes one at a time and putting them on. "I can't believe you thought I was a virgin."

"But I mean, you weren't doing anything. I thought you didn't know what to do."

I swear the woman smiles like she knows everything.

She came out of her way to come to my place so I made sure I gave her a ride home. We rode in silence for almost ten minutes. This silence was worse than the silent treatment I got in bed. I missed the way were at dinner. I tried to make conversation and all I got in return was one word answers to open ended questions. I was so focused on trying to undo my mistake of thinking she was a virgin that I forgot to turn on my radio when we got in the car.

I should've known asking her what she wanted to listen to was pointless. She shrugged each time I stopped on a station and asked if she wanted to listen to it. The oldies station was even playing one of her songs—we sang part of it at dinner!—and she acted like it was nothing when she heard it on the radio. Her jaw clenching was the only sign from her that made me know she was actually listening to me. "Fuck it," I muttered to myself and turned back to the station *I* wanted to listen to. I settled back in my driving rhythm.

She changed the radio station.

"Don't you know you ain't never supposed to touch a man's car radio?" I was half-joking, more-serious.

"Can I touch this?" She grabbed my dick.

I looked at her stunned then snapped my head back around to watch the road. "Yeah, you could touch that all you want."

She rubbed and squeezed it through my jeans and I was hard in seconds. She opened my jeans and pulled my dick out the front slit of my boxers. I think the next thing she did was the sexiest thing she did all night; she licked the palm of her hand, and my dick finally got stroked how I wanted it that night. She let out a sound that made me know she was impressed, "God, I can't resist a pretty dick..." she barely got the words out before her mouth was surrounding me. And it felt so fucking good. I was right about those thick lips of hers. I stopped, barely, at a red light. She was working that dick balls deep. That was paradise. She was even licking me right under my belly button. I didn't even know that was one of my spots until she did that. I grabbed her hair and ran my hands down her back and slipped my fingers into the back of her jeans.

"Lemme make it easier for you," she said and she opened her belt. She started taking off her jeans and the car behind me honked. Oh yeah, that's right, people 'go' on the green light. She kicked off her jeans and her panties and played with her pussy. When she started fucking herself, I could hear how wet she was. That shit was crazy. I could steer my car with my dick, that's how hard I was.

"Make a left," she said.

"What?"

"Make a left," she repeated. She took my right hand off the steering wheel and climbed on top of me. The light was yellow and I just missed a SUV that was coming in the opposite direction when I made that hard left. We were both trying to beat the red light. And dude driving the SUV saw her sitting on me and leaned on his horn. She lubed up the head of my dick by running it along her pussy then sat on it. I swear my eyes crossed and my vision went blurry. Her pussy was so tight and juicy. Forget what I said earlier, *this* was where the grass was the green and the girl riding me was way pretty. She wasn't playing. She was working her hips and sucking my neck. I was able to see over her shoulder and pull over to the curb.

Friends, don't let friends fuck and drive. "Yo, you fucking tryna get us killed..." She kissed me and that shut me up. This kiss was like our first kiss. She took control. The harder and deeper I kissed her, the more her pussy squeezed. Now she wasn't just winding on my dick but she was bouncing hard. She didn't even care that the small of her back was hitting against the steering wheel sometimes. I grabbed her hips and ass so I could feel it slap against my lap.

And she was loud. The windows were rolled up and the street was empty, but that's what made her seem louder. People in their houses would think I was murdering her. When we were in bed, she was...wack, sorry, can't think of no other way to put it. But once we got in the car, under the streetlights, she was a beast. She liked that public sex. That chance that we could get caught. I was taught to want a lady in the streets but a freak in the sheets but this shit was awesome.

She hit my hand away when I reached to turn off the ignition. Next thing I knew, I was flat on my back. She pulled the lever next to my seat and pushed on me so the seat would go back. It happened so fast. If someone walked by, they would see the headlights on, look inside and see us. Now she was working her hips up and back. And she was leaving her cream all over me. I thought about the emails and photos we sent back and forth and nothing gave me a clue it would be like this. The most skin I saw was a photo of her on a cruise with her mother and sister. She was wearing a bathing suit with a sarong. It wasn't even a bikini. But looking at her body now, she could definitely rock a string bikini if she wanted to.

She grabbed onto the handle above the car window so she could fuck up and down higher and harder. Her gold rosary dangled in her cleavage. I squeezed my ass and pressed my feet into the floor mat so I could fuck up into her.

"Yeah..." she said in response to me giving it to her and getting loud. That turned her on and her pussy got wetter and tighter. That shit felt so good and I was about to come but I wasn't trying to have no kids. "Wait, wait, wait, wait...get off..." I said. She slid off my dick and I kept stroking my shit. She hopped back into the passenger seat but grabbed my dick and sucked it. I felt the back of her throat and it was over. It felt like I was nutting in her mouth for an hour.

"You know where you are?" she asked, lifting her hips and pulling her jeans up.

I put my dick back in my pants. I sat up and looked through the windshield. And I actually wasn't sure where I was. I pulled the lever and the back of my seat popped back up. "Nah, you know how to get home from here?"

"Yeah, I know this spot. I'm like five blocks from here. I'll show you." She slipped her feet in her shoes.

"Cool." I put the car in drive and pulled away from the curb. She was buckling her belt when I asked her, "So, when I'ma see you again?" I needed a repeat performance.

She just shrugged. "I don't know."

"I could come see you during the week."

"I work," she said.

"Me too. I could come see you *after* work."

"I mean, we don't have to force it. If it happens, it happens." I had to agree with her on that one. I wanted to fuck with abandon. But I wanted us to build organically. Get to know each other.

"How about next Saturday then?"

"I can't that night. I have a date."

* * *

The Storm

The flash of lightning and the crack of thunder were timed perfectly with the sounds of T.S.O.P. Only Mother Nature could've answered our rain dance the way she did. We danced harder, the bass thumped, the rain poured. We gyrated, pulsated, our skin sticky and sweet in the humid June air.

"Are you coming?" I asked. I peered at him around the corner of the door. My eyes beckoned him to follow me into the bedroom. Or it could've been the way my lips parted slightly in bated anticipation. Without a word he rose and strode over to me taking my bottom lip between his own.

The lightning flashed and the thunder crashed as he laid me onto the bed. It felt like an eternity but was probably only a few seconds where we just admired each other. My nipples stood erect, each one vying for the number one spot. I admired his nipples and the Ankh tattooed under his left collarbone. I wanted to trace the outline with my tongue. Then down the center of his chest, over the soft ridges of his belly to the throbbing between his legs about to enter mine.

He took my breath away in one motion. He smiled as I made one of my nasty faces. One of those it feels so good expressions. That don't you dare stop stare.

The French sounds of Air faded into Love Hangover, briefly turning our party into a *ménage à trois*. Our union prepping us to rear the next generation of Black Beauties.

"Are you coming?" I asked. I barely heard his whisper before the lightning flashed and the thunder crashed. He made one of his woman you hurt so good faces. His slow withdrawal was both torture and pleasure. There it was, a trickle from deep within my yoni. A solitary tear drop, on the trail to the sheets below. So sad to see him go. And he kissed away my tears from my blue-black space.

If there's a cure for this, I don't want it either. Miss Ross and I had the same ache. Please, no bright lights, no loud noises, just the possibility of an eternity with our heads on their chests. If there's a remedy, I run from it too. Preach on, sista.

*   *   *

African Beats

The two decided to sneak into the Harlem dance studio after hours. When they got together, they couldn't help acting like mischievous adolescents instead of the 30-somethings they were. Upon entering the studio, it became apparent what drew them to this spot. The walls were adorned with masks from West to Central Africa. Eyes of the Igbo, Ligbi, Baule, Senofu and Yoruba stared back at the pair. The walls of the studio were undoubtedly held up by their strength and stature.

She raised her eyebrow to her partner in "do you feel that?" fashion. He nodded to her silent query. The spirits of the craftsmen who carved the masks, the queens and warriors who once donned them and the ancestors they represented were palpable. She gazed at a Punu mask. He ran his fingers along the smooth but weathered surface of a djembe drum as though he had made it himself. The pride in his craftsmanship was felt as the centuries old drum maker wiped his brow under the Sub-Saharan sun. The ivory Idia watched him.

He placed the drum between his knees and tapped it lightly.

Du-du-du-Boom-du

She continued examining the details of the masks but one in particular; a masquerade mask spoke to her. Literally. She thought it was him who had called her name, but in fact it was the cry of her ancestors which summoned her to that mask. Both she and the mask wore their hair high on their heads. Her long, sensuous neck accentuated. Still fixated on the mask, she started to jook to the now frenetic drum beats.

She donned the mask and entered a trance. The power of the transformation generated a split second icy chill in the studio. Stories were told and lives lived through her body, through her dance. The glow of her mahogany skin became more radiant. Her pendulous breasts, punctuated with nipples ripe to provide sustenance for the village and to relive the pleasures of her foremothers, beckoned him. Her soft belly that once carried her children until they were ready to enter the world, yet still strong and healed from the fetuses that were forcibly removed by slave doctors, undulated. Her meaty buttocks, the seat of the world, followed the twirl of her waist. Her thighs absorbed the shock of her thunderous stomps and between them was housed the power of all creation.

The slap of her bare feet hitting the studio floor made their own bass, syncopating with the sound of his powerful palms beating the drum.

Du-da-da-Doom-boom-boom

Sweat rained from her brow to the floor below while giant raindrops dampened the cracked earth of the Masai Mara. Her arms thrashed back and forth.

The studio floor became slippery from her back pressed against it under the weight of his body. The two dark figures coiled around each other. The clay covering their bodies was washed away with waves of passion, sweat and rain.

Under the gaze of the Lwalwa mask they writhe and wail. His thrust was strong and deliberate. Upon each withdrawal she readied herself for his reentry but her breath was taken away each time. He slid into the base of her womb and she drew in a breath, arching her back, pressing her chest to his. The muscles of his shoulders, back and buttocks flexed under the sweet strain of his work and from the pleasure coursing through his body. He felt the warmth as he plunged into her on every inch of his skin. Their breath still beat an audible rhythm on the drum.

Du-da-Boom-du-da-Boom

A sexy bass reverberated off the goatskin. The hollow eyes of the masks remained trained on the couple who couldn't resist the arousal piqued by their wall-mounted voyeurs.

On hands and knees, they slip and slid on the slippery surface, but their bodies still found each other. Matching the waves crashing against the shore of Gabon, the slap of their bodies was rhythmic, their cries of passion guttural and almost spiritual. In the wake of his pelvis and belly meeting her body, he is coated with her creamy remnants mixed with the seafoam covering hands, elbows, knees and feet.

Her hips rise to the heights of the Virunga Mountains. Head down and with her rear end held high for entry, she claws at the floor, wet sand being squeezed between her fingers. The sweat drips off the tip of his nose into her inviting crevice.

At the end, they lay glued together. His strong arms held her close. She ran her fingers along his slippery skin. A mask now lay next to the couple. They questioned each other how it got there, neither had taken it off the wall, he never withdrew his body from hers and neither had left the other's side.

Making a playful decision, he picked up the mask and put it over his face. His screams of terror were muffled as he struggled with the mask. They cannot be distinguished from the Angolan people begging for Nzinga's rescue.

The mask transformed his entire body into wood except for his Mandingo dick. That remained of human flesh but was rigid like the rest of his body. She couldn't resist its call. She wrapped her fingers around it and began to fondle. Then she sucked it and it throbbed, letting her know there was still life in it. She suspended herself above him for what felt like an eternity. The anticipation caused her to drip. She would free him with her nectar, causing the wood to split. She engulfed him deep inside her body and embraced his hips with her knees and thighs. The wave coursed up her spine forcing her chest forward. She arched her back and held onto her breasts.

Da-da-Doom-da-da-Doom-da-da-Doom-da-da-Doom

That wave centered deep in her pelvis. The villagers danced frenetically around the couple. She threw her head back and continued to grind against her wooden lover, letting out a passionate wail. Her climax gave rise to a response from her encased lover. His body pulsated in orgasm, splintering the wood. Their essences swirled and melded together causing a bright visible whirlwind within the studio.

Once his body was freed from its wooden prison, the mask floated from his face. She laid her breasts on his, holding onto him inside, and kissed his lips.

*   *   *

The After Party

The birthday party had nasty cake, a sound system that assaulted everyone with screeching feedback, barely any guests and no guys even worth looking at according to Eliana.

She sat gazing out the window of the cab. Simone watched the meter because she had a distrust of cabbies. To hear Eliana say it, Simone had a distrust of men in general. Yet she identified with them right down to her heavy-handed mannerisms that become noticeable after spending time with her.

Simone was pretty with smooth chestnut skin, piercing dark eyes, full wide lips and her "good hair", otherwise known as 3C. Simone schooled Eliana on the differences between "good hair" and "nigga naps". All Eliana knew was that she loved the elaborate designs Simone got braided or flat-twisted into her hair.

"Cornbread braids?" Eliana asked once.

In between laughs and snorts, Simone was able to correct her. "Corn*rows.*"

When the two women first met, Eliana never could tell if Simone was just friendly or had a crush on her and she never worked up the nerve to ask Simone which way she leaned. Her suspicions were confirmed when she met Simone's now ex-girlfriend at Fire Island during its heyday.

Neither of them wore much jewelry. Eliana wore a thin gold chain with a cross, a watch to match her mood, not her outfit, and tiny stud earrings. Her mother would beg her to put on bigger earrings after she cut her hair short "like a boy" but Eliana refused with a smile at her mother's old world views. She relied solely on her Mediterranean features to announce her gender. Simone wore a Jesus piece that was quite excessive for that night.

"Twenty-two dollars? Yo, that's crazy!" Simone shouted.

"On the meter. Twenty-two dollars! You pay! " the cabbie demanded.

Simone sucked her teeth. "This is crazy. I ain't tipping yo' ass." Simone reached into her back pocket and pulled out her wallet. She looked at Eliana. "You got enough money to get home?"

Eliana barely made eye contact with her. "Yeah," and weakly nodded her head 'yes'. She had enough money for the bus. Cab rides were a luxury she didn't think she deserved, but like tonight, there was usually someone willing to pay for them.

Simone sucked her teeth again. "You ain't got no money."

"You pay!" the cabbie interrupted.

"Yo, we tryna get our money together!" Simone barked back. "You staying with me. I ain't letting you ride home with him." She punched 'CASH' on the POS touch screen.

Simone nearly bowls Eliana over as she rushes into the bathroom. She plops onto the toilet not bothering to close the door behind her. "Yo, my stomach is all messed up."

Eliana remains at the bathroom door, fidgeting as if she didn't just take a piss. She keeps her eyes trained on the wall, or the floor tiles or the soap in the soap dish. Anywhere but on Simone sitting on the toilet. "Um, there's no more tissue."

Simone rolls her eyes, sucks her teeth again, and without hesitation, pushes her panties and jeans all the way to her ankles, steps out of them and peels off her socks. Then she strips off her top and throws it on the bathroom floor with the rest of her clothes. While she undresses, Eliana can't resist taking peeks at her.

"Shit and shower. That's the best anyway." She flushes

the toilet and hops into the tub, drawing the curtain behind her.

Eliana can't shake the image of her smooth back out of her head. Not that she expected Simone to be wrinkled and hunched over but her body looked so youthful. Early on in their friendship when Simone showed her driver's license as proof of her age, Eliana's eyes nearly popped out of her head when she did the math on the DOB. She could only hope when the 7 years passed and she's Simone's age she can look as good. "Black don't crack, sweetie." Case closed.

Eliana remains transfixed by the silhouette in the shower. Most of the washcloth disappears from view as Simone washes between her legs.

"Ellie, you gonna take a shower after me?"

She doesn't even hear the question. She can't take her eyes off the shapely, shadowy figure behind the shower curtain rinsing the soap from between her legs with the hand-held shower head.

"Ellie?" She peeks from behind the curtain. "You heard me?"

Eliana snaps out of her daze and moves closer to the tub "Huh?"

"I said, are you gonna take a shower? You know, to get clean? Wake up, girl!" She splashes water on her dazed friend.

Eliana gasps and jumps back. "You wet me!" Water trickles down her cheek. She holds her shirt away from her body to view the damage.

Simone shrugs it off. "It'll dry."

Eliana grabs the shower head and tries to take it from her. During the tussle, they splash water all over the shower walls, bathroom floor and even the ceiling. Eliana gains control of the shower head when she snatches off Simone's shower cap.

There's a tense stare down. Eliana holds the spray of water inches from Simone's pressed hair. "I'll do it..." she taunts.

"Watch it now..." There's no telling what Simone will do to protect her hairstyle.

"Why? It'll dry," she mocks. She waves the spray of water along her body. Simone flinches, still trying to protect her hair. Her friend taunts her again with a wave of the water.

The curves usually hidden under her baggy and straight-line clothing are mesmerizing to Eliana. Simone has skin models pay to be photoshopped into looking like they possess. She watches as the water flows down the slope of Simone's teardrop breasts and streams off the tuft of hair between her legs.

Simone notices her gaze. "You know, you can adjust that..." she points to the shower head. Eliana's eyebrows shoot up—a deer in headlights suddenly very aware she's standing in front of her nude friend who's made no attempt to cover up. She doesn't seem to have a self-conscious bone in her body. "If you're gonna wet me, you might as well do it right."

Eliana looks at the shower massager and the light bulb moment is written all over her expression. With one twist, three streams of water beat out of the shower head onto Simone's belly. Again, her eyes dart from Simone's breasts to her heart-shaped thighs to that mysterious triangle.

Simone closes her eyes and revels in the sensation of the water beating against her skin. Eliana inches the spray down to her crotch but hesitates. She opens her eyes, nodding to encourage her to keep going. Eliana's raised eyebrows ask the obvious, "really?"

"You gotta shower massager at home, right?"

Eliana nods. She discovered the power of her shower massager a few years ago by mistake and has used it a few hundred times since then on purpose.

"So you know what to do." Simone's naughty tight-lipped smile is priceless. She leans against the shower wall, her knees bent slightly, separating her thighs. Below the tuft of hair, her full lips part to reveal her clit dancing back and forth through the stream of water.

"Shit, girl..." she moans, grabbing her breasts. The tension in her arm magnifies her muscle tone. Her dark, nickel-sized nipples stare back at Eliana. She squeezes and pushes up her breast like she's begging for it to be touched. Eliana grazes one of her dark nipples with her finger.

"Mmm, squeeze it a little..." She's lost in the haze of her body's reaction to the spray of water. Her friend holds back at first but caresses her nipple. She pushes her hips forward under the stream of water. "Kiss it," she whispers. Eliana pulls her hand away. Simone opens her eyes and sees Eliana staring at her breasts.

"Ellie," she dips her head to place her face in Eliana's line of sight, "you don't have to... I just... I lost it for a second."

"It feels good though..." she trails off.

"What...?" Simone asks.

Eliana rethinks sharing how good it feels to have her nipples sucked while she's being fucked. Bringing up men probably wasn't the best idea. Swallowing the thought, she leans in and her lips hover millimeters away from the glistening nipple. Up close, it isn't scary. Whatever she was expecting to see or smell doesn't exist. She takes the bating nipple into her mouth softly and sucks her breast the way she'd want hers to be sucked, the way some men she's been with never did. She tickles her lips with the nipple. She loves the feeling of it on her tongue as she swirls around it. The moans that rain down on her and the pressure from the hand on the back of her head make it clear that a few hard sucks of the entire areola followed by a swirling flick on the nipple is what her friend likes. Eliana treats her other nipple to the same sweet treatment.

Simone pushes her head away from her excited chest. She searches her young friend's expression for any reason to stop. She reads the curiosity and passion in Eliana's eyes. She pulls her in for their first kiss. They suck each other's lips and their tongues dance. The scent and sounds of this kiss are softer and sweeter than any of Eliana's ex-boyfriends'. The front of her shirt is completely wet as she sinks into the comforting kiss.

Simone props her foot up on the edge of the tub and holds Eliana's wrist to keep the stream of water steady on her spot. "God, it's so fucking good..." her knees buckle slightly. She reaches under her raised thigh and slips the tip of her finger into her ass. As her pussy tingles and tightens in response to the water massage, her ass responds in kind. She's in up to her second knuckle and lets out a cry. Eliana is on her mouth again kissing with urgency as if she's trying to feel what she's experiencing through the kiss.

Pleasure courses through Simone's body; from Eliana's kisses to the wet tile against her back to the water beating her clit to the finger easing her asshole to a gape. She turns around and hikes her ass into the air, the roller coaster arch in her back and her head bowed in pleasure. All concern about getting her hair wet is a distant memory.

Eliana can't resist touching Simone's round smooth ass. It's warm, soft but it keeps its shape in her hand. Her puffy lips sit between her thighs. They're so much like hers yet so foreign. She touches her friend the way her own body craves to be touched. She explores Simone with a tentative finger from the top of her ass crack to her clit and back. Simone doesn't offer any instruction this time. She runs her finger along her slit again and this time slips her finger between her pussy lips. Simone eases back onto her finger and Eliana quickly pulls it out. She's still getting comfortable with the fact there's a woman connected to the wet hole she's exploring.

The water is one kind of wet. The slippery juices seeping from Simone is a familiar wet too. The two textures compliment each other on the tip of Eliana's finger, triggering memories of her own wet solo sessions. In the present moment, rubbing her fingertips and thumbs together, her own pussy gets wet.

Simone's fingers tug and rub on her hood and Eliana knows she wants more of the pleasurable aqua spray. She aims the *thump-bump-tack* water spray at her friend again. Simone claws at the wall with her other hand and makes no attempt to quiet her screams. She reaches around and spreads her ass open. Eliana takes in the amazing view of her asshole sitting atop her pussy and clit bounded by her thick lips all dripping wet. Her sunflower-shaped opening is tight and throbbing. She aims one of the heavy massaging streams at the target. It opens slightly allowing some water to enter her ass like a creampie. Simone fingers her ass again while Eliana points the water back on her clit. Her back arches, her waist seizes up and her thighs quiver as she comes.

Watching her friend's hole spasm is hypnotizing. Hearing her friend's orgasm cry makes her own pussy wet. Caught up in the sexual rapture Simone is so unlike the "tough guy" shield she lives behind. She lets out a satisfied giggle laced with a hint of exhaustion. She braces herself against the wall for a few breaths before standing upright. In one motion she turns and grabs Eliana by the nape of her neck and sticks her tongue deep into her mouth. After both women catch their breath, she takes the shower head from Eliana and places it back on the hook. The energy in the bathroom is charged when she turns off the water and silence blankets them.

Eliana stares at her lips and clit that are still swollen when she steps out the tub.

"It's cute, right?" Simone asks putting her hand on her belly to pull up on her lips a little.

She takes Eliana's hand and leads her out the bathroom, stepping over the pile of her clothes. Eliana watches her friend's hips rise and fall as they walk to the bedroom.

"You good?"

Eliana responds with a small, slow nod. Her skin tingles almost causing her to shiver as Simone runs her hands over her shoulders and down her arms, then interlocking their fingers. Simone brings Eliana's hand to her lips and kisses the back of it.

"I wanna see you. Is that cool?"

Eliana takes another trip over Simone's body with her eyes, worried that she won't stack up. But standing there with Simone holding her hands with a reassuring grip makes her think it won't be the end of the world.

She allows Simone to undress her. Simone smiles at the boyfriend briefs she's wearing. "Those are cute..." She traces the edge and trim of the underwear with her fingers. She slips her finger under the waist band and rubs the fingernail side of her finger against her flat stomach. Then she runs her palm over the material of the yoga bra covering her perky breasts. Eliana's nipples pebble under the material.

"Let's take this off...?" She's careful to handle her newbie with care.

Eliana pushes one strap at a time off her shoulders. Her petite breasts barely rise or fall from their high perch on her chest as she pulls her bra off over her head. She's all nipple and her breasts sit far apart because of her broad shoulders.

Simone's breasts are fleshier, medium-sized pendulums that sit lower on her chest. She catches the comparative glance Eliana passes between them. Her angelic nature is a turn-on to Simone. She kisses her again and the pair falls onto the bed. Their limbs match the black-and-white geometric design on the Queen-size sheets.

Eliana never thought this would happen, with Simone or any other woman, but she enjoys the kissing. It was going down without the aid of alcohol she was lead to believe would be the reason it'd happen, if it ever did. She was no stranger to friends-with-benefits arrangements with guys but wasn't sure where this left her relationship with Simone. The thought crosses her mind about whether or not women have one-night stands. She can't shut off her brain, as she wonders if the two of them will be kiss-and-shower buddies from now on.

The weight of Simone's body on hers isn't as encompassing as with a man. Simone feels plush with their breasts pressed together and as she holds her by the side of the waist. She doesn't have to spread her knees as wide to accommodate Simone as they grind their hips together. Missing is the tickle of body hair against her skin. Everything down to her breath felt different, lighter and sensual.

Simone's mouth journeys down her body. She licks the length of her collarbone, down the center of her chest before flicking one of her nipples with her tongue. She feels Eliana's apprehension dissolving as her body awakens beneath hers. In response, she sucks more urgently, drawing in as much of Eliana's breast into her mouth as she can, before going to the next one. They are now a darker shade from the suction. Her tongue leaves a warm damp trail down the center of Eliana's stomach, over her belly button piercing, bringing her face-to-face with her pussy. She doesn't stop her exploration. She licks the strip of material covering Eliana. Simone is familiar with that squirm and licks again, probing her tongue into her through the cotton.

Eliana shifts her hips in a way that says she wants to feel the wet of Simone's tongue or stiffness of her fingers. Simone pulls off Eliana's panties, whose heat radiates like a warm mouth exhaling on her face. She's fragrant like robust olive oil, subtle.

"You're beautiful..." She runs her fingers along Eliana's wide vulva concealing her clit in wet mystery. "I mean, everything, you, you look good. But your pussy is just..." she almost says those words into her body but holds back, grinding her hips against the mattress. Eliana has never heard her pussy described as beautiful. As long as it was clean and shaved she was happy to never hear any complaints about how dark and flat it is.

Eliana's scent and still detectable nervous quiver spur Simone into action. She plays at Eliana's opening where her juices are already flowing. "Can I taste you?"

Her answer is whisper quiet, "Uh-huh..."

Simone kisses her lightly. Her long tongue traces her lips from south to north then back again. Eliana's lips part a little more for her tongue. She tickles her with waves of her tongue before landing on her clit lightly. Eliana lets out a cute whimper. She flicks her clit with her tongue again in an attempt to get a bigger response and to make it swell. No woman can resist enough wet attention on her pussy and she hopes she'll bring Eliana to the point where any and all sounds or dirty words flow. Simone loses herself in her duty, plunging her tongue deep into the sweet and tart flavor. Eliana's hips buck. The punch to her face from Eliana's mound makes her smile.

Eliana quickly props herself up on her elbows. "I'm so sorry! I didn't mean to..." She fights the urge to be embarrassed as she's laid spread before Simone in the brightly lit room. All she can see is a head of hair, strong smooth legs and a high backside. The sight makes her throb again. From between her legs, Simone stares back and licks her lips. She lingers in one more lapping sweep with her tongue before she slips her first two fingers in and continues to use her mouth on the now puffy clit.

"Oh...god...yes..." she drops her head back and can't censor herself. She needs Simone to be in control but she doesn't need to be taught how to react. Slowly, she rocks her hips back and forth to feel more glide and slide from Simone's licks. She involuntarily puts her hand on the back of her head, holding her face to her pussy.

Simone gently sucks and releases her clit. She slides her fingers out from deep inside her. "I love the way you taste." There's that gleam in her eye that Eliana knows all too well. Simone flashes that expression when she's about to do something funny, cruel or really sweet. Eliana wonders which one it will be this time.

Simone opens her nightstand drawer and pulls out a silver vibrator. She turns one end and the toy buzzes. She brushes it along Eliana's thigh, who flinches from the tickle on her leg. "Say hello to *le petit ami...*"

Eliana's eyes widen before busting out laughing at her friend channeling Tony Montana. Simone loves the sound of her friend's laugh and seeing her body jiggle and flex while she does. She's overtaken with a surge of emotion and plants her lips on hers. Immediately, Eliana responds, taking her lips between hers one at a time, tracing them with her tongue. Her own scent and taste on Simone's face sends a surge down her body to her vertical smile.

Simone traces the vibrator over her nipple. Then along the side of her neck and tickles the tip of her nose with it. She kneads her inner thigh and kisses each. A pleading sound comes from deep within Eliana. She kisses all over her inner thighs again, every where but where her friend wants it, and is rewarded with the yearning hum from Eliana again. She decides to stop teasing her. She slides two fingers back into Eliana and rubs her clit with her thumb. Eliana digs her heels into the mattress and resumes rocking her hips back and forth. She leaves her friend's fingers and hand glistening from her leak. Her breasts heave as the pleasure intensifies and her mouth hangs open for her gasps to escape.

Simone kneels next to her hips and takes in the expanse of Eliana's olive skin. She adds the vibrator to the sensations of her fingers. Watching her already coated fingers plunge in and out of her friend's tight creamy space makes her own pussy water at the mouth. She wants to smell Eliana on her fingers for days to come. The hum of the vibrator is quickly drowned out by the symphony of the women's cries.

Simone holds the vibrator steady on her clit and fingers her at a feverish pace. Her own arousal piques when she feels her friend's deep muscle flex. She has to work harder to thrust in and out as the walls close in around her fingers. "Awww, Ellie...yeah, come for me..." She pushes in a few more times, rubbing against the ridges of her G-spot. She goes knuckle deep then snatches her fingers out while her pussy becomes a vice around them. Eliana squeals in delirium and surprise as she gushes. That scene is enough to make Simone's pussy throb uncontrollably. But she doesn't relent and holds the vibrator to purr continuously on Eliana's clit.

"Oh god! Oh god... Wait... Please...! Yes!" Stop, go— Eliana doesn't know what to beg for.

Her fingers dive back in and she works the inside. When she pulls out, another splash escapes from between her friend's legs. Simone delves into her pussy again. Eliana grabs hold of her wrist and stops her with the surest touch Simone's felt from her all night.

Eliana slowly gains control of her labored breath.

Simone moves the vibrator off her clit and places it on the bed. She waits until the aftershocks of Eliana's orgasm are over, releasing her fingers. She pulls them out slowly and palms her sopping pussy.

"That's... that's never happened before..." she says apologetically sounding like Stevie Kenarban.

Simone smirks at Eliana's body, damp from sweat and her splash. She traces her finger up her quivering thigh, and plays in the crease of her hip. Her finger travels around her belly button and the piercing before dipping into her "innie". Her next stop is a circular path under her breasts then around her nipples punctuated with a soft pinch of each of them between her thumb and the side of her first finger. Her finger creeps up her neck and rests there. She places her hand on Eliana's cheek and seals the moment with a tender peck on her lips before getting off the bed.

"I didn't know you liked me like that." Eliana inches to the edge of the bed.

"I always liked you, Ellie. I didn't know if we'd ever

fuck though."

"You... you want me to," she brings her fingers to her lips, "do that...to you?"

"You can do whatever you want, girl," she motions to her wet body. It was one of the targets of Eliana's eruption. "But I gotta take another shower."

Eliana smiles and follows Simone out the room.

*   *   *

Manu Et Le Connard

(Manu and the Asshole)

After coming in from smoking a cigarette, Manu kissed Morgan. She didn't mind the taste of it on his tongue. She caught a glimpse of their profiles in her hallway mirror as he cradled her face. She couldn't wait for his fingers to pierce the moisture accumulating in her panties.

Manu didn't bother to get dressed after his shower. He wrapped the towel around his waist and went out to the living room. She caught her breath as he filled the doorway with his frame. She scrutinized the front of the towel to preview what was to come. Her soap took on a sensual aroma on his skin and hair. The towel opened, revealing one thigh when he sat on the couch. While they talked, she kept to her side of the couch to keep her nervous energy from erupting. Manu said mid-sentence, "I want to kiss you again," and he did.

Her nerves kept her in her head instead of in the moment. She thought about whether she was kissing with enough tongue or too much lip-sucking. The soft scratch of his midnight shadow distracted her from the decision of turning her head to the right or to the left. She sucked in her stomach when his hands wandered. The voice inside her head told her to 'let go and enjoy'. She took a leap and placed her hand on the back of his head. The tickle of his hair through her fingers and the base of his skull in her palm made her feel powerful.

She felt even more powerful on her knees before him. His knees spread, head thrown back, fingers digging into her shoulders. Morgan's tongue danced around him, both wet muscles in her mouth pulsing. The faint scent of soap was washed away by her saliva. There was no pubic hair to speak of for any scent to linger on.

She matched her nude body to his as they took turns peppering each other's bodies with kisses.

His pockets were empty. Her nightstand drawer was void of protection.

"Do you have a bible?"

She lifted her head from the pillow mustering a "no" over her shoulder at him. He pulled his fingers out of her and replaced them with his body. It was in God's hands now. And so they began.

They weren't a homogenous couple and were gorgeous together nonetheless. Morgan's head reached his nipple line. Manu could rest his chin on her head with a slight bend of the shoulders and he didn't have to bend much farther to kiss her. He still surprised her with the passion of his kisses. He always left a smile on her face because he'd interrupt his own stories to kiss her then continue right where he left off, never missing a word.

Morgan was very attracted to his lean figure. His hands and long, slender, dexterous fingers matched that lean figure and were the first things she noticed about him – they starred in her fantasies. She imagined the internal and external massages she'd receive from his fingers. His jeans sat right at his waist and when he wore one of his ratty, too-short t-shirts she would catch a glimpse of his abs and the crest of his hips. There were never any underwear logos to spy. She couldn't resist tracing his 32-inch waist with her fingertips at every opportunity. Morgan was thicker and softer. He poked and squeezed her body constantly. The view of her from behind made him smile as much as her face did.

Manu's nose was rounder than she'd first noticed, not very aquiline. His nose went unnoticed because so often she stared into his bright eyes detailed by long eyelashes that waved at her on every blink. But she was all too aware of his nose when he massaged her clit with it. Manu had an olive complexion with red-orange undertones. He could pass for Italian or Sicilian, Spanish, Greek or Brazilian as well as his actual French nationality. There was no mistaking Morgan's African heritage. When she informed people of her Caribbean half it became apparent as well. The rhythm of her speech was all New York.

A few blocks ago they sat at a sidewalk café, sipped café and watched people go by. As they strolled along *la rue*, he continued his story about an octopus and a pineapple on his trip to St. Kitts in animated fashion. Morgan could barely put one foot in front of the other; doubled over in laughter, she walked in staccato steps. Manu was hilarious without even trying. Morgan reached for him to regain her balance. She wrapped her fingers around his upper arm. Through a sidelong glance she caught the slight raise of his eyebrow when she ran her finger in a circle against the skin on his inner arm. She loved discovering new erogenous zones on his body. Their sexual communication was constant, if silent at times. They'd have entire conversations in the light of day, the audience not even aware of what they were witnessing. Their telling glances were their own secret language.
The sexual charge was in the rhythm of their steps—Manu's four-count with Morgan providing the golpe beats with her shorter stride. The couple strutted to the rhythm of a bossa nova only they could hear. Morgan's glow and Manu's bravado were easily explained by their physical relationship—it was in constant supply. As they walked past the *Métro* station, a vagabond called after them. Manu saw red. The men approached each other spitting insults. Morgan's gaze volleyed back and forth between the two men. She didn't catch everything they were saying, she only caught the bad words—*fils de pute, baise toi*—the first words she learned.
The vagabond made a gesture of self-pleasure while he spoke, "...*la veuve poignet!*"
"*Nique ta mère!*" Manu shot back. His dark eyebrows became a unibrow as they were driven together in anger. She still had a grip on Manu's arm. His arm flexed in Morgan's hand as he gestured wildly.
The vagabond spat at Manu's feet. "*Cocu de merde!*" He

made a lewd gesture towards Morgan then grabbed his crotch.
"Ta gueule connard!"

Before Morgan could blink, fists were flying. Few
people got the chance to stop and watch the grappling men. As
quickly as the fracas began it was over. Manu stood over the
man and kicked him in the chest with a thud. Morgan watched
the scene, her eyes wide. Manu put his arm around her
shoulders and led her away. She could feel his heart racing
through his armpit and his breathing was a little labored. His
forehead glistened from the exertion. A man who had witnessed
the match acknowledged Manu with a nod. Morgan peered over
her shoulder at the vagabond as he lay on the ground in the fetal
position clutching his gut under the dusk sky. There was still
fight left in him as he continued to yell after Manu.

"What about him? What if he comes after us?" she
asked.

"Oublie-le."

She knew Manu was capable of violence but this was the
first time he was blinded by his temper. That sort of brutish
behavior was never accepted from her paramours in the past.
The need her former lovers had to possess her or tame her wild
streak drove her away. Yet Manu spoiled her with his macho
displays and need to protect her.

The two returned to Morgan's apartment for the night
still charged from Manu's brawl. She was aroused by his display
of force and strength. He wanted to manhandle someone.

Morgan decided to forgo her glass of *Valli Unite
Bianchino*. Manu removed a short tumbler from the cupboard. It
was a comical scene the night he struggled with her corkscrew
only to crack the mouth of the bottle instead. *"Antiquité,"* he
teased. "My grandfather used a corkscrew like this." He was
careful not to cut himself on the chipped mouth of the bottle.

The wine barely hit the bottom of the glass before it was
sloshed around his mouth and swallowed. He slammed the glass
onto the counter and refilled it. He left the kitchen carrying the
bottle and his glass. Morgan followed. As he plopped onto the
sofa she insisted on knowing what the heckler said to anger him.
Manu gulped down every drop of wine that was in his tumbler

before looking at her. He still treated Morgan like a lady, sometimes an innocent one.

"He was talking about your butt."

"You like my butt..." She turned around and swayed her hips provocatively. "So what? Another man noticed it."

"I like your butt, a lot... it's hot." He filled his glass again. It never ceased to amaze him when he saw her nude form. Morgan's body was firm putty in his hands—her pliable muscles excited him. He'd smack her ass and his hand bounced off like on a trampoline. It was ample. But her ass was "his". He'd spin her around to gawk at her with amazement and lust. "So beautiful," he announced while he lightly traced the curves with his fingers. His treatment was soft and loving compared to Black lovers who eyed her, forced her shoulders down, bit her, yet images of Baartman's showings flashed across her mind at times when she was with him.

"So what did he say that was so bad?"

Manu insisted on only giving her the clean translation. "He said your ass was too big for me, that I had a small dick and you should fuck him because his dick is big enough to fit in your ass and satisfy you."

"Whoa."

"He was rude. *Connard.*" Manu tugged on her wrist pulling her onto the sofa next to him. "Your butt, you... it's all beautiful. I love it." He handed her the glass. He held her face in his hands and kissed her.

"You want some wine?" He said referring to his glass which she held. Morgan took a sip and handed it back to him. He steadily drank what was left. She kissed his chin, swirling the wine in her mouth around his prickly skin.

The kissing led to moaning and groping. "Let's get naked," he demanded. Morgan stood to take off her clothes while he flung off his hoody and t-shirt then raised his hips so he could kick off his jeans. He didn't allow his gaze to linger on her body. He used his hands to see her this time. When she was completely bare he pulled her backwards towards the couch. He aimed his body forward so she could slide down onto him.

Morgan placed her hands on his knees and leaned

forward. He held her by the cheeks, lifting them so he could watch his repeated entry into her. Morgan was too focused on her quivering thighs after a while to focus on anything else. She halted their rhythm and turned to face him.

"I wanna do it like this." She put her right knee next to his left hip and her left knee next to his right hip.

"Like this?" Manu was puzzled. She nodded as she reached down and gingerly held him still so she wouldn't miss mounting him. That was all the convincing he needed. She snaked her hips up and down. He sunk his fingers into her hips and muttered *en français*. His fuck-face was so beautiful it was distracting. Manu's eyes shot open and he caught her gaze. He grabbed her face, silencing her with a kiss. She pressed her breasts to his, the bounce of her hips higher and harder. He slid his hands down her back and over the curve of her ass. They remained there for a few rises and falls. Then he slid his finger along a familiar path to her tightest hole. He slipped in second-knuckle deep and reacted as though he could feel it throughout his entire body.

He wanted a view of the hole he was exploring and the one he was waist-deep in. They changed positions with choreographed precision. Morgan kneeled on the edge of the couch. Manu sucked air in through his teeth and spread her cheeks apart like he was smoothing the sheets. The moment was heightened by the lights being on. Manu could see all of Morgan and that excited him. Knowing Manu could see every part of her excited Morgan. He plugged her with his thumb. They danced to their slapping rhythm until Manu announced the imminent. Being deep inside Morgan was terminal bliss.

Morgan's orgasm peaked. His shooting spasms continued until they both collapsed. Manu collapsed on to the couch. She fell over onto her side. No one spoke. There was no Magnum in sight. They had been skin to skin. Semen seeped out of her.

She lounged on her couch, one foot on the cushion with her knee to her chest, watching Manu slip on his jeans. He adjusted himself so he wouldn't get caught in the zipper. His rewarding cigarette awaited him. He didn't put on his t-shirt, just threw on his hoody.

Morgan threw her head back, basking in the steady beat of the music escaping her speakers and her afterglow in the dim living room. Manu inhaled his cigarette down to his fingertips in one and half songs.

Her knee fell aside at the sight of him. The adrenaline rush of the day was rapidly wearing off. He placed his head on her chest and she sniffed his hair.

"You ready to go to bed?" she asked. She rubbed his chest, lulling him to sleep. Below the waist, his body was awakening. They both ignored it.

"Yeah, I am so tired. Been up for almost 36 hours."

He began to drift off to sleep so they went into the bedroom. He stripped off his hoody and let it drop to the floor. He unbuttoned and unzipped his jeans. He pulled them down halfway before sitting on the edge of the bed. Morgan grabbed the foot of his jeans and he leaned back so she could pull them off.

And there he stood. He wrapped his fingers around himself, lifting his heft before letting it fall back towards the mattress. He shot Morgan one of his looks.

"I thought you were tired..." she kneeled.

"This will help me to sleep," Manu countered.

She ran the palm of her hand from the base to the tip that lay on his flat stomach. She did that a few times until he stood up without any coaxing. Morgan watched him grow. His body turned shades deeper. Almost purple. Royal. Two hands stacked, she stroked him. Manu propped himself up on his elbows watching her, his eyelids heavy with passion. He projected his wants on to her, "You want it," she shifted her gaze up his body to his eyes. He continued, "I can see it in your eyes."

Morgan didn't say a word. She let him go and waited. There was no thwack; he didn't land on his abdomen under the weight of his body.

"Come..." he motioned for her to get on the bed. As soon as she did he pushed her onto her back and separated her thighs. His tongue ran laps around her lips before his nose pressed onto her clit. Morgan was already a wet mess from playing with his heavy body. He slurped and spit on her making her body even more of a pool. Once she started bucking her hips against his chin he knew he had total control. He watched as juices ran down to her brown star. Manu teased her ass with the tip of his tongue. He waited, but only for a split second, expecting Morgan to put up a fight. He tasted her ass again and Morgan let out a glorious sound. It didn't take long for him to be able to trace her inner ring with his tongue.

Morgan was open enough for one, then two, then three of his slender fingers. He swirled them making her body speak in suction. Morgan played with her clit and her pussy and ass pulsed. Manu kissed and licked her some more reaching parts her fingers didn't.

She reached under her raised thighs and spread her cheeks apart. Manu jack-hammered her with his fingers for a few seconds then pulled out exposing the yawning hole. He dipped his tongue inside her a few more times.

Manu pressed the tip of his body against her as he kissed her. She tensed up a little and pulled away from him slightly.

"We try..."

"Not like this." She turned over and got her knees. The mattress held her head while her ass remained high. He coaxed her hips back towards him. He eased into her. She winced. The beaten vagabond from earlier that day had misspoken. Manu could barely fit inside her. She tried to catch her breath. He made her accept him before she was ready to. She could barely stand all of Manu inside her.

"Take it out..." she pleaded, "it's too much..."

He pulled out to the point where her body closed and then forced his way back in. She cried out and her body tensed at the sensation. "You don't want? You don't want me?" He slid in and out of her again. "You want... you take me..."

"Go slow..."

"Shh..." he fought Morgan's body until all of his was inside her, "take me..." They lay stacked. "...so deep..." He kissed the back of her shoulder and didn't move. Her insides were still quivering to accommodate him. "Is good?" he kissed her cheek.

She nodded slightly. "It is. But go slow... please..."

He raised his hips to start again. He did go slow. Allowed her anal cavity to enjoy the friction.

He pumped, changing Morgan's grimace to one of pleasure.

Manu's thrusts were cosmic sending her juices onto the sheets. His ass remained the only one in the air as he bounced off her rear mound. Her pleasure cries were irregular as he drove the air out of her each time he filled her. He held her lower jaw in his hand and spit wet words into her ear.

"*Je peux jouir dans ton cul? Oui? Oui. Oui. Oui...*"

He dropped her face and pressed his chin onto the back of her shoulder. He gripped her ass where it met her thighs and spread her apart. Droplets of his sweat rolled over her shoulder to the sheets below.

He was drained of every ounce he had – energy and essence.

Manu's gentle breathing greeted her when she returned to the bedroom. He didn't stir when she whispered his name. His ringing cell phone didn't rouse him either.

She sat on the edge of the bed and gently woke him. In a daze, he moved over to his side of her bed so she could slip in under the covers. He was already falling back asleep when she nudged him, "Hey, get under..." She pulled the covers back and he made his way under, his eyes closed the entire time.

Morgan set the alarm on her cell phone. Manu's melodic ringtone filled the air again. He blindly felt around the windowsill before reaching the phone and putting it to his ear. "*Allo...*" A long exhale left his body as he listened. He looked at Morgan, putting his hand on her thigh and nodded. "*Oui,*" he said into the phone. Morgan rolled onto her side, turning her back to give him some privacy. "*Pas ce soir...*" he continued in the exacerbated tone which he usually spoke to his girlfriend.

Minutes later, he turned the volume down on his phone and placed it back on the windowsill. He rolled over and sidled up behind Morgan, draping his arm around her, waking her. She had fallen asleep so deeply that there was already drool on her pillow. He kissed the back of her neck then laid his forehead on her shoulder. They always slept so soundly together.

*   *   *

Angel Lust

"I'm hungry," she continues to watch the television. "Are you?"

There is no audible answer.

"OK, I'm gonna cook us up something real nice." She hops off the couch and bounds to the kitchen. The floor creaks under the weight of her steps. She stands in the center of the kitchen for a few moments with an expectant air.

"Took you long enough," she says over her shoulder.

She remembers vividly when the two of them would cook together. She'd chop the veggies and he'd stir whatever sauce or stew was simmering in the pot.

"Gotta chop those a little smaller, babe," he ordered with only a hint of sweetness.

"It's all gonna cook together. Does it matter?"

He shook his head and stopped stirring. He knocked excess sauce off the ladle using the edge of the pot. She flinched at the sound of the metal clanging. He placed the ladle down on the stove deliberately and took a second to compose himself. "Lemme do it." He tried to take the knife from her.

"No," she resisted.

"Gimme the knife, Bailey."

"I got it!"

He glared at her for raising her voice and snatched the knife from her despite her protest. She sucked her teeth and pushed past him to the stove. "You know, if I did that," she said pointing to the ladle on the stove, "you'd catch a heart attack."

The blade of the knife smacked against the cutting board after slicing through the starchy meat of the potato. "Shut up!" he yelled. "Just shut up!"

Bailey silently mocked him. He caught her in the midst of her unflattering impression. He abandoned the potato in front of him but not the knife. In two steps he was over to her. He grabbed her by the throat and pinned her against the wall. Her cry of protest only escaped as a hoarse gasp. The force from the back of her head hitting the wall sent a bright flash across her eyes. Another contrecoup injury was the likely prognosis.

"You play too much, you know that?" He said slamming her head against the wall once more.

She squirmed trying to get out of his violent grip. He raised an eyebrow and showed her the knife. He turned on the left front burner and held the blade over the flame until the edge of it glowed. Then he ran the flat side of the metal along the neckline of her tank top resting the point of it in her suprasternal notch. This was the first time he had a weapon other than his words or his hands. She didn't let that scare her into inaction. Bailey punched him in the stomach. He chuckled at her cute attempt to defend herself. He released his chokehold but held the knife to her carotid. He pushed down her sweatpants exposing her unkempt pubic hair and bare thighs.

Her thighs were smooth up until a few weeks ago. Bailey's complexion was the color of the cream liqueur whose name she shared. It chronicled all the abuses she'd received from him like a color-coded timetable. Yellow bruises meant yesterday. Blue-green happened a few days ago. Deep purple contusions didn't allow her to forget what happened two weeks ago. He had found a new spot to cripple her.

She sat on the couch watching television. The volume was too loud and she had her feet on the cushions—she had broken his rules. Bailey couldn't breathe when he kissed her while strangling her.

"I'm sorry. I'll turn it down." She reached for the remote control. His response was to punch her in the belly of

her quadriceps. Pain receptors in her skin, muscle and bone
fired rapidly. It was excruciating. Tears stung her eyes instantly.
Bailey rubbed the spot for some relief as he took target practice
at her thigh. He pummeled her bone as he grew hard in his
pants. Her screams were arousing. He would need a release
soon. His body readied itself, clearing his pipes as precum
dampened the inside of his shorts.

Bailey had very little fight left in her for this
confrontation. He roughly tore off her sweatpants, pulling her
hips forward and displacing the couch cushion in the process.
He could examine the damage he had done to her. Her dermis
and epidermis had already started to bruise. He ran his fingers
along the length of her thigh. Then he lowered his face and
hovered his lips millimeters way from her flesh before he began
to leave a trail of kisses along her thigh. Bailey flinched.

"Why are you jumping?" he asked.

Bailey looked at him with tears streaming down her
face. Her silence, which he took for indignation, angered him.
He bit her until he drew blood. The capillaries that had already
been damaged went into overdrive sending platelets to the
wound. Blood rushed to his penis, the pressure causing it to
pulse.

He buried his face between her legs. Her salty aroma
was intoxicating to him. Bailey had given up dance and yoga
since she entered into this relationship. Three years prior, a full
split would've been child's play. He damaged her till her body
could no longer get into the contorted positions he craved. Now
the split he forced her into was painful. The sensation of his
slippery tongue on her clit was pure bliss that her body
registered but her mind yearned to forget. Tears and snot ran
down her face and her secretions ran out of her body onto his
face.

His knuckles on the fist clenching the knife pressed
deeper into her neck while he undid the button of his jeans. She
mustered all the strength she could and carefully shook her head
'no'. The sound of his zipper opening ignored her plea for
mercy. She tried to pry his hand off her throat but he spun her

around and yanked her by the hair pulling her head back past the comfortable angle. It looked as though the back of her head was resting between her scapulae.

An awkward sound came out of her as he entered her. After a few thrusts he moved her over the stove and continued to drill her. He entered her with enough force to scar her insides, carving her vaginal walls claiming her as his property. Her labia caressed his genitals. He let go of her hair and put down the knife so he could grab her buttocks. He separated them. If he had another penis he would explore her other warm, tight orifice as he had a few violent times before. He had left her anus torn and bleeding and didn't allow her to go to the emergency room for the stitches she needed.

This evening in the kitchen, Bailey was spared. He only concentrated on abusing her vagina. With each thrust she pushed back against him engulfing his body deeper into hers. Bailey had to push against him to avoid the flames. This reminded her of the last fight they had in the kitchen. Her head was submerged in a sink full of soapy water and dirty dishes. As he plunged into her, her head plunged into the water. She gasped sucking in a mouth, nose and lungful of water. She refused to accept that her demise would come from the element of water or fire.

She remained silent; he was stealing his sensual gratification from her already. She wouldn't give him the satisfaction of hearing her cries of ecstasy. Her heart and mind abhorred what was happening to her. But his body could feel her reaction. The space he entered betrayed her. It was throbbing, swollen and lubricated. He moaned and the sticky, slurping sound her body made while taking him in grew louder. She battled the quivering muscles of her quadriceps that threatened to buckle her knees at any second. Bailey threw her head back in reflex to the passion. Her back arched. He was getting ready to spasm and howl. The angle of his thrust was more in and out instead of the down and in stab that caused her fluid to flow. He adored her wet velvety heat. She avoided the dry heat of the open flame. She pressed up to prevent her tank top and breasts from resting in the flames. The aroma of the stew on the opposite burner and singed hairs on her arm mingled. Bailey gripped the edge of the stove as she would bed sheets while in throes of passion. Her body rebounded more in response to his thrusts. Her fingers found the knife.

"I love trying new things," she says as she uncovers a saucepan on the stove. "No more of those thick heavy stews that you like. They take *forever* to cook. Who has all day to stand over a hot stove stirring and stirring and stirring..." she scoffs, "It's enough to drive you *insane.*" After the steam clears, she takes a look and a lingering whiff of the thick fillets of salmon simmering. She dumps some chunks of potato in the pan.

Bailey stands there, staring into the pan. She goes over to the freezer and takes out a pack of frozen veggies. "Nope, I don't wanna hear it. Frozen vegetables won't kill you." She rips open the bag and dumps half of the contents into the saucepan. "And look at that. No chopping. No clean-up!"

She has a satisfied crooked grin on her face. "All the knives are dirty anyway and I do *not* feel like washing." She combines all the ingredients, spooning some of the sauce on the bottom of the pan on top of the potato and veggies. "I think it's gonna taste good too. Definitely edible." She covers the saucepan.

"I love that you have so much confidence in me in the kitchen." She places the spoon down on the stove between the burners where it is sure to leave a stain. "Go set the table..." she smiles.

After fixing two plates of brown rice with salmon and potato and veggies, Bailey tosses the spoon into the sink full of dirty dishes.

"Ok babe, it's ready." She walks from the kitchen into the dining room. She places her plate down at her place setting and the other in front of his seated corpse between his dead purple hands. The body was a few days from the point of tumescence. It wore the same wife beater and jeans, now bloodstained, he stopped to undo instead of chopping the potatoes the day before. The aquamarine death stain could be seen on his belly and the wound on his chest.

"Look at you. You're a mess." She scowls at the corpse for not cleaning himself up for dinner. She picks up the cloth napkin at his place setting and opens it with a flick of her wrist. She tucks it into the top of his wife beater like a bib, gently, as not to disturb the rigor. "But, I do love a wife beater...stained with blood – as they should be." Bailey sits, whips open her napkin and places it on her lap.

She smiles at her dinner mate. "Eat up."

She takes a bite of food and suddenly cuts her eyes at the *memento mori* sitting at the table with her, his head slumped to the same side he once wore his penis. She eyes the body's lap. His post-mortem erection has subsided. The thought that beautiful virgins had satisfied his angel lust angers her. But she knew his semen was no longer viable.

She'd been destroyed by him to the point that she could not bear children. She plunged the knife into him with the same force he would penetrate her during his lusty rages. The sound of the knife cutting through skin, muscle and adipose tissue was like the familiar sound of her sticky pussy sucking on his penis even when she failed to will her body not to.

In that split second between life and his realization of his impending death, she thought she saw the little death of orgasm in his eyes. She was fortunate that when he stumbled backwards, his pants down around his still flexed thighs, that he landed bent over the kitchen island or she would have a hard time lifting the dead weight. There he was, his ass with male pattern body hair, exposed. His testicles hadn't dropped yet, his scrotum still tight. There she was still gripping the knife, nostrils flared, lips pursed, her masseter rock hard. She quickly pulled up her sweatpants and talked herself out of the maniacal things she wanted to do to his still gasping body.

Bailey inched up slowly behind him. Her heart rate quickened and a new wave of vaginal secretions seeped out of her. She was so conditioned from the harrowing time with him that fear aroused her and she hated it. She circled his body tentatively until she could see his face. She knew exactly what to do in a situation like this to save his life. He held her hostage at home whenever they had a bout, denying her the medical treatment she needed. Bailey grew adept at treating herself. In the process, she'd learned tons of medical and first aid information.

Bailey leaned in and heard him gurgling as the hemopneumothorax brought him closer to his final breath. She looked into his dilated pupils one last time. She could still smell the sex on him as she brought her face closer to his and whispered into his ear, "I said no." She could only hope that it was true that hearing is the last sense to go when we die.

* * *

Smokey Rhythms

Remember the New York City when you could smoke in bars? Everyone was drawn to the danger of the city. Witching hour strolls with the brown paper bag wondering what you'd trip over at the next alley. Prostitutes worked the streets. AIDS was no longer a "gay disease" so condoms met their limp end on sidewalks. My heart-rate quickened when I spotted him from down the block. He was standing up against one of those giant green metal dumpsters you always find dead bodies in. He was moving slightly, not rhythmically, but it was visible. I wanted to be able to catch the eye of the working girl giving him head if I could. He was just taking a piss. Having a hard time with it though. Realized he looked a little older than my Pops. Probably had prostate problems. I did catch his eye.

I went out a lot back when New York was, for lack of a better word, gritty. Took home memories of those all-nighters on my leather jacket. I could smell the events of the evenings in my jacket weeks later. The cigars, cigarettes, weed or cologne from my partners. It wasn't a New York full of flower children practicing commune love or the key party 70's but love was freer back then. Folks were quick to hit a vein and pass the needle. I lost underwear in taxicabs. I had a lot of cocaine-fueled marches across the Jews' Highway and took shits on Kent Avenue. Prudes may call our generation "reckless" but we were living life with the information and means that we had in the best fucking city in the world. With no regrets.

There was no sign on the building on Grove Street. Just the faint buzz of a horn escaping out to the street. If a cabbie

zoomed by fast enough it'd drown out the musical beacon. The
club had just the right balance of smoke, whisky and static in the
air. By the time I got in, the stage was empty and the spotlight
waited for the next act. I walked past the bar and took a seat at
an empty table in front of the stage. My selfish side likes to be
fed. I like to feel they're putting on the show only for me.

He took the stage. In two steps his long legs carried him
to the mic. He took a seat on the edge of the stool and propped
his right foot up on one of the rungs. He wore dark colors and a
leather jacket of his own. I watched as he ran the fingers of his
left hand along the strings to the head of the guitar. Those
fingertips stained from spliffs rolled and puffed moved with
such grace, almost psychedelic slow motion, as he played. I
shook a new cigarette out my pack and slid my hips forward in
my chair. My knees fell apart as I focused on the fact that his
knees were apart as well. I lit my cigarette. Just then his lips
pursed as he sang. The image of kissing him flashed across the
screen of my mind. I wanted to taste him. That sudden charge
of sexual tension escaped my body as I exhaled slowly, the only
sign being the smoke bellowing out my nostrils. My second drag
was deep and deliberate. I blew it out my mouth and my lips
hung open. My mouth an opening to let my motives out or an
entryway for him.

The cocktail waitress placed a drink on my table. A
drink I didn't order. She pointed to the bar and whispered to me
that the man at the end of the bar had sent it over. I turned
around to see who she was pointing out. He raised his glass to
me. All I noticed was his wristwatch and that only one of his
fingers wasn't adorned with a ring. I hate a man who wears gold
jewelry. They're usually minute men in the sack. All flash, no
substance. Huffing and puffing, asking if it's good for you
because if you say yes it helps them stay hard. The jangle of their
jewelry is so distracting. They're making such a ruckus and
oozing globs of come before I can make up a lie to boost their
ego. I pushed the drink to the edge of the table and took
another drag.

I couldn't see the musician's eyes through his aviator
glasses, glasses he must've been wearing because he thought he

was too cool for the spotlight, but I was sure he was watching. I didn't want another man's drink. I watched his mouth as he formed his vowels in his song, the emotion in his brow when he held a note longer than five seconds. That caused me to play with my cigarette. There was less smoking and more licking and tongue-twirling and lip-dangling. I wanted a part of his body on my lips. I wanted to make him sing.

I stood outside the club making small talk with some of the other buzzed smokers. Then the door opened and what emerged first was the neck of a guitar case, like an erect penis. It was the musician and we locked eyes immediately. He was six feet if he was an inch and with artistic handsomeness.

"Hey, you gotta great sound." I took a drag off my cigarette. Held it in my mouth just long enough and blew it out as he started to speak.

"Can I bum a cig?" he rasped. His speaking voice was a shocking contrast to his singing voice but it complimented his bulimic figure. I stuck my fingers into my inside pocket, pulled out my pack and handed it to him. I saw there were only two cigarettes left when he took one out.

"Keep it."

He flashed a crooked smile with the cigarette to his lips. The artist struggle was written in the lines on his face. I handed him my lighter. He lit up and took that first drag. The expression of satisfaction washed over him. I saw that look earlier when he finished his set. I hoped to see that expression again later.

"We gonna stand here all night?"

I shrugged at his gruff question. "We could go wherever."

He started walking down the block. I was a step and a half behind him.

Everybody followed their crotches to New York in search of fame, riches, sex and drugs. Those same performers had to walk to and from their gigs cause they didn't have money for a cab or the bus. I've seen dudes shoveling a meal in their faces at the Mission then keeping up with Joneses and sweet talking their way into a loft for the night after schmoozing at the

SoHo galleries. Can't blame them, I eat good when I go to the Mission.

We got to his walk-up apartment on 5th between Avenue B and C. The building and his apartment were slum glamorous. The door required an extra lift and shove to close. The graffiti artists used the stairway and hallway as their canvas. They didn't quite have the skill level as the ones who covered the subway cars but I guess the East Village was the training ground. Feral cats quieted the neighborhood with their infant wails.

My musician was a magnificent lover. The gold Magnum condom wrappers littered his bedroom. He was worth his weight in gold. Fantasies of being handled like his beloved instrument were fulfilled. He traced my vertebrae like the frets of his guitar. I did hum. His work rained down on me, his sweat refreshing. There was a rhythm to the slap of his balls against me and the suction of my gape. He barked commands at me in a harsh whisper. He told me where to place my hands on his bony terrain, how tightly to wrap my legs around him and even demanded complete stillness at certain moments. The desire to comply with his wishes while he made me want to scream in pleasure and leave my handprints all over his body was the ultimate test in self-control. Trying to prevent myself from pulsing around him while he entered me was a test of wills. Who would win in the battle of mind versus body?

The next morning we lay in bed. I woke up with my head on his chest and my arm draped across him. He had one hand behind his head and the other held his cigarette. I was instantly intoxicated by his scent. I didn't have time to think before my nose led me to his armpit. He smelled like a man. And now he was forever imprinted on my brain because of that scent, his unique essence. I wanted something in my mouth. I reached for his cigarette. He pulled his hand away only so he could be the one to put the cigarette in my mouth.

It was still not light out. Pre-dawn. There's nothing like the stillness of a Sunday morning. I was headed uptown to catch the L on 14th. There was a hunger in my belly that I would have to quiet with a smoke until I got home. He was smoking the last cigarette from the pack I had gifted him with last night. A certainty washed over me that that wasn't the only thing I left him with from our meeting. As I approached the corner of 6th and Avenue B, there was a man sitting on an upside down bucket under a wooden scaffold. I saw a plume of smoke waft over his head.

"Hey," he raised his chin in response, "can I bum a smoke?" I asked. He looked like a courtroom sketch you see on the evening news – lined faced, lopsided eyes, uncommon skin complexion. I was sure from his sidewalk perch he'd witnessed more than any of us could fathom.

"Sure," he took a cigarette out of a fairly crushed pack. "Here you go, buddy."

*   *   *

Unforgivable

But you and I, we live and die, the world's still spinning around, we don't know why
                    - Noel Gallagher, Champagne Supernova

He agreed with the way I described myself in my Craigslist ad. I used words like "hot", "tight", "young" – shit, I'd always be young. I don't usually tell my age in my ads. This time I did. But I always make sure I include the "B". For some dudes it's a red flag, for others it's a fantasy come true. They'd never admit to their friends that they fuck with Black girls, but they love that shit. I've been called jungle bunny, exotic, sweet, juicy—the list goes on and on.

I had his picture in my phone so I could compare it to the guy who showed up at Starbucks. He was pale and not 5'10". I love how guys add on an inch or so to their heights. We all give the side of us we want other people to want. So who am I to argue? If he wants to be 5'10", I'll let him be 5'10". I'll be hot, tight and young for all the lonely men I meet.

Express yourself, don't repress yourself

"You're even more beautiful in person," his gaze was intense. I don't get uncomfortable easy but I had to take a step back from this one.

"Thanks." I coo like that means something to me too. I'm not looking for a love connection when I go on my dates. Whatever gets me my money.

"I hope you don't mind that we met here instead of at
the hotel. I just wanted to feel each other out first." He flashed
his coffee-stained teeth. "Your skin is so soft..." he rubbed my
arm, but was staring hard at my tits. I didn't shrug him off but I
had to get into work-mode.

"My legs... are really soft too." I crossed my legs, jutting
out my hip and mesmerizing him with the curves of my thighs.
He leaned forward and crept under my skirt with his fingers and
that's when I slapped his hand away. "The hotel?"

He stood from the table abandoning his coffee and
scone. "After you." I'm sure he didn't want to eat that dry-ass
scone anyway.

We had a second floor room at the Carlton Arms Hotel.
There was no bathroom, a full-size bed, wire hangers dangling
from the ceiling and a sink. He kissed me as soon as we got in
the room and put my hand on his dick. He musta been hard for
the entire walk over there.

"Suck it. I need you to suck it," he tugged on my bottom
lip. He unzipped his pants and let his dick peek out. Like it really
looked like it was peeking. I was about to ask where the fuck the
rest of it was. The clang of his belt buckle and the thud of his
wallet when his pants landed around his ankles reminded me I
had money to make. His dick was short and fat and I liked the
smell of soap on his balls. He'd make an obedient client. The
ones that get cleaned up for you tend to do whatever you want.

His come was bitter and thick. I held it in my mouth just
long enough to get him through his aftershocks then spit it out
in the sink.

His body was even paler than his face. He wanted me to
make fun of him while he jerked off. "Sometimes..." *stroke stroke
stroke* "I can come four..." *stroke stroke jerk jack* "five times a
day..." He came so hard that he caught a cramp in his stomach.

"Not bad for a black girl."

Those words would stay with me forever.

He kissed me again. I pushed him away running my shy
girl routine.

"Bring that ass over here."

I sashayed over to him and all of a sudden he ain't love me no more. Now he was calling me a "fucking freak!" and a "black motherfucker!". I made him stop saying those things to me. During our tussle I ended up behind him and dragged him down onto the bed between my legs. My crotch was pressed hard against his back. His struggle grew more animated. I wrapped my legs around his waist, locking my ankles and wrapped his tie around my fist.

This happened a couple of times before – they pass out, I grab their money and cell phone so they can't call the cops as soon as they wake up and I'm good. They don't know my name and are always too embarrassed to report it. This pale white boy, I strangled him and bear hugged him with my thighs. I could feel the life seeping out of him. Every time he exhaled I pulled harder and squeezed my legs tighter. I was trying to get my knees to touch. *Anaconda* Soon he stopped struggling and I could smell his shit and piss.

Not bad for a black girl

I once heard about this trick who got revenge on her john even in death. He was out to make his own ghetto gagger video. Spit was all over her face and going up her nose while her head hung off the bed. When he choked her, her throat got tighter. She tapped him on his arm giving him the signal that she was gonna vomit but her throat felt so good so he kept fucking her face. While she died her cadaver spasms left deep bite marks on his dick. He waited two weeks to go to the doctor cause how was he gonna explain that? I hear they had to cut off his dick cause of the infection.

How many lives are living strange?

I counted three hundred and fifty dollars while I left the hotel. I guess he was planning on tipping me or catching a cab back to wherever it is he came from. It wouldn't take them long to find him in that ninety degree heat. I took the coins he had in his wallet too. One was a JFK half dollar. Ain't seen one of those since I was a kid.

Ask not what your country can do for you...

Yeah, easy for him to say, he was at his sexual peak when he was killed. He had a wife and lovers on the side. I ask all the time what my country can do for me, wondering about the next time America's gonna fuck me over. I'm left spread, torn and sore every time Uncle Sam is done with me. He bites my nipples till they bleed and I've shit liquid for days after he tore my ass up. I'm AWB – American While Black.

Sirens were going off in the distance. Sounds of summer in the city. I had no intention of facing the cops over my latest CL conquest. They're only here to protect themselves and serve their libidos. Always shoving their nightsticks up someone's ass. They get off on that power, leaving white stains on the inside of their NYPD blues.

The church steeple fucked the sky. I didn't even know that I had turned onto that block till I was in front of the church. I know a sign when I see one.

Forgive me Father for I have sinned...

I could see enough of him through the partition in the confessional booth. I didn't get the answer to "why do we die?" but he told me to accept it and it was a journey we all must take.

"Champagne Supernova."

"Yes, you and I must live and die."

I like music and movies that no one else even cares to know. Leave it to a man of God to be the only one to get me.

"If I've killed a man, do I deserve to die?"

"One should never take the life of another."

I wondered if this man could understand crimes of passion.

"Yeah... but I did. Do I *deserve* to die?"

"Are you saying you murdered someone?" he waited. "If you've murdered someone, you have to go the police."

"I'm not going to jail."

"That's the right thing to do."

"I'm confessing to you, Father. Lemme get it off my chest and I'll be good."

"What you've done is wrong. You've broken man's law and God's law."

His accent came out as he scolded me. That partition is the only thing that stopped me from bending over for my spanking.

"You ever spank anyone at Sunday school?"

"No...I have not."

"I thought they do that in church. Or maybe just the nuns do that on TV."

"Television is for entertainment."

"And education."

He didn't respond. "It's delightful, Father, how someone's ass feels when you spank them."

I slammed my palm against the partition. "Their flesh quivers from your touch."

He remained silent.

"And their screams could be pain... or pleasure."

I smacked the partition.

"So you spank them again..."

I smacked it again.

"Your hand... and their ass gets so warm from the spanking." I kept my hand up against the lattice.

He placed his palm on the other side of the lattice. We didn't have a good view but we stared deep into each others eyes.

I lowered my hand.

"You've always been in the church, Father?"

"I've devoted my life to the Lord."

He didn't strike me as a little willy loving priest. "Have you ever been with a woman? Haven't you ever wanted *flesh?*" He took a breath. "I mean to just be with someone. Your part *deep* inside their part..." I leaned in, grazing my lips against the lattice, "You think about that sometimes, don't you?" I waited. "Father?"

"Yes..."

"Do you touch yourself?"

I could hear him shift on the bench.

"There must be mornings when you wake up and you're so... *hard.* Morning wood is a gift from God. Let's you know you're alive." I whispered through the lattice.

I could make out his eyes darting around. I didn't let him answer, but I let him think.

"So you lust after God? When you touch yourself? Are

you thinking about Jesus? Or are you thinking about someone like me?"

He cleared his throat and moved his hand to the side of his face. I was sure he could see my lips through the partition.

I closed my eyes and kissed the partition. I relived my many first kisses right there in that confessional. *Father, May I?* The warmth of the Father's lips spread to mine as he pressed them against his side of the partition.

"It's almost spiritual...a kiss..."

"Yes, it is," he let the words slip out.

Express yourself don't repress yourself Madonna whispered to us. I was suddenly transported to a peep show booth. A glory hole would be divine intervention. I'd get on my knees and pray for that. *Worship the Father...May I?*

The following Sunday I went back to the church and witnessed Father DeMaria lead his faithful. I was falling in love with the sound of his Latin tongue.

The church emptied out and descended into silence. I didn't move an inch. It was hard not to notice me sitting there.

"Hello, I'm Father DeMaria. Are you a visitor to the church?" he said as he walked down the aisle towards me.

I shook my head and he slowed down.

"Can I help you with something?"

I eyed the length of his body. Then I eyed the pew closest to him and tilted my head, motioning for him to have a seat. Get comfortable. Let me have some fun with him.

"Ok," he walked into the pew, "perhaps you would be more comfortable if we weren't facing each other?" He sat down. He was two pews in front of me. "Do you need to unburden yourself?"

"I've already confessed to you, Father." His body told me he knew exactly who I was now. His spine straightened and the back of his neck blushed.

"You were at mass."

"I was. Couldn't take my eyes off you."

"You listened. Received today's message."

"Love."

He whipped his head to the side, "What?" His eyes shot downward.

"Your message was about love." I stood up and walked toward his pew.

"Yes, love and compassion. For we all make mistakes. And in a world where we are tempted," I sat down next to him. But I left enough space where a 400-pound man could squeeze in between us, "it's important that we learn and practice forgiveness." He looked straight ahead.

"Why does God tempt us?"

"Your fellow man offers temptation. But it is through your faith in God that you will be able to resist. You must have faith..."

Well I guess it would be nice if I could touch your body, I know not everybody has got a body like you

"Do you think about our kiss, Father?"

I saw him side-glance quickly and he shifted on the bench.

"I... I have thought about it."

"What are you thinking when you do?"

"I've thought about what you may be doing, how you are handling what you shared with me... that day..."

"That hasn't crossed my mind since."

"Wondered if you would return for confession..."

"So we could be alone again?"

He raised his eyes to the statue of the crucifixion.

"So we could be close?" I slid a little bit closer to him. The muscles in his jaw were flexing. "Are you thinking about it now?"

"That. And other things."

"Am I the first black girl you've kissed?"

"You are."

Doesn't matter that we had that mesh between us. That was a kiss. I thought about it a lot since that day. It meant something.

"Say that again."

"You are the first," he looked at me finally, "you are the first woman I've kissed."

He was fucking me with his caring eyes. I hate that feeling. When dudes fuck you up with *feeling*.

I tucked my hand between my thighs like I was trying to warm it up. I saw Father DeMaria scoping out my lap. I inched my hand further up my skirt until I reached my warmth.

"Do you wanna see me, Father?"

My dates beg to suck me or love it when I fuck them in the ass. Well, the ones that know I have a dick. His nod was almost undetectable.

I hiked up my skirt just a little and let the church air kiss my head. If I had blinked I would've missed the look of surprise on his face. His jaw loosened. I closed my eyes and let him watch me play with myself.

Breathe

Breathe

Breathe

"Have you ever seen one before?" When he didn't answer, I opened my eyes and turned my face to him. "Have you ever seen one like mine?" I continued to massage myself.

"I... I have not."

His curiosity was so hot. I pulled my skirt up a little more so he could see more of me.

"I wanna see yours."

He shook his head. "I can't. It wouldn't be right." He was still shaking his head.

"Please..."

Father DeMaria kept glancing at my busy hand. "I mustn't..."

"Please, Father, I beg of you..."

I'm not sorry. It's human nature

The Father had a semi spilling out of his open zipper. "Touch yourself."

He slowly wrapped his fingers around his uncut dick. He kinda reacted like someone else was touching it. I kept my mouth shut and let him get used to his touch. I didn't want to distract him. We sat in that pew jerking and throbbing. I didn't break the silence of our sacrament.

He finally looked at me again after what felt like an

eternity of our silent stroking. His dick never got all the way hard but I could see he was wet. He studied me. My dick in my hand, his dick in his. "You're beautiful."

His words fucking set me off almost immediately. I came in my hand. The statue of the crucifixion seemed to glow with each pulse.

I cleaned myself off with wet naps and hand sanitizer. Father DeMaria had an earthy-scented come. Like how it smells right before it rains.

"Please, you mustn't speak of this."

I slid off the bench and kneeled on the prayer pad. I made the sign of the cross and brought my prayer hands to my face.

Blessed am I.

That was the first time I was inside a rectory. It was less holy than I thought it would be. Like a regular home. Like I didn't consider priest to be regular men. I got a good look at his face as we stood in his bedroom. We were about the same height. His skin was healthy. His jaw was strong and square. I could see the shadow of his five o'clock shadow.

"What do you wanna do first, Father?"

His eyes stopped darting around the room and found mine. But he didn't answer.

"Where do you wanna start?"

It looked like he was trying to figure out where in the room or where on our bodies he wanted to start.

He kissed me. Closed mouth. Pressed his face against mine. I opened my mouth a little and waited for him to follow my lead. He grabbed my shoulders and pushed me away.

"Think about our first kiss... do it like that."

He stepped back up to me and took my face into his hands. "I imagine kissing you like this..." This kiss was softer and lighter. It even reminded me of our first kiss in the confessional, this time without that barrier between us. He tilted his head to the left and this time he opened his mouth just a little. I didn't want to scare him away with my tongue. So I just closed my lips around his bottom lip. He was less forceful when he stopped this kiss. He ran his hands over my shoulders and down my arms. "Please, will you take this off?" He started taking my shirt off but stopped himself. "Off."

I took my shirt off.

"Beauti—"

Full. His mouth was full of my B-cup before he finished the word. He locked his arms around my thighs and picked me up. My crotch was pressed against his chest. He held me up sucking my tits until his arms were shaking.

The Father removed his collar. He was figuring out what to do with it I could tell. He put it on the arm of his chair. He unbuttoned his shirt and let it drop to the floor. I unbuttoned my skirt.

"Wait..." he got all the way naked and then sucked on my tits again. Jesus...

Then he really kissed my black girl lips again. My woman lips. His mouth tasted somber. Like lettuce.

"Your skirt." I took off my skirt and stood there in my panties. He didn't say anything so I took off my panties too. Obviously he saw it. I was standing there butt naked. The room wasn't dark. He kissed me again.

He pulled me down on top of him on the bed. I straddled him. He was gripping my breasts and his hips were bucking slowly. A little while longer and I could feel his hard dick behind me. Now he was squeezing his butt and pushing his hips up more. I don't bottom for my dates. I never have. I kept thinking about that as I reached back and held his hot dick steady. "No." He let go of my tits and got me to get off of him. "I want to do what we did...in the church. I want to do that again."

His dick was bobbing. I started first. Watching his 7-inches swell was a gift from God. He was panting heavier and he was treating his dick like it didn't belong to him. He was rough. I was worried he'd rip his foreskin.

"*Dios mio...*"

He was sweating now and moaning loudly.

"Shh!"

"*Ay...ay que sucio...*"

"You gotta be quiet..." I wasn't trying to get caught.

"...*tan bueno*... *Ay*... *tan bueno*... *sí*..." I put my hand over his mouth. Father DeMaria grabbed me by the wrist and put my hand on his neck. "*Ay sí*..." He held my hand there. He dug his heels into the mattress and bucked his hips while he was jerking off. "*Sí, más... más!*" He pushed down on my hand.

I squeezed his neck. "More?"

He nodded.

I had both hands on his neck now. "Tighter?"

He raised his eyebrows and I could feel his muscles tense as he tried to nod.

I applied more pressure to his throat.

"Tighter?"

He looked so pathetic. He was pleading with his eyes. He wheezed out a '*sí*'.

I squeezed harder. I wonder if he saw God.

* * *

The Right Wrong Number

I am a walking orgasm. My laugh surrounds you in warmth like a deep throat with no gag reflex. That's how I'd describe myself if I listened to all the babbling men spew after sex. Men say the darndest things with a finger in their ass tapping on the prostate drum.

"I'm so sorry..." Edgar pleaded for forgiveness as I wiped his come off my wall. He moaned and strained. His ass gaped and pulsed but his dick stayed true to form while I sucked it. Because he kept squirming he was jamming the top of my mouth and getting extra sensations from my top teeth. But he didn't seem to mind. It added to the taboo nature of our meeting.

It was rare that my landline rang. Only bill collectors or my older family members called that number. This wasn't an 800 number and Nana's name didn't show up on the caller ID. I was tempted to go back to my movie but I answered the phone anyway. "Hello..."

On the other end, the male voice went on in a language I didn't catch at first. It was almost melodic, a bit guttural and totally foreign to me.

I interrupted him, "Hello?" If he heard me say it in English maybe he'd understand that I didn't speak his language.

"Oh! This is not Ruby?"

"No, it's not Ruby."

"Ah, my apologies. I dialed the wrong number. This is America?"

"Yeah, New York."

"Oh, I meant to dial Boston. 781."

I smiled to myself. "Sorry, you dialed 718 instead."

"Ah, so many numbers."

There was a pause in our conversation. The actress on television was wearing a baby tee with no bra. While filming, she got turned on because by the end of the scene her nipples were hard. Her co-star wasn't outwardly attractive but I bet they had tons of sexual tension on the set.

"New York is a beautiful city. Very big," he said.

"Yeah, it is. You've been here?"

"For a few visits. Beautiful women, as well. You speak like a beautiful woman."

It turned me on that he found my voice beautiful. I shifted position on the couch. He didn't seem worried about running up a long distance bill and I felt a phone sex romp brewing. Of course I had no clue what he looked like but there was his voice. There was a level of bass to it that told me he had sufficient testosterone coursing through his veins to engorge his penis on command. Yet his accent made me think he was simple even though I knew that probably wasn't the case. Would I fuck a simple man? Did Jenny fuck Forrest?

"I will visit New York. Thursday." My nipples perked up at this information.

"What about Ruby in Boston?"

"Ah, my call was to inform her that I would no longer be making my trip to visit her."

"Will you tell her about your visit to New York?"

"She is aware I meet new girlfriends on my travels."

I had plans for this one. My intuition screamed at me: he's a woman explorer! And my ego was stroked at the thought that he'd tell another woman that he left NY exhausted and satisfied. "How do you fuck your girlfriends?" I asked absentmindedly running my finger along my labia. In any language, they understand the word 'fuck'.

"I fuck my girlfriends in the pussy, in ass, in mouth." His tone changed to match my now aroused state.

I kept my questions on the topic at hand. I had no

desire to know too much about my wrong-number woman
explorer. As with most of my playmates, his last name was
irrelevant. What he did share with me during our phone call
were the details of tasting his come and how he would edge for
hours.

      "I can't wait to feel your dick in my ass."

      "Ah, you like to ass fuck?"

      "Yes."

      "Good. As do I. We will enjoy each other on
Thursday."

      Thursday happened to be Thanksgiving. So I rushed
through the three dinners I was invited to, telling each one of
my hosts about the other two stops I had to make, all while
presenting my bottle of wine with a smile. They were all very
understanding. By the last one, I sat grinding my clit against the
seam of my pants, squeezing my thighs together and ate very
little. I was so wet from the anticipation of meeting Edgar, the
Dane, with the French-German accent. I fantasized about him
French-kissing my pussy until I covered his face with my come.
It had been a few months since I had a dick in my ass. I don't,
no, I can't grant backdoor access to most people. They don't
know how to treat it. But I can count on one hand the blessed
souls who have ventured back there and it's been glorious.
Edgar spoke like a man who knew what to do with a tight,
wanting asshole.

      I had a small orgasm while I sat there eating pumpkin
pie with my aunt. All I could think about was lying on my
stomach, reaching around spreading my cheeks while Edgar
licked my ass and darted the tip of his tongue in and out of it.
His rim job was exquisite. His tongue was long and teasing. My
back arched and I pulled harder on my ass cheeks when he stuck
his finger inside me. I don't think they could get any farther
apart. He pulled his finger out at a tormentingly slow pace on
the last thrust. Then I felt the fat head of his dick press against
my asshole. There was a little give but my ass pushed back, not
allowing him in all the way. He didn't move. He kissed the back
of my neck and ear until my sphincter relaxed. I engulfed

Edgar's dick about halfway down as he broke the seal and my
asshole closed around him. He pulled out again and the base of
his head hitting my ass ring over and over felt amazing. I
couldn't wait for that to happen for real.

"You always did love my pumpkin pie. Ever since you
were a little girl," my aunt said. I had been sucking that fork
long after all the pumpkin pie was gone. I had to get home.

Edgar decided to take the subway to my place. That
would take a lot longer. I just wanted to fuck already. He
explained he wanted a New York experience and loved the
subway. Well he'd have a lot of time to think about me and what
I'd let him do to my body. Missing were the jostling of strange
bodies against one another during rush hour, hands and fingers
grazing accidentally and then lingering in their touch. That
Thanksgiving evening he rode with the tired women in their
nurse whites. Eyeing panty lines draped over robust bottoms.
The question was what was under those panties. Could be
shaved pussies or the ones with extra long labia minora, the kind
you could almost wrap around your finger. I watched as my
pussy lips got fatter and spread while I shaved. Edgar had made
a very specific request for baby smooth lips but hair on the top.
I rinsed off and slipped on a pair of jeans.

I dimmed my 60-watt light bulb to about 20 watts.
Couldn't tell the difference between night or day when I set the
room up like that. I don't like to hook up in complete darkness,
especially not the first time I'm with a man. I'm turned on by
the visual just as much as they are. I like to watch them undress
and see their expressions as they undress me. Their eyes widen
in excitement like they did when they unwrapped the best
Christmas present in the world. My nipples salute them when
they unhook my bra and drop it to the floor. There's always that
split second where their gaze darts back and forth between both
of my breasts, taking in all the stimuli. In that split second,
they're deciding which tit they want to suck on first. Then
there's that moment when they just say, "Fuck it" and grab both
tits, push them as close together as possible and attempt to suck
them both. With the lights still on, I can memorize which side

they wear their dick on before they pull off their boxers or
boxer briefs. At my age, men in briefs will dry up my pussy on
sight. Makes me think of boys and I don't do boys. I love *men*
with all my pussy's soul. A dude with no underwear sends my
mind into overdrive thinking about all the random places I
could just whip his dick out and get to sucking.

There was a knock on my apartment door. I knew it was
Edgar. Someone must've let him into the building or left the
doors unlocked. Visitors had been coming and going all day for
Thanksgiving dinners that the other tenants were hosting. Edgar
had sleet and freezing rain glistening on his head, shoulders and
the front of his peacoat. His scarf was wrapped tightly around
his neck and chin. This was a total departure from who I was
used to fucking. Blond hair, square jaw, thin lips. He was very
attractive. Almost too attractive. Model good looks yet still
masculine. In silence we stood there studying one another. His
eyes darted down my body and lingered on my cleavage as I
inhaled. It was very possible he was wondering what our
contrasting skin tones would look like with our limbs tangled. I
stepped aside to let him in. He stomped out his boots on my
welcome mat and brushed the shoulders of his coat. He had the
air of the weary traveler seeking something to warm his insides.
He stripped completely naked right there in my foyer. He
wanted to take a shower to clean up and warm his blood. I told
him to help himself to a towel from my linen closet.

Sitting on the far end of my couch, he had to take a few
extra steps to reach me. His balls didn't hang extra low but his
dick had a fat head. My suckling reflex kicked in as my lips
parted. And I couldn't wait to feel his light dick plunging in and
out of my dark asshole.

"Do you like me?" Edgar presented his naked body to
me. I had seen very few white men naked. In person, that is. He
didn't have a porn star's body but I was turned on by it. He was
slim, toned, with narrow hips. His kneecaps were perfect
anatomical diamonds. I liked that his stomach wasn't sunken in.
His swimmer's shoulders were so broad they looked painful. His
creamy skin looked almost tanned under the glow of my yellow
dim light. A few months from now I could imagine he'd have

tan lines.

I didn't stand, just traced my finger along his neck and down the center of his chest. His dick was now dancing for me. My finger swirled around his left nipple and he threw his head back while the head of his dick pointed more in my direction. My finger was a snake charmer or a magic wand. I could make his dick do as I pleased without even touching it. I slithered my tongue into the mouth of his dick. The wet surprise thrilled him. My mouth was stretched from his girth. It took a few moments before I became comfortable maneuvering my tongue around him and gliding him in and out of my mouth. I sat on the edge of my couch, knees spread with my feet together, and rocked my hips back and forth with each bob of my head. Dick-sucking of my caliber required the whole body. He caressed my chin as he fell under my spell. I had yet to touch his dick or balls with my hands. They were on his hips and thighs. The more I felt the blood pulse through his dick and his muscles clench under my grip, the harder I sucked. I pressed my fingers into his skin. I wanted to leave marks on his creamy skin, to scar him, to make sure Edgar never forgot me.

"Please, I must sit..." he said breathlessly. I ignored his request for a few more seconds practically holding him up by the hips before abruptly ending the blowjob, my mouth releasing his dick with an audible "pop". Edgar nearly collapsed onto the couch. I slid off the couch and onto my knees in front of him. His dick had grown considerably from when I first began to taste it. It would be a challenge getting fucked in the ass with that dick knowing the head would give me the most pain and pleasure. I wrapped my brown fingers around the base of his dick to get a feel of his girth. I licked the underside of his dick lightly. He bear hugged me with his deceptively strong slender thighs. From the way they trembled, I knew he wanted to burst but was holding it back. The pressure from his squeeze and then the release gave me a momentary high. I tightened my grip around him and his brow furrowed in pleasure.

He let out an indescribable sound then managed to say, "Wait." He got off the couch and went to his heap of clothes in the foyer. He returned carrying a rubber cock ring. He stretched

it to its limit and put it around his dick and balls. I barely gave
him a chance to get comfortable in his seat again before his dick
was at the back of my throat. It was so stiff. I could feel the
tight skin on the head glide against my tongue. His knee was
next to my ear and he bore down on my shoulder when I did a
trick with my tongue every few licks. His heel pressed against
my back. The ridge of his dick became more defined. I could see
the landscape of his dick with my tongue and feel his balls
cushion my chin on every other thrust. Spit rained out the sides
of my mouth down the length of his dick, coating his balls and
parts of his thighs. His sounds made the crotch of my jeans wet
from my excitement.

"Fuck my ass." Edgar told me. I played around his
asshole, making him wait for it. "Yes. Do it." I spit on my finger
and pushed into what felt like a virgin ass. When I stopped to
wait for his ass to let me in he insisted I keep pushing. There
was no way I could fuck him so I just moved the tip of my
finger inside him. He let out an incredible sound. The head of
his dick was somewhere between a dark red and deep purple. It
was so engorged it looked like it could actually explode. That
piqued my morbid curiosity. I looked up at him as I ran my
lower teeth up his dick head lightly as I closed my mouth. He let
out a harsh breath and smiled at me. His neck and chest were
flushed and his lips were fuller now. The sight of the redness on
his chest made me want to slap it to see how much redder it
could get.

My palm stung. His eyes were wide with disbelief. He
was butt naked with this woman's finger in his ass and she just
wailed on him so hard his eyes watered. I shook my hand out to
get the tingling to stop. Behind that shock in his eyes was
definitely some fear. Edgar didn't say anything in any of the
languages he spoke so I slapped his chest again and his dick
almost tapped against me when it bobbed. Too bad for him I
saw that reaction. He squeezed his eyes shut trying to will his
body not to react. I slapped him again and this time I ignored
his body's limits and pushed deeper into his ass. Precum ran
down his shaft. I slurped and wiped the drool from my mouth
with the back of my hand. I raised my hand to slap him again

and he blocked me. I could feel my nostrils flare. I reared back again and he raised his hands to stop me again. "*Warten...*"

"English!" I demanded and readied to slap him again.

This quadrilingual man couldn't find the words. His eyes weren't focused. His mind was racing. "Wait, please!" he held my wrist. "I don't want to come yet." He was trying to catch his breath and looked at me pleading for mercy and for more. He squeezed my wrist a little tighter. He was subtle about it. Then he started twisting it. I shoved my finger in and out of him and his man pussy got wet all over my fingers. He grabbed his knee that was thrown over my shoulder and held it to his chest. I stroked his dick with my other hand while massaging him on the inside. As I felt him about to bust, I stopped. I slapped his chest again. Blood rushed to his chest in the form of my hand print. He would come when I let him come. Edgar said something in French or German or Danish before saying, "Again."

That command was a switch and my finger started up again in his ass. I eased two more fingers into him. I sucked him because I was beginning to miss the feel and taste of him in my mouth. His dick smelled like my spit. He barely said two words in English past that point. When he was about to come I stopped sucking his dick. Instead I stroked it hard and fast. I wanted to see him when he finally did come. I thumped and rubbed his insides as he bore down on my finger, his whole body following as he slid halfway off the couch. Edgar grabbed his dick from me and only after three or four of his strokes he came. It was the most amazing come I'd ever seen. He shot up over his shoulder and hit the wall, completely clearing the couch by inches. As the power of his come spasms lessened the rest of his come landed on his shoulder, the arm of the couch and in his mouth.

Fully clothed, I felt like I had been fucked. My heart raced and my breathing mirrored his. The inside of my jeans were slick. He still hadn't moved and his dick was still hard. He very well could've been stuck in that deep crouch. On the phone he told me that he would often come hard enough that it would land on his chest or even in his mouth. I got the chance to see it happen that night. I watched him savor his spunk. He probably did his laundry with a sense of pride since his loads were full of come-crusted socks and t-shirts. Edgar held my wrist to guide my finger out of his ass. He slowly made his way to his feet and twisted my wrist. I bit my bottom lip. I knew then he could dish it out as good as he could take it. He walked to the bathroom, slightly bowlegged on his tip-toes. The come on my wall had started to liquefy and trickle down, taunting me with the message, "Edgar was here."

* * *

The Ride

The bead of sweat rolled down the center of my back. I imagined it was his finger or better yet, the tip of his nose tracing my spine to the rise of my ass. I put my right foot in front, shifted my hips to the left and squeezed my thighs together, trying to generate some heat and friction. Anything to make this subway ride more enjoyable.

The low, scratchy sounds of merengue buzzing from the headphones of the man standing next to me penetrated my body. I moved my hips subtly to the 2/4 tropical rhythm. He caught me. Took out one earbud to ask me if I like the song and to say it looked like I could dance it well. He had no idea. He cocooned himself back in his music placing the earbud back in. He looked sidelong at me and I noticed he was dancing now too, for me, the movements of his hips hidden from the other riders because of the rocking of the train. My private dancer had limber hips, loose so he can hit all sides when he fucks. What rhythm. I shifted my weight again, to generate heat from the other side between my legs.

The train let out a good number of people at 125th Street. Between the shuffling of bodies and the musical chairs, I got a delicious whiff of a man who didn't look like he belonged in the neighborhood. He wasn't wearing scrubs so I assume he missed his stop. He had downtown good looks that should have kept him on the train. I watched him for as long as I could see him on the platform. Yearned to be his uptown girl. To wear him out all night and send him on his way in the morning.

I took a seat. We had a good stretch of express rocking between here and 59th Street. I made sure to sit up tall in my seat. Ass all the way to the back. Get the seam of my jeans between my lips, so my clit could roll over it, back and forth.

There were no buskers or preachers or wannabe teachers to contend with on my ride. I was too deep into rush hour that I'd missed the construction workers. My urban cowboys decked out in steel toe boots and dungarees. Their work jeans worn down in just the right places to entice. Shoulders broad enough for me to wrap my legs around.

The man sitting across from me watched. Maybe he knew what was going on in my panties, or maybe he just thought I was cute. He was a "suit" buttoned up with a tie, jacket on his lap. *I see you. You were looking at my face. Now your eyes are glued to my chest.* I glanced down, and my nipples are hard, breasts undulating. At the slightest breeze they react.

On this morning with thoughts of him on my mind they beg for a flick of a tongue. For a suckle. He loves that little squeeze and release I do involuntarily, sometimes not, when he's inside me. Kitty holds on tight when she feels him pulling out. Then he puts it back in its rightful place and she throbs some more, swallowing him. Peristalsis of the pussy. I pretend I'm scratching my scalp when I bring my hand to the back of my head, but I'm really imagining he's behind me, with a hand full of my hair, arching my back, demanding to know how deep I want it. And the "suit" watches.

Yeah, take this vision with you to work. He'll probably jerk off in his office thinking about me at lunch. *If I could park myself under your desk, what a wonderful world it would be.*

Grandma down on the other end of the car is having herself a coughing fit. She's probably leaving a different sort of wet spot on that seat. Wouldn't it be great if they would reward women for childbirth and making it to the Golden years with orgasms every time they cough, sneeze or laugh instead of a leaky bladder? Shit, they'd be laughing all the time. *Tell me a joke won't you, sonny? I love to laugh.*

The suit wasn't in particularly bad shape but the gym head sitting to his left eclipsed him. The logo on his duffel read

'Gold's Gym'. The bulge in his sweatpants said he had to use condoms that come in a gold wrapper. I convinced myself that his post-workout musk was intoxicating. Little does he know a secret admirer of his at the gym stalked him until he could steal his jockstrap and get a whiff. I was unapologetic while I stared at his crotch. He spread his legs even wider for me and continued to read *Muscle & Fitness*.

We continued to head downtown. *Mmmm*. There it is. I could feel that trickle from deep inside. My precum. I took advantage of the space on either side of me and parted my legs a bit. I made room for the imaginary cock-pounding I was craving. The man seated at the perpendicular seat lowered his newspaper and peered over his glasses at me. He must have heard my moan. *Music to your ears or familiar sound?* He's a man who's ridden these same trains in the 70's to and from jaunts to CBGB or Studio 54 I surmise from his pinky ring and cat daddy reading glasses. I bit my bottom lip at the thought of him growling during the third orgasm I milk out of him in one session. But that's all I was gonna get. The thought. My stop was next. That first visit I make to the ladies room, I'll take a whiff of my panties while I stoop over the toilet. Remind myself why it's not always so bad to have to go to work in the morning.

★ ★ ★

Lay Your Hands On Me

Short, sassy and sexy. She's a metropolitan cosmopolitan. She eats and breathes the rhythm of this city. And she holds power and her future in the palm of her hand like a middle-aged man's dangling balls.

When she was younger, Morgan didn't like her name. Now she loves the sexual ambiguity of it. Before her clients meet her, there's all sorts of images conjured up in their minds. There's no telling what will turn someone on.

Tim imagined being face down on the massage table, drooling on the face cradle as he peeks at her toes, wishing he could suck each one of those pretty little piggies. His Morgan is 6-feet tall and blond. She turns him over to massage the front of his body. As her strong, feminine hands tickle and knead his thighs, he'd be excited, his dick growing hard under his towel. Would she like it? Will she take the towel off and suck his dick? In his fantasy, Morgan continues to be a consummate professional and massages only parts not concealed by the towel.

"Tuesday at six-thirty."

"Yes, that works for me. Will this be a half-hour or hour massage, Mr. Dominick?" the real Morgan asked over the telephone.

"Let's start with an hour. The longer the better. And please, call me 'Tim'."

"Anything you want, Mr. Dominick."

Tim Dominick sets up a few more appointments while on speaker phone, that way his hands can continue to stroke his dick and tug on his balls held in place by a silver ball ring. The massage he's eagerly awaiting continues in his imagination. By now, his dick is fully hard. No way to conceal it and his fantasy Morgan massages up the length of his thigh, fingertips reaching under the towel but not even grazing a pubic hair.

"I have to touch you," Tim says breathlessly.

"You know that's against the rules."

"Please, let me touch your legs. Two hundred extra."

Morgan smiles at the extra money she'll make, not at the nervous touch from Tim. His other hand reaches under the towel and can be seen rising and falling along the length of his dick. It's when Tim Dominick reaches under the 6-foot tall and blond Morgan's skirt and feels a matching dick and a set of balls that he loses it right there at his desk. He tries to maintain his composure in the conversation but the business associate on the other line senses something is awry.

"Tim, are you ok?"

"Yes," he exhales the word harshly, come running down his hands and dick.

"Are you sure? Should I call for help?"

He strokes his Morgan under her skirt while he continues to spasm at his desk. "I'll...I'll call you back."

There are definite perks to having a corner office, one being the executive washroom. Tim Dominick got cleaned up and splashed cold water on his face. As he stared deep into his eyes in his reflection he could hear his therapist reassuring him that there's nothing wrong with his fantasies. Although those scenarios may be triggers for his solo loving, he's never once acted on them with a partner. Even if they were to discover down the line that he were trans-attracted, that was OK. I'm OK, you're OK, right, Doc? He fought his desires as hard as he worked to conceal his Baltimore accent. He resisted the urge to beat himself up. He worked his way up the ranks over the last twenty-two years to become CEO. He had an ex-wife who got a good chunk of his earnings every month. The girlfriends he had all depended on how much he was willing to spend. And to keep up appearances, he was willing to spend a pretty penny on designer clothes, weekend jaunts and breast implants. But the natural, everyday woman he would watch from the back seat of the company car excited him too. Tim wondered how many of those college girls fucked their professors for A's or how many girl-only orgies took place in the dorms. He would see Black women with skin so smooth and find himself foolishly fantasizing about how sweet their skin must taste. Or maybe they were coffee flavored. On his way back from the airport after his last business trip, he requested his driver take the long way through Flushing so he could select one Hindu beauty for his dreams. Her nude body would tremble as he ran his tongue from her jeweled bindi to her chin, between her breasts, dip into her navel and then park on her sweet spot.

That night was the first time she had called his name. The bed creaked while Tim fucked her from behind. They were both sweating and surprisingly around the same age.

"Yes! Yes! Tim! *Yes! Yes! YES!*"

His breathing was high-pitched and shallow. Fucking Hindus, Blacks, college girls and ladyboys fueled him. Then he came inside her. His abs spasmed. There was silence for a few moments and nobody moved. Tim wiped the sweat off his face. He kissed the middle of her back then pulled out of her. His chest puffed up when she fell over onto her side, exhausted.

"I can't believe you came inside me."

He shrugged. "We're clean. And there's no chance of you getting pregnant." Hurt was etched on her face as he climbed off the bed and left the room.

"Have a good night, sir," his driver said while he closed the back passenger door.

"Thank you, Don. I'll see you in the morning."

He had his driver take him to his other apartment, the party house, if you will. The party house in the city. If walls could talk...

6 P.M.

He had just enough time to shower and shave before his massage appointment.

There was a knock on the door. Morgan was instructed not to ring the buzzer. He rose from his chair wearing a white undershirt and dress pants, belt and button undone, and opened the door.

Morgan stood there; her folding massage table nearly touched the ground as it hung over her shoulder. His 6-foot tall, blond fantasy was shattered. Morgan stood five-foot-three because of the shoes she wore that day. She was brown skinned and curvy.

"You look nothing like I imagined." Tim said.

"I never do," she walked past him into the penthouse. Her scent was intoxicating as it wafted past him. He shut the door and she turned to face him, smiling. Morgan's smile disarmed him instantly. He ran his eyes all over her body. Her jeans hugged her small waist and full thighs. When he took a second look at her chest he could see she wasn't wearing a bra. If the straps of her tank top were to fall off her shoulders, he'd have full view of her full breasts.

"You're cute," he concluded. His semi-erection was tingling already.

"But *not* what you imagined." He shook his head slowly, suddenly aware that he may have offended her. "I never tell my clients what I look like. I let them take whatever they want from my voice and my name. When they meet me, if I fit their fantasies, so be it. If not, I'll fulfill new ones." She flashed that smile again, this time with a hint of mischief. She had been in this situation before. Tim Dominick was like a lot of Morgan's other high-end clientele. They think they're supposed to be attracted to a certain type—the runway model, the NFL cheerleader or the 40-year old botox queen. They could never seem to figure out why their dicks got hard at the sight of Morgan. They wanted to be the ones to make her smile that smile after they've made her come a few times. They wanted to be the ones to come all over her ass. With that in mind, she turned her back to Tim and walked farther into the penthouse. He watched her ass just like she wanted.

"Is this a good spot?" she asked.

"Yeah..." he snapped out of his leer and started to head over to her to help with the massage table. "Yeah, sure. You can set up there."

One, two, three, the massage table was set up and she

turned to him again. "I usually massage my clients in the nude," she said deliberately, her eyebrows raised.

"Really...?" he stood close enough so he could inhale her scent again. It wasn't a perfume he was familiar with but he would be from now on. He leaned in and took a long whiff at her neck. Morgan could smell the cognac he had as an appetizer. She didn't know where this massage was going to go. She'd done everything from sports massages, happy endings, to three-hour full-service sessions—if the price was right.

She slipped out from between Tim and the massage table and walked around to the opposite side.

"In the nude, Mr. Dominick."

He chuckled when he realized he would be the only one nude. His dick mocked his foolishness with a twitch that almost made him catch his breath. He wished it wouldn't be that way. He knew her nipples weren't pink, but he wanted to see them anyway. If she sported pubic hair, and not a smooth Brazilian wax, it was black, coarse and curly like the hair on her head and he wanted to play in it. Tim wanted the sound of his hand spanking her ass to echo throughout his penthouse.

All Morgan could see was his face as she held up the towel. From Tim's vantage point it looked like she was wearing a terry cloth face veil. They never took their eyes off one another while he got undressed.

"They need to make dick cradles on these tables too." Tim tucked his semi-hard dick between his legs before lying down on the table. Morgan draped the towel over his ass.

"Actually," he raised his head so Morgan could hear him, "You can start with my ass."

"Anything you want, Mr. Dominick."

He had told her time and time again to call him 'Tim' and she wouldn't. He liked her stubborn nature. Or it was more like disobedience. He would be sure to reward her for it financially. Morgan removed the towel from his ass. She poured massage oil into her hands and held it there to warm it up before placing her hands on him. Her hands were small and soft. He couldn't see, but was turned on by the vision in his mind's eye, the contrast of her brown feminine hands on his chalky masculine ass.

It wasn't until the massage was well underway that he realized he hadn't turned on any music. It was silent but for the ticking clock and his breathing. He had a surge of insecurity that he tried to quiet by talking.

"So, how long have you been doing this?"

"Twenty minutes," Morgan answered.

"I meant how long have you been giving massages?" Tim clarified unnecessarily.

"I started when I was 23."

"And now you're..." Tim dragged out the words waiting for Morgan to fill in the blank.

"Older." Tim's back heaved as he chuckled. Morgan would maintain the mystery. When she was ready to create a bond with him she would, on her terms.

Tim watched her feet through the face cradle as she shifted her weight and worked out the obsessions he carried in the muscles of his back. His skin drank up the oil. His imagination took off as he envisioned her feet in those Converse sneakers. His 6-foot tall, blond Morgan's toes were long like her body with hot pink nail polish. The Morgan of his reality would look best with deep maroon nail polish, complementing her dark brown toes. That color combination made him think about chocolate-covered cherries. He had to see her in a pair of thong sandals and deep maroon thong underwear to match. He shifted his weight as his dick reacted to the thought of her ass swallowing the thong in one gulp.

"Can I see your feet?" the question escaped him on a breath.

"Yes you can, Mr. Dominick." She continued to massage him while standing at his head. She made no attempt to fulfill his request.

"*May* I see your feet, Morgan?"

"Yes, you *may*." She stepped on the back of one sneaker with the other and slipped her foot out. Then she stepped out of the other sneaker. She worked her stripped tube socks off. Her toenails weren't colored but they sported a coat of clear nail polish. Her feet were flat and her toes looked strong, not too long, not too short, but just right for a footjob.

Morgan wiggled her toes before walking her body and hands down his body back to ass. "I have a question for you, Mr. Dominick."

"Ok, sure."

"This penthouse...Do you live here all by yourself?"

"Yes and no. I don't live here full-time and when I am here, I'm never alone," the suggestive tone of his statement was more for his excitement than hers. But he hoped it would excite her anyway.

"You've had other women here?" The tone of her voice was apprehensive, her expression was smug confidence.

"How does that make you feel?"

"Jealous." That answer was the farthest thing from the truth but Tim was the kind of man who needed his ego stroked more than his dick, that much she knew.

She squeezed and separated his ass cheeks and it sent a deep pulsing through his belly. "You play with those other women?" Morgan ran her hands from the back of his thighs, up and over his ass again.

"I do."

"Do they play with you?" Morgan slipped her finger through the silver ring and wiggled his butt plug. Tim was a man who had top-of-the-line taste. Morgan took a quick glance around Tim's penthouse and the butt plug was no surprise. He didn't skimp on watches or cuff links and his time with Morgan would run him four-figures. He spared no expense on backdoor tools either. She could tell it was a stainless steel, heavy model that cost almost a grand and she was thumping it against his drum when she jostled it.

Morgan controlled him by the ass. "I...play... They usually don't. It's hard..." He had to stop to take two labored breaths, "phew..." he swallowed hard, "to find someone to play. Sometimes."

"That's unfortunate." The pulsing deep inside him hit a place full of loneliness. "You should really find someone who doesn't scare easily." She stopped playing with his toy. His dick was so hard but there was no where for it to go. Her little fingers grazed his balls and he wanted more.

"Can I turn over?" he asked.

She considered giving him another grammar lesson but had sympathy for the man who was getting uncomfortable lying on his stiffness. "Of course." She stopped rubbing his ass. He missed her touch already. Tim flipped over onto his back and saluted her with all his glory. For a split second he was self-conscious as he watched Morgan look at his body. Were his almost-six inches enough? He didn't want to believe the stereotypes but he could only imagine the big black dicks she was used to handling or riding or sucking with her thick lips. This massage could end right now and she could climb on the table and ride him till they both exploded.

He suddenly grabbed her and pulled her towards the table. Morgan reacted quickly, digging in her heels so she wouldn't be pulled down on top of him. Neither of them spoke. He hadn't paid for this. Morgan touched and he received. That was the deal. Stay closer to me, he thought. Just...stay. Morgan was no where near 6-feet tall and on the opposite end of the spectrum from blond but he wanted her. Needed her almost. Tim knew he'd broken the rules by touching her but his body acted before his mind could stop him. His lips ached for a kiss. His balls ached for a release. His soul ached for a caress. He held her tight around her waist; she was a perfect fit in the crook of his arm. Morgan didn't break their gaze. She gave Tim a chance to realize his mistake. His hand wandered along the side of her body, above and below her waist.

"Mr. Domi—"

"I know," he released his grip on her and she took a step away from the table. "I'm sorry."

She hadn't stormed out and Tim exhaled. That meant his apology was accepted. When she looked into his eyes again, he could tell it was time for Morgan to get back to work.

"Will I be massaging here," she ran her fingers along his thigh, "or here?" She wrapped her fingers around his dick, ran her hand up to the head and released it.

When he opened his eyes after that surge of pleasure he noticed her nipples under her tank top. "Your nipples are hard."

She looked down at her chest as though she were surprised she had breasts. She placed her hands on either side of her breasts and pushed them together to get a better view. "I guess they are," she said, leaving oil stains on her top. Her cleavage was inviting. He stared at it, wishing he were riding her chest. Her cleavage also resembled the crack of her ass. And he would love to just rest his dick there after coming. The heat of her ass liquefying his thick come.

"Do you mind?" Morgan asked. He must've been making her uncomfortable he thought, and suddenly didn't know where to direct his eyes. She let go of her breasts and held her hands up showing him her palms and wiggled her fingers. Tim watched her. "I need to get some of this oil off my hands." They both knew full well soap and water was the only way. But for now, his dick would do. She rubbed and stroked his dick, scissoring it with her fingers in a futile attempt to get the oil off her hands. He added his own hand to the massage. She saw his scrotum wrinkle like a time lapse video pulling his balls into his body. There was a hint of a smile on her face. He was going to come soon. And then Morgan stopped.

"I have to change my top. This oil is gonna set in." She crossed her arms and pulled her tank top over her head revealing the brown breasts he envisioned. When she put her arms down her nipples saluted him, her breasts sitting high, her belly soft. He only had to stroke himself a few more times before he came.

"That's *my* job." She raised her eyebrows. The tsk-tsk was all in her eyes.

Tim stopped but didn't let go of himself.

"Remove your hand, Mr. Dominick." Tim, his name was *Tim* Dominick! His dick landed on his stomach when he let it go.

"Thank you." Morgan pressed her hips against the massage table. With her four fingers pressed tightly together she made her way under his dick. With it resting on the back of her hand she massaged his stomach. She worked the area from his belly button to the base of his dick. She did this until he softened and the massage felt like just that, a massage. This was

nothing his fantasy Morgan would ever think to do. He didn't
know it's what he needed until his mind was free from thoughts
of expense reports, layoffs and trans women.

"Can you reach the oil?" The bottle was on a curio
table. If he'd rolled over it would easily be in reach. He didn't
look to see where the oil was.

He answered with a defiant look in his eye. "No."

Silly man, she thought to herself and climbed onto the
massage table with a nude Tim Dominick. She straddled his
waist. In order to reach the curio table she'd have to lean over
his body. So she did. Her breasts hung down and her nipples
grazed his. She needed more reach so she pressed her bare skin
to his. Memories of her arrival at his apartment came flooding
back when he got a whiff of her again. With her arm
outstretched he could see the toned results of carrying the table
and working over the tight muscles of her clients.

She grabbed the bottle of massage oil. She placed her
opposite hand on his chest to brace herself. "Got it..." she
whispered into his ear before straightening up. He wanted her to
say that again, or anything for that matter, so he could feel her
warm breath against him one more time.

Morgan didn't bother to warm up the oil this time. She
squeezed it right from the bottle onto his chest. She played in it,
making sure to coat all of his chest hair.

"Thank... you..." she breathed into his ear again as she
pressed her chest to his to place the bottle of massage oil back
on the curio table. He turned his face to hers and their cheeks
touched like nuzzling lovers. He was years removed from
intimacy that made him feel secure. Morgan touched him, let
slip signs that she enjoyed the sight of his naked body. Her belly
pressed into his when she inhaled leaving no space between
them. There would always be distance between them, no matter
how much he paid. His lips parted at his intent to nibble her
earlobe. He fought the urge to wrap his arms around her as she
lay on top of him. Asking the cost to taste her may send her
running. But if he was given the chance for a meeting of his lips
and her heat, the opportunity to spread her meaty thighs and
feast until they both dripped sweat and sticky, that would be his

sales pitch. A standing weekly appointment would easily fit into his budget. He had the prowess to make her want less of his money and more of him, he was sure of it.

Morgan let him soak up the moment. She sat up and the oil that transferred from his chest to hers magnified his yearning to touch her. It wasn't long before she was in work mode. When she wasn't making eye contact with him, he was mesmerized by her breasts. He wanted to hold them and find out how sensitive her nipples were using his tongue.

"You're tight..." she found a sore spot with her nimble fingers. Tim thought about making that same observation upon entering her wet pussy for the first time. "You spend a lot of time in front of the computer, don't you?" Tim made a futile attempt not to wince.

"Yeah..." Whatever else he was going to say was forgotten when she really dug into his tight muscle. That torture went on for a few more seconds until she brought him down by making circles on his chest with her palm. She circled his nipples with her thumbs and got the response she was looking for. He inhaled deeply, holding the breath in, and arched his back. It wasn't long that his dick bobbed up and down again.

"Touch me."

"I *am* touching you."

"No, please, touch *me*..."

Morgan raised her hips and scooted down to straddle his thighs. Now the dick that was lightly tapping against her from behind was in front of her. She interlocked her fingers and held it. She crossed her thumbs and began milking him. He locked his knees, squeezing his thighs together. He could feel the heat from her crotch and ass on him. His eyes were on her and her eyes were on what she was doing. When she bit her bottom lip it set him off. He grabbed his dick from her hands and jerked off feverishly. He clenched his ass so the butt plug could massage him on the inside. There were only thoughts of the Morgan who was straddling him when he came all over himself.

Morgan smiled. Her work was done. She pulled out a package of baby wipes from her bag and wiped Tim's belly.

"I'll do it," he said.

She handed him the wipe. "Ok, Mr. Dominick." She left the pack of wipes next to him. She slowly walked along side the table, pausing briefly at the foot of the table to scan his oily, hairy landscape and then sauntered off.

Morgan stood topless at the sink washing her hands. Tim came into the bathroom and stood behind her. They looked at each other through the mirror. He held up two crisp hundred dollar bills, folded them and slipped them into her back pocket. He patted her ass and kissed bare shoulder.

"Thank you very much, Morgan."

"Thank you, Tim."

* * *

Double Penetration

She loved to sit at the end of the bar in her favorite bistro when they had the sliding garage door open. It afforded her a great view of the neighborhood comings and goings. She kept an eye on the flirty waiter, fellow imbibers and the people strolling by on the street. The restaurant sat at one of the few five-corner intersections of the city. Not *the* Five Points, but close enough.

He headed back to his apartment after buying some fruits and veggies. His black tank top with the oversized arm openings revealed his nipples and muscular lats. He carried the signature light red plastic bags city folks are known to get from the Chinese or Korean fruit stand. His triceps flexed under the weight of his purchased produce.

She saw him.

He saw her.

She became oblivious to what her friend was saying. She spun completely around on her bar stool to watch him walk by. They eyed each other the entire time until they were out of eyeshot.

"You know him?" her friend asked.

"I want to."

They locked eyes when he took a seat on the other side of the U-shaped bar. She did a better job paying attention to her friend this time but noticed he was only toying with his french fries and didn't order a drink. He'd changed his clothes in the twenty minutes that passed since he walked by the restaurant. Less of his brown skin was exposed now that he wore a t-shirt.

She had on a "laundry-day" outfit. There was nothing flattering about the clothes she wore that day.

He stepped outside to greet friends from the neighborhood that were walking by. Her friend excused herself to go to the restroom. With a few moments to herself she had a decision to make—speak now or forever hold her peace. He didn't lose sight of the reason he came to the bistro. He noticed she was now alone at the bar. She took a sip of her drink.

When he wasn't looking, she watched as he wrapped up his *tête-à-tête* on the sidewalk. As he reentered the bar, she beckoned him with a come-hither. Her woman's intuition was spot on about the American man of European design. He had indeed come back to the restaurant for her.

He did the gentlemanly thing and entertained the object of his desire and her friend that evening. He could wait a while longer to get her alone. He added to his stash of stolen glances at the bar with a stolen kiss from her after he walked the two ladies to the subway station. Their pairs of thick lips melded together. Her body softened in his arms imploring him to hold her tighter, press every inch of his body against hers. She descended the stairs underground on wobbly legs, high off his fumes. His kiss and embrace were intoxicating. She knew nothing about him but her body, her soul was already attached to his kindred spirit.

The kiss, the taste, the possibilities fueled feverish sexting. The pair made plans to see each other the following night. After dinner, he led her to his third floor apartment. He pressed her against the wall as they made out. His briefs were damp with excitement from grinding against her, feeling her nipples on his tongue, and him demanding her to tug on his hair.

"Turn around."
She did.
"Put your hands over your head."
Obeyed without question.
He tied her wrists together with her bra.
"Don't move."
She remained perfectly still.

She didn't look over her shoulder to see what he was doing behind her despite how much the anticipation killed her. She sized up his apartment and reasoned she could make it to the front door in five bounding steps if need be and wouldn't think twice of running out half-naked since it was the middle of the summer.

Truth be told, she didn't want to go anywhere. He dropped to his knees behind her and pulled her hips away from the wall. He lifted her ass cheeks and introduced himself. He didn't even stop to think about it. She stuck her ass out even more in reflex, bracing herself against the wall with her bound hands over her head. Her breathing quickened. His tongue never touched her pussy yet it was soaking and aching to be penetrated. Her knees buckled because of the passionate licks and swirls from his strong tongue. He held her up because her quivering legs couldn't hold her steady. She didn't move her hands from over her head to wipe the tear of pleasure that streamed down her cheek.

TWO YEARS LATER

The rain that had been falling for about fifteen minutes was more nuisance than soaker. Most people refused to open their umbrellas. She had her hood on while she waited on the curb. She looked up from her cell phone to check if there was a long enough break in traffic to make it across the street before she was given permission by the traffic light. When she looked the second way of both ways they locked eyes again.

He rode his bike with the flow of traffic. Once he recognized her hooded face he skidded to a stop. She took the few steps to meet up with him. The excess material of his drop-crotch pants draped over the banana seat. His fruit sat a little under his waistband. During their time apart, they had absolutely no contact. But the mere thought of their night and morning together produced a physical reaction from both of them. Those flashbacks hit them everywhere.

Their second meeting was a block and a half away from

his home. He was living in a different apartment now, on the second floor instead of the third, in an uptown neighborhood instead of downtown. And the bistro where they'd met was now out of business.

He led her into his studio which tripled as his bedroom, office and workshop. Images of dragons and hares, his sketches and *Penthouse* tear sheets were layered on his inspiration wall. Tools and jewel cases were on one of his many work tables. He had an urge to kiss her but before he could act on it she dropped out of reach when she flopped onto his leather futon. Kissing hello was not their style. That's what he deserved for even thinking about it.

He uttered an urgent "hello" into his cell phone when it rang and excused himself into the next room. She took a slow survey around his room. Her examination was just on the surface—photos on the walls and the works-in-progress on the tables. Wrappers and takeout containers left clues of his late night snacks and meals he inhaled at odd hours. She made her way to the window. Windows were her Achilles Heel. She wondered where birds flew to or how a squirrel's den was decorated. She'd take quick jaunts into the lives of other New Yorkers by watching them through their windows. Most memorable are the one penis, the hetero couple fucking doggy-style and the middle-aged woman on the toilet that she spied.

She turned around at the sound of the wheels of his computer chair rolling along the hardwood floor and saw him pushing the chair tight against the desk.

"Explain this to me," she pointed out the window with her thumb.

He joined her by the window to see she was referring to a neighbor gardening in a backyard of a building facing the other block. He'd almost stood behind her and wrapped his arms around her waist. He side-stepped quickly. He expressed that gentrification and the gentrifiers annoyed him. Some of his irritability may have been displaced. She was standing inches from him and asking fucking questions instead of touching him. His chest was solid and inviting; she could've rested her head on it. She wondered what the fuck was wrong with her for having the urge. She smelled sweet and warm. She insisted on bending over to peer out the window trying to see something around the corner. He peered down at her ass that insisted on being so generous.

"You need to touch this." He had the waistband of his pants down below his balls. If he hadn't said anything she wouldn't have noticed. He was stealthy.

"I do?" She played coy.

He waved it at her. Damn if that fat brown dick didn't get her every time she thought about it the last two years. Damn if he didn't know it.

She ran her finger from the side of his thumb, down along the top, to his head. He was so warm to the touch. She taunted him with her eyes letting him know she was only going to touch it.

"Kiss it."

She licked her lips. She bent over and planted a wet, closed-mouthed peck on the base of his second skull. She straightened up again.

He waved it at her again. Twitches of frustration fired in his brow and the corners of his mouth.

"What?" she feigned cluelessness, "You want another kiss?" She took him in her hand.

He expressed his growing tension through his grip on her shoulder. He was moaning a few seconds later when she engulfed him in her mouth. She got off on having her mouth full of his texture and heat and also on the control she had over him. Memories of his girth came flooding back to her. He grabbed her hair and face-fucked her so gently that she wanted more. There weren't any blinds, shades, curtains, plastic bags— nothing—over that window. The gardening neighbor would witness quite a display if he looked up from the damp earth at that moment.

He reached over her back and slapped her ass hard a few times. She ignored her gag and took him in deeper, her hand covered in spit. He suddenly pulled her throat off his dick and brought her back to standing by her hair.

He stared at her, her lips swollen. Those fucking lips.

"Fuuuck..."

If he let her at his dick again he wouldn't be able to hold back. She reached down and stroked him with her wet hand.

His nostrils flared. "Shit..." He snatched his body from her grip and took a few steps over to one of his tables. He swatted away letters and magazines, receipts, fur swatches and fabric and found gold. He tore the wrapper open with his teeth and rolled the condom on hastily while he walked over to her. She was only able to open her jeans in the time it took him to get back across the room. He spun her around and pushed down her jeans for access.

Her snug body hadn't changed in two years. She screamed for more and deeper until he was spent and they changed positions. He took a spot on his floor and she smiled at the sight. She was quite pleased and he was still hard for more. She teased his body with her tongue. When she released his sack from her mouth she licked his taint. His balls rested on her nose as she wrote the alphabet with her tongue. She gave him a handjob while she sealed her lips on him and sucked on his g-spot. Her first finger on her other hand tickled his asshole. This was a woman who could walk and chew gum at the same time.

"Put a finger in..." He raised his knee a little to prove he was serious in his request. She pushed her finger into his body. It closed around her first knuckle like a scalding vice. His body didn't trust her as much as he apparently did.

She was very careful when entering a man. Being the recipient for the majority of her sex life, she was empathetic to that whole region of the body. Warming that hole up the right way made it a gaping, creaming heaven. She tested his patience with her one-finger, two-finger then three-finger dance. He was patient with her as she learned what his body liked and what it'd allow. He let out throaty sounds that she found melodic.

They fought, twisted, breathed, waited, lotioned, and nothing—her whole hand couldn't get inside him. His ass didn't loosen to allow more than the four fingers that struggled to fit but his body was still capable of an earth-shattering orgasm.

That was the reintroduction that they needed. The conversations about gentrification and jewelry no longer had the irritating sexual tension underlying them. She was in no rush to travel home with rush hour commuters so they continued to talk and laugh as they ate a bowl of strawberries.

LESS THAN TWO WEEKS LATER

She battled with the decision to text him for another play date. All she could think about was getting fucked by him. The weight of his body, tugging on the curly hairs on his chest until he winced, and trying not to give him the satisfaction of wincing when he had all of his body inside of her. When she finally sent the text, he pinged her back almost immediately telling her to come over and bring toys. She filled her backpack with dildos, vibrators, lube and condoms. The red satchel which held her 9-inch ringer, Mr. Johnson, had gotten stuck in the teeth, as if in a last-ditch effort to not be taken along.

When she walked into his place she wrapped the longest of his free-form locks around her hand and gave it a slow tug, tipping his head back.

"You're fired up," he commented.

She responded with a raised eyebrow and biting her lip. There was more she wanted to tug on but she'd wait. He slap-grabbed her ass as she walked farther into the room. It was hard not to notice the bag she was carrying. She looked like she was going camping.

"All that stuff's for me?" he motioned to her bag as she took it off her back and placed it on his futon.

"As requested." She bent over to untie her sneakers. The view of her ass took all of his focus. He parked himself right behind her. He bit her neck when she stood straight up. The pain he inflicted felt good.

"You wanna watch a movie?" he sat at his computer.

"What kinda movie?" She also wanted to ask if he really meant that they'd watch a movie. She came over with their play date front and center on her mind.

"You like foreign movies?"

He began Googling. She stood behind him occasionally

reaching around to point out something on the screen and eyeing his thighs and crotch too. She played in his hair without thinking. She combined some of his locks at the roots. This was a different level of intimacy for them. She enjoyed feeling his wool on her fingertips. He took his hand off the computer mouse. All the tension left his body and his neck could no longer hold his head up as she hit the sweet spot in the middle of his scalp. He let out a contented sigh.

This went on for a few silent minutes. Soothing him was soothing her. One minute they were ravenous to the point of being rough and then the next they purred and petted each other. She ran her fingers along his hairline and thought it'd be nice if her lips were against his forehead.

The moment was lost when he shrugged her hands off as though he were bothered by her touch. He was annoyed at himself for sinking into her energy, getting so comfortable and enjoying her touch above his waist. He pushed back his computer chair to stand up almost hitting her in the gut with it. He turned his 30-inch monitor towards the futon. She asked the back of his head what movie they'd be watching but he remained mum and left the room.

He returned with two glasses of water and handed one to her. This was the first time she'd seen any kind of house wares in his possession. She found herself studying the glass, impressed at the set he'd chosen. "I didn't poison the water, you know."

"No, it's not that," she smiled, "It's just—" she was talking to his back again so she shut up. He lit incense to kill the metallic stench in the air. He turned off the lights in the room. She didn't know what to make of his "bowerbirding". He'd never set any sort of mood before. He made his way back to the futon carrying a folded blanket he'd fished out of the closet. "It gets cold in here sometimes," he shook it open and draped it over her lap. She hid her surprise.

They spoke sporadically during the movie. She glanced over at him every once in a while and spotted him out of the side of her eye doing the same. She took her hand from off the seat and wedged it between her thighs. She wanted to fuck until

she was sore. But she was melting in the moment sitting there
with him. It was dark, her shoes were off; no pedicure on her
feet. Her pants were open; her soft belly spilled out. It wasn't
love but she'd take it.

The movie ended and he hit ESC to send the screen
back to the desktop. That bluish-white glare illuminated the
room and his smooth brown skin. He tugged her over to him
and they made out like lusty teenagers. She held out for as long
as she could before her hand landed on his crotch. He grew to
more than a handful and his kisses went from sweet to spicy. As
much as they loved to fuck, they could kiss one another all day.
The decision had to be made between swirling her tongue in his
mouth or around the head of his dick. His kisses were more
intense because of her strokes. She eventually tore away and slid
off the futon onto her knees in front of him. He took off his
pants and slid his hips toward her. She ran her tongue along his
inner thigh from his knee to his sack. He wrapped his hand
around his balls and the base of his dick. It stood mighty. She
mentally prepared as she knew a sore jaw was inevitable. She
slapped his hands away. As she did her job he clenched his ass
and rocked his hips up. She responded with moans that vibrated
against him. He responded with another rock of his hips. She
had him and loved it. She held his hips to still him. She was
driving now.

"You wanna start with the small one or the big one?" In
her right hand she held Mr. Johnson, a few flesh tones lighter
than they both were. In her left she held a less-lifelike, ornate
dildo which was ribbed for anyone's pleasure.

He pointed to Mr. Johnson.

"You wanna start with *this* one?" she asked
incredulously.

He shrugged and continued to make the open futon.

Maybe it wasn't that big she considered as she studied it.
It was a little longer than his dick but the thickness was pretty
much the same. She'd only spent time with Mr. Johnson a few
times since bringing him home a few years ago. Her eyes were
bigger than her pussy when she picked him out of the display

case at the boutique.

He took off his shirt. She stripped down to her panties and smelt how turned on she was thinking about what lay ahead. She awaited his primal sounds and seeing him come hard and strong again. Mr. Johnson wouldn't let them down.

"You got lube, right?"

She squeezed some lube onto the dildo and worked it on with lewd flicks of her wrist. She squeezed more lube onto her fingers and massaged his pucker, inside and out, while swallowing his dick a few more times. There was no denying how incredible it felt as his legs rose higher into the air, and he pulled his knees closer to his chest. She took her mouth off him and slid her fingers into him again. He battled with his pleasure and frustration. She knew that look on his face. Spit ran down her chin when she wrapped her lips and tongue around both his balls. His knees touched his chest, fell to the sides, one up, one down—he didn't know what to do with his legs; every position felt amazing. He jerked his throbbing dick hitting against the top of her head a few times.

She backed her face away from his body with his balls still in her mouth until the very last inch, stretching his scrotum. His voice was shaky.

That's when she pushed Mr. Johnson against the resistance of his muscle. Once the head of the dildo made it past his tight ass ring she stopped. The grimace on his face wasn't one of pleasure just yet.

"Keep going..." All-or-nothing is how he lived his life.

"You sure?" Her forearm burned from fighting his body's urge to push the dildo out.

"Push..." He demanded. "I'll tell you when to stop."

She held her right wrist with her left hand and applied steady pressure. Her upper body inched forward as her butt lifted off her heels. Less and less of the dildo was visible. She felt his end point. He didn't demand more this time. His breathing had a pleasant labor. She slowly pulled the dildo in the opposite direction and his face softened. She had a pretty good idea of the sensations he was experiencing. Feeling a man pulling out of her was equally as thrilling as him plunging into her. She pushed the dildo back into him and with a slight twist pulled it out. She slowly sped up her thrusts. His guttural growls sounded so pretty. His dick drooled precum onto his belly.

"Take it out."

He lowered his feet to the sheets. He flipped over onto his hands and knees. The hairs in his crack glistened. They propped his hips up on three pillows. She drew a circle with her palm on his ass cheek then gave it a good whack. She pressed Mr. Johnson's head to his asshole.

"Spit on it."

He turned his head to the side when he heard the pop of the bottle opening.

"Spit on my ass."

"I'm gonna put more lube." She squeezed a slippery coat on the dildo.

He held his cheeks apart and rocked his hips in frustration. "No. Spit on me... Spit on my ass."

"I don't spit."

"Come on, just do it. It's my fantasy."

"It's your fantasy to be spit on?" They knew little of one another personally but the learning curve of their sexual proclivities was exponential.

"Do that for me. Just spit on me."

She couldn't do it. Spit just wasn't her thing. Seeing it done in porn was murder to her lady boner. But she was gung-ho about pegging him with abandon. She leaned forward running her hand up his back and pressed the head of the dildo against him again. "I'm not spitting on you." His body didn't resist the penetration as much as the first round. He quickly forgot his demand. His squeals were familiar; she'd made those sounds before. He snatched the dildo from her and fucked himself at a pace she was probably too afraid to do. Watching him was a thing of beauty. Instead of touching herself she caressed his ass and his waist and his back and his dangle. She kneeled next to him, kissed and sucked on his neck and ear.

He pumped the dildo into his ass vigorously. Mr. Johnson was covered in the cream of his sweat and pleasure. She placed her hand over his to learn his movements. He slowed down just enough to drag his hand out from under hers. The swirling flick of her wrist became automatic. She worked him over. He fucked her hand back, bracing against the mattress. Her pussy was drenched from hearing the sounds he made that couldn't be faked and watching his ass open for the dildo, feeling his resistance and give. She tilted the dildo ever so slightly and his body trembled. That was the green light. She didn't let up.

He came up on his hands and knees and through his wheezing and sighing she made out that he wanted her to stop. He couldn't handle much more without coming all over the sheets.

She pulled the dildo all the way out of him. "I hope you have some energy left for me."

He turned to her with that slick satisfied look on his face. He noticed the sheen on her chest from a mixture of sweat and shea butter. Her nipples were solid. She had a look on her face like she'd just been fucked. "You turn me into a fucking animal," he pounced on her like one. He kissed her, sucked on her neck and tits. She dropped the dildo in the onslaught. He removed her panties from her body, ripping them in the process. He roughly pushed her legs farther apart. She granted him such liberties with her body. She was on her back clutching the sheets and his hair while he ate her pussy.

"You taste so fucking sweet..." His words sent another flood out of her. She was intoxicated hearing him savor her juices, lapping up every drop.

She needed him inside her. She tickled his balls while he rolled on a condom. He got on top of her and they did what they do best. He felt her tightness stretch to accommodate him. He hit all sides, went in just-deep-enough. She bit his shoulder, scratched his back and dug her nails into his ass.

When they kissed it took their union to a whole 'nother level. From the waist down they connected for release. They lingered in their kisses sensually, lovingly, vulnerably. She sucked on his tongue and lips and felt him throb inside her. He fucked her as deep as was physically allowed.

He felt her pussy announce she was close to coming. He

steadied himself on his knees and steered her by the waist while he fucked her. She rubbed her clit. Now he knew for sure she was on her way. He threw his head back and squeezed his eyes shut to hold back his nut. She pulled the sheets completely off one side of the futon. Right when she started to cry out incoherently, he stopped. He was breathing heavily, looked at her and pulled out.

He let out a sharp exhale. "I don't want this to end... not yet..." He sat on his heels.

She sat up. "Wanna watch me play with myself?" She'd already started. She could put on a great show for him and the ending was guaranteed. He couldn't get enough of her. He grabbed her by her damp armpits and pulled her on top of him directing his dick back into its rightful place.

This leg of their marathon was aggressive. They fucked each other with an underlying thread of anger. She rode and *wined* on him and her pussy massaged him in appreciation.

"Yeah, get that shit, yo," he slammed up into her. "Come for me, aight, I want you to come for me," he grabbed her hips. It wasn't clear if he was egging her on or himself. He made that almost-there sound. Her pussy wonderland felt great but it could feel better. He pulled out of her and stripped the condom off. He put her back on top of him. She was well aware of what he'd done but was too wrapped up to stop. They slammed into each other over and over...

"Let's do this." She didn't or couldn't form words in the midst of it all. "Let's go half on a baby."

She'd heard what he said, word for word, but couldn't stop fucking him back.

"You ready? You ready? Let's do it..." He had a vice grip on her ass, slamming into her.

She didn't respond to his questions because she was on her way to fulfilling his first demand; she was going to come all over him. He made that "I'm almost there" sound again. Her hips bounced and the slapping flesh rang out. At the very last second he pulled out. She snapped back to the present with a sense of relief. She straddled him with her hips hovering over his gusher, watching his glorious come face.

She went into the bathroom after he was done cleaning himself up in there. She was in that combination drained-energized mode, feeling invincible, tired, happy, taller...

He was still naked, sitting on the edge of the futon, tapping and swiping the touch screen of his phone when she came back into the room. The smell of sex was heavy in the air along with the aloeswood and patchouli incense she'd become nose blind to. An internet radio station was playing on his computer.

"How do the trains run around here now?"

He didn't look up from his phone. "I don't know. What you worried about that for? Just catch the train in the morning."

"Oh." He was still focused on his phone. "Ok."

She took her phone out of the pocket of her jeans thrown on a chair. She climbed onto the futon and went behind him to the window-side. "Thanks for letting me stay."

"Uh huh." He immediately felt awful for making his invitation seem like he was doing her a favor. He really did want her to stay. If he appeared busy, he wouldn't have to face the woman with whom he was so exposed.

He walked across the room and turned off the light. He climbed onto the futon and they lay there on opposite sides, their faces illuminated by their cell phone displays, catching up on what they'd missed when they occupied each other.

She finished first and turned off her phone display. He was done soon after. He let out a loud yawn and stretched out on his back. She studied his sex-softened and sleepy profile and wondered if his half of the baby would include his round nose. She rolled onto her side and pulled the blanket over her. He sat up and stretched for his computer mouse turning off the music.

"You can leave that on."

"Yeah?"

"Yeah, it's nice to fall asleep to music sometimes..." She needed the music to distract her from her thoughts. He didn't want a song to come on that could make him emotional.

He looked at the back of her head and her curvy form under the blanket. He tucked himself in next to her and threw a few more inches of the blanket over her. She smiled to herself at the gesture.

Aside from the faint music, the room was quiet. He stirred again, moving over to her and rolled onto his side to face her. He draped his arm over her as he fit himself to her curves. She sunk into his warmth. That moment sure beat having to wait on a deserted subway platform or fighting sleep on the train to Brooklyn. It wasn't love but she'd take it.

* * *

Speed Play

"Here's your ballot," the cheerful plus-size woman at the registration desk hands the man a notepad as she continues with her explanation. "You'll mark off which dates you are interested in seeing again after today. Each woman has a number. Any questions?"

"Just one, what's *your* number?"

The host giggles. The charm bomb strikes again. "You silly!" He may be silly but he's down for bouncing off her cushion all night long.

Mark enters the main dining room of the restaurant which has been reconfigured for the speed dating event. And with Mark's looks he'll likely be snapped up at the speed of sound. In the world of singles in his city, men are outnumbered by women. The world is his for the taking, at least for tonight since he's at an event to actually meet someone with similar intentions.

Mark is 6-foot-3 and a solid two hundred and ten pounds. He works in IT consulting but looks like he should work in the mail room. The blue collar sex appeal works to his advantage and he flaunts it. He learned in college that looking like a dummy with smarts was his key to success. Professors and the women who gave him pussy were always sucked in to the illusion—this isn't a man I have to fix he's already "there". He has no children or emotional baggage that they can discern before their intense passionate flings die out.

The room buzzes with conversation once the event is underway. Couples sit face-to-face at the dating stations getting to know as much as they can about one another in five minutes to decide if they want to see each other again. Countless friends-with-benefits and marriages can trace their origin stories back to this speed dating event. There's an attractive mix of Black and Latino men and women paired up. It makes you wonder why any of these people are single if even for the sole purpose that they'd look scrumptious in their leaked sex tapes.

The signature voice of D'Angelo singing the line 'How does it feel?' echoes throughout the room. The event host bounces to the center of the room. "Ok, fellas! Time's up! If you'd like to see your dates again, don't forget to mark down her badge number or," she makes air quotes, "digits, so we can arrange your real-life dates." She chuckles, proud of her form of branding for this event. "Now, move to the," more air quotes, "dating booth, to your right and begin your next date!"

Mark's next date is with Jehina. She's caramel, almost a golden hue with blond dreadlocks. Her burgundy stained lips excite him. He leans forward with his elbows on the table. Jehina's textbook posture accentuates her breasts, making them appear a full cup larger. She maintains expectant eye contact with him. He checks off her number on his ballot before the first word is even uttered.

At the neighboring dating booth, Roz, 31, is engaged in intense conversation with an average-sized man, light-skinned, named Chase whose prominent feature are his bulbous eyes. His gaze can penetrate anyone when angered but melt your heart when he's in the mood to play. He's a departure from her previous speed date with a man who looked like he had a history of doing gay porn.

"I sing. It's my life force," he explains to Roz in response to her 'what do you do?' query.

"That's an interesting way to put it, your life force."

"Think about it, the breathing, the energy transfer, the emotions, the healing power. It's all there when you sing. And the healing power of music has been proven."

Roz has had her fill of men who tread the surface and don't dive deep into life. She was getting the impression that Chase could handle emotions without feeling like it would challenge his manhood. At 28, Roz already had her own business, had sold two previous entrepreneurial ventures for a substantial amount and had traveled the world via airports and her pussy.

She leans back in her seat to take in more of the scene before her. "I could see you singing your children to sleep one day. Or singing your daughter down the aisle."

Chase hadn't even thought that far ahead in his own life. But he's at speed dating to see if there would be any women he connected with to possibly get there. "Roz, I'm gonna go ahead and check your badge number right now." He makes the notation on his ballot with a playful flourish.

Roz reaches into her handbag. Earlier she'd reached in for a stick of gum. This time she pulls out her business card and slides it stealthily across the table. "Chase, I'm gonna go ahead and give you my number right now."

Chase's eyes dart around the room while he picks up her card and slips it into his pocket.

D'Angelo summons the singles to make their way to their next dates. Mark studies the woman sitting two booths away, overlooking the date he's standing in front of. He tries to catch Chase's eye in the hopes they can switch places but he's already sitting with his next date. Mark sits down across from Roz. They eye each other while the host of the event gives a pep talk. Once the timer starts on their date, they continue to stare at each other.

"Hey."

"Hey."

"This is a cool event." She places her hands on the table, interlocking her fingers.

Mark nods. "Yeah, it's good to see all these beautiful people together."

Roz twirls her thumbs as if hitting a mini speedbag. Not that the man sitting across from her isn't one of the beautiful people but it appears both of them have run out of steam for the evening.

"Listen, I kinda already met someone tonight I'm interested in. I mean, sure, I could meet more than one person, it's just..."

"Oh! You have? Great! Me too... I already know who I want." Mark quickly amends his statement so it doesn't sound as one-track as he may have meant it. "I already know who I'd like to see again for a real date, you know?"

"So we don't have to pretend? Nice." Their expressions dissolve into relaxed smiles.

Roz and Chase return to her downtown high-rise apartment. She turns on a few lights but not to their full wattage. In the dim light, Chase scans the room like a lemur on the lookout for fossa, checking out the luxury furnishings and overall upscale quality of the apartment. The double glass doors leading to the terrace are closed but the curtains are open allowing city lights to cast shadows throughout the room.

"So what do you like on your tongue, Chase?"

His back stiffens and his arms drop straight to his sides, "I was taking a look at some of your art—wait, what?" he cocks his head to one side. "Did you just ask what I would like on my tongue?"

Roz takes out a bottle of Johnnie Walker Blue and places it on the bar along with two glasses. "Hey, while you're over there, turn on some music." She motions with her chin to the control panel. Chase scans the console with his fingers until he finds the power button. The Roots "Break You Off" begins. "How fitting."

"Very." He approaches the bar. "I need a splash of water in mine." He fends off her protests by putting up his hand. "I know... but I need to protect my instrument," he touches his throat.

Roz resigns with a nod and adds a splash of water to his drink. She joins him on the other side of the bar. "Cheers! Or *Salamati* as they say in Iran." They clink glasses with lusty eye contact.

"You've been to Iran too?"

"Yeah, I spent time traveling through Iran, Turkey, Cyprus and Greece."

"That is outstanding." He sips his whisky.

"Well now, I have another question for *you*..." she places her drink down. "I've never had Johnnie with water. How does it taste?" She fans her fingers on the back of his head and neck and pulls him in for a kiss. When his body crashes into hers, his drink sloshes around in his glass, a few drops landing on his hand and wrist. He blindly places the glass on the bar then picks her up and sits her on the bar. She loves the feeling of her hips and thighs spreading out over the cool marble. She wraps her legs around his thighs and they explore each others mouths, necks, and bodies. She pulls her shirt off over her head without disturbing a single hair in her auburn-highlighted twa. His hands and tongue are on her bare breasts before she can bring her arms down. The next song that comes on the shuffle is "In the Morning" by Ledisi. Couldn't be more perfect for the moment.

As quickly as his mouth finds her breast, her hands wrestle with his belt buckle and pants button.

"I'll give it to you..." he says half in her mouth as he kisses her again and unzips his pants. His hands send his pants down and her hands bring his dick out from his underwear.

She breaks the kiss to look at him. The two have their foreheads pressed together as they gaze down at his body.

"It's pretty..." He's a little over 7-inches and fat. She strokes it, "wow..." Her fingers swirl under his balls.

"Yeah?"

"Fuck yeah..." She's stroking him again.

"Are you pretty?" He cups her crotch with his hand and sticks his tongue in her mouth again.

Mark and Jehina enter from the foyer. "Oh! I'm so sorry!" Jehina shrieks and hides her face against Mark's shoulder. There's a mass scramble to avoid eye contact and cover up exposed body parts.

Roz drapes her arm over her breasts. She shoos Chase from in front of her so she can jump down while he's buttoning his pants. She turns her back to the others and puts her top back on. Mark and Chase don't speak while they eyeball each other.

"Um, where's your washroom? I'm gonna go freshen up."

"Third door. End of the hall." Mark says. His date makes a hasty retreat from the living room. Mark is staring at the man who's concentrating on him that he doesn't even sneak a look at his date from behind as she walks away. Instead, Roz does the scoping of Jehina's hourglass figure accentuated by the electric blue pencil skirt she's wearing. She has a body that would make a man forget his baby in the backseat.

Roz unnecessarily adjusts her clothes. She has the focus of someone rehearsing lines from a play. "Chase, this is Mark. He lives here too."

"Hey, how's it going, man?" Chase extends his hand. The men shake hands.

"He's my husband." Roz watches the impact of the bomb she just dropped. Chase drops his chin, squeezing his eyes shut and tries to shake his head clear. When he opens his eyes again he looks directly at Mark.

"Hey, dude, I'm so sorry. She didn't tell me she was—"

"No, it's ok, I knew she was here with you." Mark smiles.

Roz and Mark say "we got him" with their shared glance. She places her hand on Chase's back. "I brought you over here thinking we all could..."

"Whoa! Whoa, whoa, whoa, whoa..." he backs away from the couple. "I'm gonna go get some air." He rushes out to the terrace.

Roz doesn't have to say a word to express that that didn't go as planned. "What did *your* date say?" she asks.

"I didn't tell her yet."

The battle to give Mark a piece of her mind or to hold her peace is written all over her face. She exhales audibly for nearly 7 seconds.

"That's the dude you want tonight?"

"Yeah." Her tone says she doesn't appreciate her choice being questioned. Mark's never had an issue with her dates before. As he reaches for his wife to make peace, they hear the bathroom door open.

"I'm gonna go talk to him." She makes her retreat to the terrace.

Jehina peeks into the living room from the hall. Mark smiles and waves her in. "The coast is clear."

"Sucks we walked in on your roommate like that. Hope

we're not in the way of him and his date."

"Actually, *he's* not my roommate. I live with her."

Slight discomfort flashes across her face. But her acceptance of the living situation is written in her expression soon after.

"She's my wife."

"Naw. How the fuck you gonna bring me home after meeting me at a speed dating event for single people? And hold up! She was in here messing around with some dude! Yo... ya'll are some freaks!"

"I brought you home with me because I want you. I'm not a freak."

"But ya'll are married. Like what the fuck yo?"

"Right. Happily married for 8 years. I love Roz with all my heart. She's all I need in a woman," Jehina rolls her eyes, "but that doesn't mean I don't want other women. I'm human. And I'm a fucking *man*."

"Yeah, and just like a fucking man, you gotta fuck around." She crosses her arms over her chest.

"Aight be easy. I'm not fucking around on my wife. I would never do that."

Her upper lip curls like she's been hit with a whiff of something rotten and her eyes hop around the room looking for the source of the rank odor. "Well I guess if you're gonna cheat, you might as well have it out in the open."

"It's not cheating *because* it's out in the open. We don't have secrets."

Jehina looks towards the terrace at Roz and Chase. "So you're telling me you're fine with your woman fucking other dudes?"

"She's not *mine*. I don't own her. But yes, I'm fine with it. She's very in tune with who she is sexually. And ya'll women be wanting *a lot* more than one man can give."

Jehina can't help but crack a smile at that tidbit from Mark because it rings true for her. "So ya'll just get horny and swing?"

"We're in an open marriage. But yes, sometimes we swing."

She uncrosses her arms and drops her bag onto the couch. "And ya'll thought it was a good idea to go snag some fresh meat from the butcher shop." She shakes her head.

"Aight, full disclosure," he sits on one of the bar stools, "yes, we went out tonight because we wanted to play. So we registered for the speed dating. That way we could meet people who had something going on in their lives and in their heads and who we also wanna fuck."

"You checked off my number before you even spoke to me. Don't think I didn't see that."

"I *said* part of the criteria was it had to be someone we wanted to fuck. And you fine as all get-out, girl."

They laugh. Mark waves her over to the bar and takes her hand when she's within reach. "We can go slow. Whatever you wanna do. But I was hoping we all could play tonight."

Her eyes dart back toward the terrace. "He's not bad looking..."

"See...?"

"But I'm not interested in another woman's coolie. No disrespect to your wife, *at all*, it's just not my thing."

"You've never explored with a woman?"

"I guess that's one of the things you forgot to ask me on our date," she mocks with wide eyes and a neck roll. She picks up one of the glasses of Johnnie left on the bar by Chase and Roz.

"Wait... I didn't pour those."

"You're talking about me eating a woman's pussy. Does it really matter?" She takes the glass to the head.

Chase lights a cigarette. His shoulders are up at his ears and he's hugging himself despite the 70 degree temperature outside. He glances at Roz when she joins him on the terrace.

"Why do you smoke? You're a singer."

He takes a long drag from his cigarette and lets the smoke escape his full, pursed lips. "I only do this when I'm nervous."

"You must be nervous a lot." Roz is enthralled at his expert handling of the cigarette.

It takes Chase a few seconds to catch her meaning.

"And that's why I sing." He flashes a half-smile.

"Ah, vicious cycle." She glances back into the apartment at the faint sound of her husband and his date laughing at the bar. When she turns her attention back to Chase, he's also watching the scene in the apartment.

"Hey, I need to apologize to you. I should've told you what was going on before we got to this point."

"You're a woman who knows what she wants. And you got it. I'm here," he takes another drag of the cigarette.

Roz struggles to read the expression on his profile. "So, um, my husband and I were looking to play tonight."

"I liked playing with you."

She looks back into the apartment and sees Mark has his arm around Jehina. He's whispering something in her ear and judging by the smile on her face, Roz knows her husband's date is gushing in her panties. He has a way with words and his hands that women can't resist. Jehina exudes a demure aura that coming from the right woman is like catnip for Mark. Nibbling on her neck is just icing on the cake. One down, one to go. Roz turns her attention back to Chase. He quickly turns his attention back towards the night skyline of the city.

"I gotta be upfront though." She props her elbows on the railing. "I don't think you're gonna be able to play one-on-one with Mark."

"Why would I want—"

Roz cuts him off with a shake of her head sparing him from hemming and hawing his way through a bogus explanation. Chase turns his whole body to face her. "How'd you know?" he puffs on his cigarette.

"I could just sense it." She shrugs.

"Even though I was hooking up with you?"

"Doesn't mean you don't want to hook up with him too. It's cool. Someone of us are bi. No crime in that." She watches as he takes a deep breath, his shoulders shrugging even higher. "Plus it's not like you ran outta here when we told you. I think you were hoping it was more than just a swap." Since the couple decided to explore other people together, her husband has never played with her male dates. He had no issue being naked with another man, being ringside while they smashed her till she screamed like a banshee but that was as far as he ever went.

"So he's never... ever?"

Roz sends her eyes skyward in a moment of total recall. "Well, this one time, at band camp..." Chase laughs before she breaks and laughs too. "But seriously, when we first got into the lifestyle we went to a festival. Turned out to be this pansexual event. At night, they had bonfires and skinny-dipping but there was also a boom boom room."

Chase perks up even more at the mention of the boom boom room. She nods in agreement with his excitement as she remembers when. "Yeah, so there was this dude who really liked me, but," she turns her head towards to city and lowers her voice a bit, "he also wanted to get fucked by Mark."

The gleam in Chase's eye is undeniable as he drops his arms for the first time. Roz stomps on his dreams the way he extinguishes a smoldering cigarette butt. "He teased and denied both of us that night." She shakes her head. "I would've loved to have seen that." She turns and leans against the railing, facing the apartment. "He's a great fuck."

Chase takes the last drag of his cigarette, the embers racing towards his fingers as he cradles his body even tighter. She's thrilled by the roll of his hip when he crushes the cigarette under the toe box of his shoe. "I knew I liked you."

"Yeah?"

"Yeah, you have an intuitive, nurturing energy that I was attracted to tonight. I could tell you live by that 'one love' philosophy."

"We both read each other tonight."

He practically melts into a puddle when she places her hand on his back. He puts his arm around her shoulders. "Wanna know how Dunhills taste?" he lifts her chin and they pick up where they left off on the bar.

Mark and Jehina are rounding the bases on the couch. He's already stripped down to his underwear and has helped her out of her blouse and bra. Her back arches when he eases her nipple into his mouth. She squeezes him tighter with her thighs in response to his suckling. He moves attentively down her body. His fingers travel under her skirt and under the front of her cotton panties. His pelvis presses forward when his finger parts her pussy lips. He's eager to put his dick where his finger is exploring. He kisses her softly and she sucks on his tongue.

"Yeah, go slow... like that..." She grips his wrists as she trembles. He slowly pulls his finger out and wastes no time putting it in his mouth.

His eyes light up. "Damn, you delicious…" he sucks his finger some more. She's wearing her skirt like a belt by the time he grabs her by the hips and whips her body around so he can bury his face between her legs.

Roz leads Chase back into the apartment and immediately they're mesmerized by the scene playing out before them.

Mark comes up for air. "You ever tasted yourself?" His shiny face is a familiar sight to Jehina that is long overdue. Her bed has been cold for a long time.

Roz kisses his shoulder and she feels him up with the reach-around. "Her pussy looks so hot, babe," Jehina's golden pussy with her trimmed natural dark brown hair is almost too much stimuli for her.

Jehina draws her knees together slightly at the sight of Roz kissing and sucking on Mark's neck. Having a man's wife at the party while she receives some of the best head she's ever had is new territory for her. It doesn't help that it looks like Roz is about to dive headfirst into her pussy.

Mark stands, "Taste..." and he kisses Jehina. She kisses her juices from his lips, chin and cheeks. She flinches at the sensation of Roz's hand on her thigh but he reads her sudden movement as hunger for more. He drops to his knees and licks her again, stiffening his muscular tongue and dipping it into her.

"Gimme some..." his wife's lips are parted waiting for him to give her a taste of his date. While the married couple shares Jehina's flavor, she guides Roz's hand off her leg.

"You *are* sweet, hon..." Roz smiles at her. She stands and brings Mark to his feet too. She notices Jehina's hips and belly relax at the sight of her husband. She takes hold off him in his boxer briefs, her fingers and thumb no where near touching as she wraps them around him. Jehina's eyes dart back at forth like she's tracking a fast-moving target. Roz rakes her fingers down the front of her husband's body biting her bottom lip and grants Jehina permission with a nod. The two women bond while they run their hands on Mark's chest.

Roz purrs approvingly at the sight of Jehina working her clit in a circular motion. Jehina's jaw drops but then she smiles slyly at being caught.

Mark is wet in Roz's hands from the stroking. "You wanna see him?" she asks Jehina.

"Yes, please!"

"You ready to show her, baby?" she continues to stroke him, "You ready to show her what you got?" She pushes the waist band of his boxer briefs below his ball sack. He salutes both women with his rigid 9 inches, the head shiny from his precum.

"Shit..." Jehina thinks for a second that she's bitten off more than she can handle but she's too fired up to stop now.

Roz follows her gaze to Chase who's rubbing himself over his pants. She reaches out to him, inviting him to come closer. "Get over here. I know *you* wanna play... " She playfully runs her tongue along her teeth while stroking Mark sharing her true meaning with Chase. And he loves her for it. He wraps his arms around her. She tips her face back towards him and they kiss sloppily.

"This is Chase," she looks down at the other woman. "You might remember him from earlier..." she teases. Up close, Jehina realizes she really likes his face, his large eyes giving him a piercing gaze. There's sexual prowess in his eyes. His lips are swollen from kissing Roz.

"Taste my husband, beautiful." she points Mark's dick down towards Jehina who takes as much of him as she can into her mouth.

"*Nnnnh...*" Mark feels like he's being wrapped in a hot towel. His sounds trigger Chase, who gropes Roz's tits from behind while she grinds her ass against him. "I want summa that..." the wet whisper in her ear is proof of his hunger for her husband.

She turns to face Chase and frees him from his pants. "This is gonna be fun." Her comment's directed at his dick. He steals glances at Mark who's lost in the sensations as Jehina runs her tongue up, under and around his dick and balls. Her burgundy lip stain is all but gone and is replaced by the blood rushing to her lips. Mark has two handfuls of her golden locks and rocks his hips into her face. She does a good job holding him deep in her throat until she has to back off for air.

The sound of the wet release draws Roz's attention. "Damn, she got you, baby."

"You think you can do better?" Mark challenges.

"You mind?" She checks with Chase about stopping their slow grind.

"Nah, I got her," Chase lightly rubs Jehina's chin and is lucky enough to graze Mark's balls in the process. Even as Jehina takes her first taste of him, he looks right at Mark. His gaze drops to witness Roz swallowing most of her husband's dick on the first try. He makes a mental note of how Mark likes it. He has the same tight grip on her dreadlocks Mark had earlier and his ass clenches while she controls him with dick-length sucks. Raunchy and nonsensical words escape his lips while she goes berserk on his dick.

For a few seconds, Roz absentmindedly strokes her husband as she watches Jehina devouring Chase. She can't help but reach for Jehina's upper inner thigh. Mark strokes his wife's head to get her attention and narrows his eyes at her. She gets the message and takes her hand off Jehina's thigh, albeit after another caress and squeeze. He just had to choose a date who didn't want to play with her—that made her want her more.

Roz goes to a curio cabinet and returns to the party with a handful of colorful packets. She showers the couch with the condoms as if they've been beaten out of a piñata. She has a one-track mind of getting pounded by both of the dicks in the room that night and hopefully a taste of pussy direct from the source.

Before too long, Chase rolls a condom on and is pushing Roz's shoulders down to the couch. "You want this deep, girl?" He slides in with an 'oooh' at how snug and wet she is.

Mark sits on the couch and Jehina still has him in her mouth. He enjoys his momentary role of cuckhold as Chase drills his wife. Roz joins the party when she can, slurping up and down the side of her husband's thick dick. She's aware of how deftly Jehina avoids touching her lips to hers while they both fellate her husband. Ordinarily, she'd steal her kiss anyway but she's getting off on her hard-to-get routine. The reward will be so much sweeter when she willingly gives it to her.

She revels in watching Jehina ride her husband's dick. The slap of her hips onto his thighs acts as a metronome for the room. Her sweat mixes with his. He slaps her ass hard and feels a surge of her warmth surround him. He slaps her ass again. "You like that shit, don't you?" he slaps her again as she continues to bounce up and down on his lap. "Let her do it..." he hisses at her and slaps her ass again. She's too far gone in her trance to object. "Go for it, babe..." he eggs on his wife. Roz rubs her ass before slapping it with an open hand. She feels the reverb of Jehina's jelly all the way up her arm.

Before she can think, Chase pulls out of her and pushes her face into the couch next to Jehina's knee. His strong tongue on her asshole takes her breath away. His spit and her unstoppable flow leak down her thighs.

"Yes! Yes! Yes!" Jehina is the loudest person in the room. She coats the base of Mark's dick and balls with more and more of her pussy cream. Chase locks eyes with him over his wife's hump. His gaze remains steady on him as he fucks Roz's ass with his tongue. It's unnerving to Mark, those doe-eyes begging for more, begging for more from *him*.

Jehina slows her bounce a bit, "You good?" She rocks her hips trying to wake up Mark's softening dick.

Her hushed urgency snaps him out of the stare down with Chase. "Yeah..." he slaps her ass again, "get it... go for yours..." She revs up her hips again.

Basking in her afterglow, Jehina throws her head back over the arm of the couch and opens her mouth for Mark to drop his balls in. She lightly taps her pussy with her four fingers through her subtle aftershocks. Roz touches her thigh and can feel her orgasm has cleared all the resistance from her body.

On the next pass of her hand, she ends up with Jehina's juices on the tip of her finger. Jehina moans on Mark's dick. He smiles at his wife knowing the more she touches her, the better his blowjob and teabagging will get. She traps Jehina's fat pussy lips and clit in the V of her fingers and slides up down before slipping the tip of her finger into her wet muscle.

Jehina lifts her head briefly to see Roz is the one reigniting her. Roz sticks her finger back inside, daring her to say something. Jehina's mouth hangs open while she fingers her slowly; pulling out every few thrusts to ice skate over her lips and clit with her tender fingertips. Jehina drops her head back and sucks Mark into her mouth. Roz withdraws her wet finger and runs it along Chase's lips like she's applying lipstick. She kisses him and sends him over to Mark with a jut of her chin.

The two men stand dick to dick over their Goldilocks. Roz licks the length of Jehina's pussy then blows on it. An arousing sense of pride washes over her as she tastes her husband's date. From the sounds of things, Jehina is enjoying the taste of Roz's date too.

She takes a break and Jehina lets out a whimper in protest. "I'll be right back." She gives her thigh a reassuring squeeze before getting off the sofa.

She returns carrying a lifelike dildo. The way she caresses it would make any man envious. The real men in the room have their dicks pressed together by Jehina who licks the underside of both their hoods. Mark is in his own world and misses the look shared between his wife and Chase. Chase stands dick-to-dick with Mark and his smile says that counts for something. If how she's felt all evening trying to get a taste of Jehina is a fraction of the pent up energy Chase was experiencing wanting to taste her husband she knew something would have to give.

She kneels on the couch between Jehina's gaping thighs licking her pussy a little more then rubs the head of the dildo along her wide slit. Jehina answers by rocking her hips up and down. She presses the head of the dildo at her pussy opening and waits. Her hips rock some more, impatient.

"You want this, hon?" Roz is going to make her say it.

Jehina nods and mumbles her answer while switching back and forth between the two rock hard dicks.

"Yeah? You want it?" She rubs her clit as she pushes the dildo inside her. The job Jehina is doing on the men becomes disjointed as her concentration is tested. "Mmmm... you're pushing me out..." She's steady as she fills her with the dildo repeatedly. She squeezes one of Jehina's tits then slaps it lightly. "Let me in..." she coaxes. She rises up off her heels for more leverage.

Jehina has completely abandoned the men as she crescendos, a tight grip on her breast. They keep their dicks hard, masturbating at the women's heads.

"Huh? Like that? Want me to fuck you like that?" she swirls the dildo on each in and out. Roz leans over her bringing her lips tantalizingly close to hers. "Look at me..." Jehina struggles to lift her heavy eyelids. "Look at me when you come..." The scent of whisky and her husband commingle on Jehina's breath as she quietly exhales her orgasm.

Roz is on the brink herself, the evidence leaking down her thigh. She stretches her body over Jehina's to lick the two throbbing heads. She spends a little more time on Mark's dick out of habit.

"So fucking... yes... Jesus..." Mark barely finds the words for his wife.

"Can you tell when I'm sucking you or when she's sucking you?" She sucks Chase waiting for his answer.

"Fuck, it *all* feels good..."

Without question she kisses Jehina, lingering for a second to let her think about it, no tongue but open-mouth. She slowly pulls the dildo out of her. "That was beautiful, wasn't it baby?" That question is for both her husband, his shoulder bouncing as he strokes himself, and the woman under her. "Damn," she examines the creamy-coated dildo, "look at that come..."

Chase grabs her wrist and puts the dildo in his mouth. The married couple exchanges a stunned glance as he takes the dildo from her and works it at all angles.

"I bet that'd feel good to you too, babe..." She nuzzles her face next to Chase eyeing her husband, getting a small taste of the dildo. "You probably wouldn't even be able to tell the difference."

Chase bobs his head a few more times only leaving behind his saliva on the toy.

"You like the taste of pussy," Mark baits Chase in a pussy-loving bro moment.

"I like the taste of pussy *on* dick." Chase twirls his wrist, waving the dildo by his face.

Mark's stroking slows to a crawl then halts as his gaze floats from mouth to mouth to mouth. His wife had a knack for picking people who know how to party.

*   *   *

Sand In My Shorts

He had the body of a bronze statue.

"My god, he's beautiful," I said as I turned to my husband.

"You should go say 'hello'" Alvin suggested.

Those words were music to my ears timed to the rhythm of the beautiful stranger's dick sway. I was hypnotized by it as he approached us. We were at a clothing optional beach. I'm so glad the living sculpture chose the no-clothing option. Alvin and I sometimes go completely nude. On this day we wore barely-there swimwear. Beachgoers on the shore of Rio would love us, as they have before. The bright green of my string bikini clashed beautifully with the deep red undertones of my brown skin. Alvin held his meat in the bright white casing of his bikini briefs.

The beautiful stranger walked by as Alvin and I watched his broad shoulders and back provide a canvas for the sun's rays. His ass was perfect. Perfect.

A sly grin crept over my face. "What're you smiling at?" Alvin asked.

"Think that's a virgin ass?"

Alvin let out a moan which told me he was praying the answer was 'yes' and he'd be deep in it sooner than later. I wondered if anyone or anything had been deep in the stranger's ass. I whispered into Alvin's ear about the possibility of sitting on the face of the stranger we both were lusting after while Alvin fucked him. Alvin had the power and desire to be inside every living person we came across.

A warm breeze blew in off the ocean but it wasn't enough to cool us down. We imagined out loud all the tastes, sounds and touches of having the stranger on all fours. I'd lay under him with his dick deep in my mouth knowing exactly how Alvin would look with his head thrown back and neck veins bulging while the stranger ran his tongue over the bulging veins of Alvin's black dick.

I took off my sunglasses and said hello to Judah at the sun shower. "I don't want to be strangers anymore." He took off his sunglasses and his eyes told me he felt the same way.

"My husband would like to get to know you too."

"All right… Take me to him," Judah said without batting an eye.

We took the high-knee walk back to Alvin. I sat in my beach chair. Alvin rolled over and sat up on the towel. Judah sat facing me on the edge of the beach chair next to me. His dick and balls rested comfortably on the chair. Alvin eyed the body of Judah that matched his own.

"I don't even want to know what Sam said to you to get you to come over here." Alvin said.

"She said 'hello' and her ass said 'follow me'" Judah answered. I was sure he also heard my ass say "grab me", "spank me", "taste me", "enter me". I already knew what I was getting with Judah. Even his soft dick was a lot to wrap my thoughts around. And I knew the three triangles that barely preserved any decency I was going for that day on the beach would betray me. Hard nipples teeped the bikini top and my spreading, swelling pussy lips would start to peek out either side of the crotch of my bikini. "I hope I heard correctly," Judah added.

I nodded. "Loud and clear." I flashed him a smile then shared that smile with Alvin.

"You have a beautiful mouth," Judah said.

I gave him a sidelong glance while I bit my bottom lip. Alvin reached up and started rubbing my foot. That meant he was putting a lot of strain on the material of his briefs. Another man found his wife desirable. Another man who he'd have the chance to experience and who could also make his wife scream and come. Alvin interlocked his fingers with my toes.

"Her mouth is amazing," Alvin bragged.

"I'll tell you if it is," Judah said the last few words into my mouth as he kissed me, his hand turning my face towards him. His mouth tasted of Gatorade and a marijuana dessert. His kiss was forceful and passionate. Strangers don't kiss with that level of passion. I felt the warm dampness of Alvin's mouth on my toes. He was losing control like he had countless times before. He would taste my toes until he had no choice but to taste my pussy. His hands traveled up my legs pushing my thighs apart. My legs fell open and my feet hit the sand on either side of the beach chair. Sand stuck to my wet toes. If it were a few hours later, sand would be sticking to all parts of all three of our bodies. We could each relish in the sensual commotion of four hands and two mouths on our bodies with the soundtrack of waves crashing against the shore and the moon shining above. The crotch of my bikini barely covered my pussy in the bright mid-afternoon sun. Alvin's finger grazed my pussy lip then slipped under the fabric. I moaned into Judah's mouth when my husband's finger rubbed my clit. Judah kissed and sucked my neck and his fingers slipped under my bra to find my nipple. The splash from Alvin's finger fucking me grew louder. Judah flicked my nipple with his tongue. That's when I whispered into his ear, "Let's go home."

He looked at me with a subtle smile acknowledging my request. He took Alvin's wrist and pulled his fingers out my pussy and put them in his mouth. I watched as he ran his tongue around and between Alvin's fingers never once taking his eyes off him.

In the shower I had four hands sudsing and groping my body. I'm usually drained after a day in the sun, but I was getting my second wind. I had the energy to feast on the two black dicks saluting me while I kneeled on the bed.

"Taste him, love." Alvin took Judah's dick into his hands and fed it to me. I took in as much of his ten inches into my mouth as I could. As my juices trickled down my leg, Judah

reached over me and played in it. His fingers explored my
warmth until it started to tug on his fingers. He ended his
exploration after he collected a big enough sample from inside
me to suck off his fingers and be satisfied. Then he took his dick
out my mouth, took my face in his hands and kissed me. He
enjoyed my mouth and the taste of his body in it. Judah climbed
onto the bed and lied down. He grabbed my hips and pulled me
over his face before I had the chance to turn around. The way
he took charge reeked of testosterone, pure unadulterated
manliness. There was no escaping his grip. Judah positioned my
pussy on his face. I watched his balls retract after the faint tickle
I gave them with my fingertips. I knew he wanted to house his
dick in my mouth again. It was easier to deep throat him at this
angle. But it also made it hard to concentrate, the way his tongue
circled my pussy and slowly slid in and out of it. I was on the
losing end of this multitasking challenge.

Alvin stroked his hard dick to the sight of our two
brown mouths pleasuring each other. It wasn't long before a
mouth was pleasuring him. He hovered over Judah's face and let
him tease and suck his balls and dick, making it wet before
piercing the warmth of my pussy. Years of marriage had made
Alvin an expert on my body. He'd given Judah a cheat sheet. He
was eating my pussy like a straight-A student. My moans
conducted the symphony of tongue and dick.

Alvin backed off his sweet plunging when he felt my
quiver and Judah slipped out from under me. Alvin loved when
I come on top. In that position, he was awed and overcome by
my powerful femininity. There was always that moment where I
stopped focusing on "us" and I became my main objective. And
as powerful as my orgasms were, I became weak and needed
him to hold me up or would just collapse onto the wide expanse
of his chest. He took his spot under me and dug his heels into
the mattress so he could fuck up into me. I twirled my hips once
with his dick inside me before kissing him. He spread my
cheeks. That sent a shock coursing through the center of my
belly and a wave of juices out my pussy. Judah pressed against
my asshole while Alvin held the door open. My pucker relaxed
while Judah made a steady entry.

They alternated in and out of my body. All I could do was tell myself to breathe. It was sensory overload. Alvin and I had invited others to play with us before, but the strength of my husband and Judah was unmatched. It felt so good and necessary to scream from the sensation of their dicks hitting my g-spot from two angles, stretching my holes that wanted to gape to accommodate them yet at the same time tighten to come around them. The rhythm Judah played on my anal drum made me cream. He grew even stronger with his thrusts. Alvin moaned as my pussy contracted and he could feel Judah's dick rub against his through my insides. Soon after, Judah's thrusts became spastic and the weight of his body on my back grew as he came. He pulled out of my gaping ass, collapsing onto his own with his dick still throbbing. The only thing the three of us did was breathe.

"You came in her ass?" Alvin asked. He couldn't see him but I'm sure the words struck Judah with the same sting I felt.

"I'm sorry, man," he exhaled. "It just came outta nowhere," he touched my ass. "She has a great ass." He climbed off the bed and went to the bathroom.

I could feel a different sort of tension in Alvin's body while he lay underneath me.

I don't know if the sound of the water running in the bathroom was enough to drown out Alvin's anger.

"Babe, it's ok," I said to him. I was still straddling him but he slowly went soft while still inside me.

"He wasn't supposed to come inside you."

"We never said there were any rules," I said in a hushed tone. Alvin took a few more irritated breaths before I asked him, "Do you want him to leave?"

"No, I'm not done with him."

I kissed Alvin. "Play nice." I climbed off him and went to the bathroom to squeeze what I could of Judah's deposit out of me.

Judah had just finished sink-washing his dick. My focus was on his chest. This was the first time since I saw him earlier on the beach that I really studied his body; the definition of his abs and serratus, the kink of his chest and pubic hair, the point of his chin. Then I broke the rule Alvin and I knew was on the books. I wanted to be with Judah. Alvin was nowhere to be found and I acted on the urge. Like the passion of our first kiss, Judah felt natural. We kissed and smashed into the walls, sink, towel rack—anything that was in our way was bowled over. His body asked and mine answered as he picked me up and I wrapped my legs around his firm waist. The door to the bathroom slammed shut as he slammed me up against it and buried himself deep inside me.

"Shh..." he quickly kissed me to muffle my cries. He had picked up on the unspoken rule we were shattering. He was in so deep. I wanted him at first sight on the beach that afternoon. Alvin and I were husband and wife. Any lover we took, we took together. Being fucked against my bathroom door with the love of my life in the next room was wrong, no matter how good Judah's warm breath felt on my neck. I pressed my shoulders against the door and arched my hips forward. Judah accepted the invitation and drove into me balls deep with a violent grip on my waist. We locked eyes. His stare was daring me to break the silence I was forced to keep. My mouth hung open, face contorted in pleasure but no sound escaped. I wanted this man, this moment, all to myself.

"We have to stop," Judah said into my neck before licking it. I squeezed my pussy when he started to pull out trying to keep him inside for a few more moments. I knew he was right to withdraw. What we had done was wrong. This was a party for three.

I cleaned up quickly but there was no way to hide my puffy lips or flushed skin. Alvin sat back on his heels while Judah, on his knees, skillfully navigated his dick. Alvin finally opened his eyes and looked at me. He pulled me in for a kiss. The same angry kiss I get from Alvin after an argument or when he's had a bad day.

"You wanna see me fuck him?" Alvin spit the question at me and I knew he knew what happened in the bathroom. He was still pissed that Judah left remnants of himself inside me. Moments earlier he was close to doing it again. I was close to letting Judah fill me with his come pressed up against my bathroom door.

Judah presented his ass to both of us. "On your back," my husband barked.

The power play began. Alvin wasn't only angry but he was displaying his dominance. He was the Alpha male and he had to be sure Judah knew and respected that fact. Our lifestyle had always been adventurous and relatively free of drama but Alvin had his moments of extreme possessiveness. He was two grunts away from lifting his leg and pissing on me, marking his territory with his musk. Now he let it be known he owned me and Judah. Judah spoke volumes with his eyes; he wasn't going to give Alvin the satisfaction of hearing him moan in pleasure. He knew he was being punished, yet that wouldn't change the fact that he enjoyed being surrounded by my wet pussy. He was fucking me with his eyes right in front of my husband. He braced against Alvin and the mattress so he wouldn't rebound against the pounding he was receiving. Judah took it like a man. He silently massaged his dick as it ebbed and flowed from hard to soft. With his other hand, Judah reached out and ran his fingers down the front of my body. Alvin threw extra force behind his thrusts.

"Sit on his face," Alvin told me, "I want him to taste my wife."

It could've been the thought of getting my pussy licked or the gruff sexual state Alvin was in that made me put my fingers into my slippery pussy. I slid them out, straddled Judah's shoulders and watched as my sticky sweetness stretched between my fingers. Judah lapped me up like a parched captive. The sound level raised a few decibels in the room. Whether it was my husband or anyone else making me moan like I did, it still turned Alvin on to hear the sounds of his wife. Alvin decorated Judah's balls and sculpted center with his release. The Alpha male had spoken.

* * *

Two Way Threesome

I heard the elevator reach my floor. That meant my favorite show was about to begin next door, my saving grace from horrible reality TV. Wednesday night. My neighbor's husband starts his work week on Wednesday night. I met the couple in the elevator soon after I moved in. She's a fashion designer. He's an ER doctor. He does three twelve-hour shifts then he's off till the following Wednesday. She doesn't like to be alone. So the stranger shows up. I figure he's a Sergei or a Jacques. That's the name I'd call out. He's so very handsome. Dark. Thick black hair, smooth face.

He exits the elevator and walks straight to her door. No knock. No doorbell. After a brief pause he turns the doorknob and disappears into her apartment. I watch the empty hallway for a few more seconds through my peephole hoping he would reemerge, change his mind. No such luck. Music plays. Sounds like Jamiroquai. I wonder who makes the musical selection for their trysts. I would've chosen some Oasis; "Fucking in the Bushes," how appropriate.

I went into the kitchen to put dinner on. I sliced the chicken breast thinly after cutting off the fat. I coated the first piece of chicken in egg and milk. The mixture had the consistency of semen. I brought my nose to the bowl and inhaled. The scent was similar – that heavy protein smell. I'll swallow semen but would never consider tasting what was in that bowl. The first piece of chicken got a generous coating of breadcrumbs and I put it down to rest.

I could hear her moans. She was calling his name this time. Couldn't quite make it out over Jamiroquai going goo-goo over his cosmic girl. Sounded like a three-syllable name. So he wasn't a Jacques or a Sergei. But he and Jesus were doing a number on her. I envisioned he had her bent over the arm of the couch. Or they were both on their knees, her on all fours. That was one of my favorite positions. I was getting moist between my legs. Chicken goes in egg and milk. Chicken goes in bread crumbs. Chicken placed onto the plate with the rest of the breast pieces awaiting the hot oil. The monotony of my work allowed my mind to wander. Was he holding her by the hair? Did he grab her hips and pull her back into him? I coated my frying pan with about an inch of oil and turned the heat up. Oil dripped down the side of the bottle as I replaced the cap. I wiped it off with my finger and considered using it to massage my clit.

The chicken breasts were a golden brown. Two shades lighter than my own. I got splashed with hot oil that popped. I wiped the oil off of my arm. It hadn't stayed on my skin long enough to leave a mark. I took the chicken breast out the pan and blotted them with paper towels. My neighbors were probably using paper towels to clean up his come. At first, the paper towel was rough against her inner thigh. As he would fold it over to uncover a clean section, the sharp edges were dampened by his sweaty palms. I covered the bottom of my baking pan with pasta sauce and then put the chicken breasts down.

I loved the way my body sunk into my couch, right between the cushions. The perfect cradle for my ass. I could lie in the couch watching television and my nipples would get hard. I was triggered by the comfort, I suppose. It fascinated me how much glistening, slippery liquid seeped out of me after I'd come.

The back of the couch was just the right height to throw my leg up on. My other leg hung off the couch, my foot on the floor. My clit was now swollen under my fingers. My neighbor probably has a big one as well. I've seen her commit just one fashion faux pas: she'd just come back from a run and had major camel toe. The seam of her spandex shorts disappeared between her meaty labia. She works out without underwear like I do. I love the smooth curve of my ass under my spandex shorts. And there's always the chance I'll climb my way to an orgasm while on the Stairmaster. I said hello to her that morning as I always do, but couldn't help but stare at her crotch. It spoke to me.

I could feel my juices trickling out of me and down to my ass. I should've put a towel underneath. The louder she moaned, the wetter I became. I've tried on several occasions to come at the same time as she does. I can do it when I'm watching my favorite porn. The one where the coquettish "young" woman takes it up the ass like a pro. The actor's money shot coincided with my climax. I could hear my neighbor nearing the finish line. Her animated purrs became intense, growls almost. I was nowhere close, but I kept the rhythmic massage going on my clit until there was silence coming from next door. The droning of didgeridoo entered the air. The stranger would be leaving soon, so I had to be ready. I threw on my cut-offs and a tank top. I tied up the garbage in my kitchen and waited by the door.

About two minutes passed when I heard her door open. I counted to five then opened my apartment door. He looked my way then back at the elevator. I held the garbage bag at arm's length as I walked past him to the garbage chute.

"Gotta throw out this chicken skin."

"So you're the one cooking what smells so good," he said, following me with his eyes. I smiled. In reflex I held my breath as I opened the chute and dumped the bag.

"You just moved into the building?" I asked, feigning ignorance that I prayed he'd see right through.

"No, I'm just here visiting a friend."

"Oh... I like visitors." My eyes gleamed in response to his. "Did you have a nightcap already?"

"No, I haven't actually." He turned completely around to face me. I ran my eyes down the length of his body, studied his shoes, ogled his crotch, and then landed on his full lips.

The elevator dinged and the door opened. He followed me into my apartment. I was sure that my neighbor was watching us through her peephole.

Angelo was his name. He swirled his Jack on the rocks.
The ice cubes clanged against the glass. I had examined his
hands and fingers from a distance. They were well manicured
and clean. I wondered if they still smelled like my neighbor. She
was probably next door, not yet showered, with his deposit still
leaking out of her.

"Will you visit me again?" I asked.

"If this visit is worth while."

I sat in lotus position on the couch. My left lip peeked
out from my cut-off shorts. He noticed it. My four-day shadow
was apparent. Prickly to the touch. He sipped his drink and
trained his eyes back on my crotch.

"Should I have shaved?" I asked.

"No, it's fine the way it is."

"You don't shave, do you?"

"I'm a man."

Good answer. I wondered if the same thick hair that
covered his head covered his body. I saw a few strands sticking
out the top of his shirt. My neighbor had helped him get
dressed. Made sure to leave the first three buttons open. Made
my work easier. I leaned forward, and took a few of his hairs in
my teeth and tugged. I could see his skin and follicles bulge up
under my pull. He sucked in a deep breath through his teeth and
he opened his legs for me. I put my elbow on the prominent
bulge between his legs. I put a little more weight onto his crotch
and he made that sound again.

"*Mi piace molto,*" he moaned. I adjusted my contact with
his penis and grabbed it and his balls with my hand clawed. Like
a vice, I took all of my fingers and squeezed. Lightly at first,
then harder. If he didn't slide his hips forward, I would've
detached them from his body. Angelo stared at me wide-eyed
and smiling. He opened his pants. His penis stood up like one of
those inflatable dolls with sand at the bottom.

When I put his cock in my mouth I could smell and
taste her. It was a sweet flavor, like she had a diet full of oranges
and cherries. I sucked till her scent and flavor were gone. I kept

sucking till I could taste his precum. I wanted to taste all of him.

I took his balls into my mouth and juggled them with my tongue. Then I tasted his ass. He squirmed. I tugged on his cock like a cow's teat. I used his drippings and my spit to lubricate my longest finger. I fucked him with my fuck-you finger. These animal sounds emanated from him. I knew when I moved from my spot, there would be a puddle.

My neighbor was mesmerized by what she heard. I was sure of it. She never knew Angelo could make sounds like that. She never knew that sounds alone could make her touch herself.

He slid off my finger and turned around to me. "Let me see you."

I stood up for him. He didn't say anything. I turned around for him. Still silence. He grabbed me by the waist and pulled me to my living-room floor.

"I want to see you!" He pushed me onto my back. His intention was clear. I had my hands around my ankles and my elbows on the back of my knees.

"*Bella.*" He feasted on me while he stroked his cock. When he entered me, his eyes were closed and the veins in his neck popped out from his exertion. My screams were answered by his. He muttered something in Italian and grabbed my hair low, by the scruff of my neck like I was a baby kitten forcing my chin to my chest. He held me there till I heard him come. I was filled with his warmth. When he pulled out he wiped the head of his cock clean and sucked his fingers.

"Would you eat milk and raw egg?" I asked.

His face contorted in disgust.

I nodded, "Me neither."

His arms and legs wrapped around me like an orangutan. I didn't recall his limbs being so long.

The next morning we got ready for work. Without any words we relived the night before. "I'll go get the elevator." He let himself out my apartment.

I gathered the last of my things – my keys, chapstick, cell phone – and threw them in my bag. Then I took the same path he did out my apartment.

Angelo and my neighbor stood side by side at the elevator like two statues. They didn't utter a word. When the elevator announced its arrival with a ding, she walked in first. He was second. I followed. She went to one side of the elevator and he stood on the opposite side. Neither of them pressed the button. So I stepped forward and pressed 'ONE' and 'Door Close'. I took my spot between them. We looked like the letter "M", with me being the lowest part in the middle. I watched the numbers light up, then go off in descending order. I swear I heard a collective sigh when we made it to the ground floor without anyone joining our party.

He exited the elevator first. We all exited the building.

"I'll talk to you later, love." He gave me a kiss on the neck.

"Have a good day." He walked down the block with such a confident swagger; his shoulders and hips swaying just right. It reminded me why I loved to watch him so much. My neighbor took my hand and gave it a squeeze. We held hands till the last possible second as we headed in opposite directions. She winked at me.

"You taste delicious," I told her.

* * *

About The Author

Abigail Ekue is a writer and photographer based in New York. She uses her body to live and therefore, write. Her interest in biology, anatomy, physiology, health, fitness, psychology and sociology fuels her writing. She is a NATA Certified Athletic Trainer with a B.S. in Sport Sciences.

Her written work and insight have been included in *AskMen*, *Maxim Magazine*, *San Francisco Chronicle*, *VICE*, *Sensheant Magazine*, *Clutch Magazine*, *AM New York* and *SheKnows*.

She also runs the semi-regular advice column, "Ask Abbie", where she offers her own brand of advice and insight on health, fitness, body image, sex and relationships.

Abigail has been a guest on numerous radio shows, participated in literary reading events and facilitates erotic and creative writing workshops. She has work, knowledge and opinions to share and isn't afraid to tackle the taboo... and she still has to finish her erotic adventure thriller.

www.thedarkersideoflust.com

www.abigailekue.com

www.ingramcontent.com/pod-product-compliance
Lightning Source LLC
Chambersburg PA
CBHW070013120726
47909CB00003B/913